War Party

A John Tall Wolf Novel

Joseph Flynn

Stray Dog Press, Inc.
Springfield, IL
2019

Stand Alone Novels
The Concrete Inquisition
Digger
The Next President
Hot Type
Farewell Performance
Gasoline, Texas
Round Robin, A Love Story of Epic Proportions
One False Step
Blood Street Punx
Still Coming
Still Coming Expanded Edition
Hangman — A Western Novella
Pointy Teeth, Twelve Bite-Size Stories

Dedication

To the psychology professor at Loyola University
who persuaded me to follow my passion
rather than become a lawyer.

Acknowledgements

For Catherine, Caitie and Anne for helping me to limit the number of glitches in this book and keep my overhead low. Otherwise, I'd have to charge a whole lot more for these books. Any errors that remain are strictly my responsibility.

Author's Notes

This is a work of fiction. Neither the characters nor the Native American reservations named in the story are real. The Bureau of Indian Affairs, of course, exists within the United States Department of the Interior, and within the BIA its Office of Justice Services is "responsible for the overall management of the Bureau's law enforcement program," but my research turned up no one who has the job description I gave to John Tall Wolf. This mixture of fact and fiction falls under the heading of literary license. If you're a purist who demands complete realism, I recommend you stick to nonfiction, and good luck finding an author in that field who doesn't make mistakes or omissions.

As to a white male writing about Native American characters, that involves a bit of license, too. From my point of view, that license is rooted in our common humanity. If writers were to focus only on characters who shared their own backgrounds, we would establish a regime of literary apartheid.

AL
Reader Discretion Advised
Contains Adult Language

Stray Dog Press, Inc.

War Party
A John Tall Wolf Novel
Published by Stray Dog Press, Inc., 2019
Springfield, IL 62704, U.S.A.

Author website: *www.josephflynn.com*

Flynn, Joseph
    War Party / Joseph Flynn
    244 pg.
    ISBN   978-0-9908412-5-8
    eBook 978-0-9887868-7-5

Printed in the United States of America

PUBLISHER'S NOTE
This is a work of fiction. Names, characters, places, and incidents are either the product of the author's imagination or are used fictitiously; any resemblance to actual persons, living or dead, events, or locales is entirely coincidental.

Book design by Aha! Designs
Cover photo © 2013, Catherine C. Flynn

War Party

A John Tall Wolf Novel

— CHAPTER 1 —

New Orleans, Monday, August 19th

In the midst of a steamy hot start to the work week and the tail end sludge of the morning rush hour, all the traffic lights in New Orleans turned green. Every driver who was in a hurry to get somewhere, and that was pretty much all of them, suddenly had the right of way, and was aghast to find the sonsabitches on the cross streets apparently thought the same thing. It would later be said, with only slight exaggeration, that the screech of braking tires and clang of colliding cars could be heard all the way to Baton Rouge.

In short order, the howling and whining of ambulances and police patrol cars added to the ruckus. The various emergency service vehicles were not only foiled in reaching their destinations, they thickened the overheating stew of gridlock. Worsened tempers, too, with their added hubbub.

In the spirit of the moment, every driver in the city seemed to lean on his horn.

The cops, many of whom were now out of their cars, might have begun to direct traffic manually, if they hadn't had their hands full breaking up fistfights between motorists who were as overheated as their cars. Blood flowed at several intersections. For just a moment, many combatants held their punches as a number of gunshots sounded above the general din.

Those caught in the automotive pandemonium who had any sense retreated to their cars, locked themselves in and ducked below window level. This pragmatic approach to survival only guaranteed that a resolution to the citywide impasse wouldn't happen anytime soon.

Almost none of the people in their stiflingly hot metal cocoons noticed that aside from the traffic signals there wasn't another light on in town. Ninety-odd percent of the city's power grid had been taken down. An absence of electrical power in a modern city, of course, was always seen by some as a license to commit mayhem. Conditions grew worse.

Beau Duplessis, a security guard at the Thibodeaux State Bank on Rampart Street, had only to look at the mess outside the main door to know something bad was happening. Cars all jammed up, people going crazy. A retired NOPD patrol officer, he had first-hand knowledge that criminal behavior was more communicable than the Ebola virus and was often just as deadly. When the shit started to fly, the first thing you had to do was set your defenses and be ready to —

Wonder what the hell else might happen.

Like having a bunch of guys on black motorcycles wearing black helmets that covered their faces roar up to the front of the bank.

Pull itty-bitty machine guns out from under their black jackets.

Whip off their helmets and, good Lord, they were Indians. Faces covered with war paint. Long hair tied back. Some of them wearing eagle feathers. Beau almost soiled his britches then and there. But his training and a sense of duty kicked in.

Not that he had any intention of going for his gun. No, sir. If he started swapping shots with those guys, they'd put more holes in him than Katrina had put in the levees. He lunged at the front door. If he could lock them out, that might be all that was needed. The bank's doors and windows were made of a polycarbonate resin. Ought to stop the slugs from small grease guns.

Beau hit the door a heartbeat before the first bad guy did. He pressed the button to shoot the bolt but it didn't respond. He did lose a little something in his underpants right then, but he tried to throw the lock by hand. An Indian pushed back on the door, and he was bigger than Beau.

By now, the thirty-seven people in the bank, clients and staff, had caught notice of the struggle going on at the front door. Shrieks rose from several women and more than a few men. The other security guard on duty, Harold Murtree, might have rushed to Beau's side, lent his weight to a push that would have allowed the door to be locked, and changed the whole course of the day's events.

Only Harold was too busy pulling off his uniform cap and shirt and disposing of them in a waste paper receptacle. With only a slight hesitation, he put his gunbelt and sidearm in the bin, too. Now he was just another guy in a pair of slacks and Doctor John T-shirt. The maneuver might have been a clever ruse, have the robbers think he was just another civilian; he could go for his gun at an opportune moment.

But Harold raised his hands in an attitude of surrender. Sweat beaded on his brow. He whispered the first prayer that came to his mind.

The only other person acting in a peculiar fashion was a man in his mid-twenties. He had a gleam in his eye and looked as if he was watching the coolest TV show that had ever aired, not a crime that might take his life. He reached a hand into a pocket of his jeans and came out with something he held close against his right leg.

By then, Beau's resistance was overcome by a second Indian pushing on the other side of the door. The robbers poured into the bank, leaving two of their number outside to guard against a threat from the street and to protect their motorcycles.

One of the robbers rewarded Beau's attempt at heroism with a blow to the jaw from the butt of his weapon. The former cop went down in a heap. Several people moaned, anticipating that the guard would be killed for his resistance.

That didn't happen.

One of the robbers held up a sign printed in large block letters. It said: EVERYBODY GET DOWN.

Everyone did just that.

One member of the Indians' war party kept watch over the people now lying on the floor. Made sure they stayed put. Several of the bank customers were sobbing softly, trying to keep the volume down so they didn't call attention to themselves. Others murmured prayers, but these were muted, too. Men in warpaint with automatic weapons inspired the urge to become invisible.

After his first visual sweep, the robber tasked with watching the bank's cowering customers relaxed and turned his attention to the other members of his tribe to see how they were doing. He didn't notice the young man who aimed his mobile phone at him and got busy shooting a video of the robbery.

Four Indians were cleaning out the tellers' cages. The war party's chief directed their movements with hand signals. The young guy with the phone captured that and the deft choreography of the men grabbing the cash. Taking chances that made him shiver, the young guy made sure he got head shots of every Indian in the bank.

Seeing the one that was supposed to be watching him start to turn his head back to where the biggest knot of customers lay, the young man pulled his phone down under his chest and lay still with his eyes squeezed shut. He started to pray, too, that he wouldn't be shot. And neither would anyone else.

He didn't need a bloodbath to make his movie a hit.

A moment later, his prayer for salvation seemed to be answered in the affirmative. He heard several motorcycles roar away. He opened his eyes. The robbers were gone. Everybody else was still on the floor. The young man looked at the time signature on his phone.

His video was less than two minutes long.

The robbers had done their work that quickly.

Came, stole and took off. Without saying a word.

The young man jumped to his feet. He was the next one out the door.

Marcellus Darcy stood outside his car on Rampart Street just up the block from the bank. The heap's air conditioner wasn't working, but what could you expect from a government fleet vehicle? Marcellus watched his hometown go crazy. Not for the first time. Katrina was the mother of all social collapses, of course. You could hardly blame New Orleans for that. A biblical flood came along with no ark in sight, people anywhere would get excitable.

Civil unrest in the Big Easy usually manifested on a smaller scale, though. Often on or near Mardi Gras. White off-duty cops beating up black transportation workers. Revelers of any color shooting one another. The sorts of things that while regrettable were comprehensible within the contexts of alcohol consumption and racial or personal animosity.

What was happening that morning, though, was already way beyond street corner brawls or shootings. It looked to Darcy as if every damn car and truck in the city had been all but welded bumper to bumper and people were fighting mad. Several of them within his view were punching and kicking each other.

Fortunately, the combatants seemed both equally matched and inept.

No knockouts, no stompings. No mobs beating on particular individuals.

As a U.S. postal inspector, Marcellus was a sworn federal law enforcement officer. True, his normal duties were to defend the nation's mail system, its employees, infrastructure and customers. But he carried a badge and a gun, had the power of arrest and served federal search warrants and subpoenas. The Postal Inspection Service was the oldest federal law enforcement agency in the United States.

So, at the moment, it was a matter of personal judgment as to how he should exercise his authority. It was only when he saw a big red-faced guy in a suit going after a kid who looked barely old enough to drive and weighed maybe a buck-twenty sopping wet that he knew he had to get involved.

He ran over to the fight taking place next to the unintended coupling of a Ford Focus and a Mercedes SUV. Darcy saw the kid duck a roundhouse punch that would have killed him had it landed. He then kicked the big lug right on a kneecap. The guy howled and his arms shot out as he sought to balance on one foot.

As luck would have it, one of the big guy's hands found the kid's mop of hair. He grabbed hold and lifted the kid off the ground. Held him at a level just right to punch his lights out. Still standing on one leg, the big man cocked his right hand. There was no chance any mercy would be shown, especially not after the kid kicked his opponent's other leg.

Marcellus arrived just in time to catch the big guy's wrist.

He was even bigger than the guy with the Mercedes.

That was disconcerting enough to the red-faced guy.

He goggled at Marcellus and dropped the kid. When Marcellus put a handcuff on him he said, "Hey, wait a minute."

Marcellus didn't. He got both of the guy's hands cuffed behind his back.

The red-faced guy cried, "That little shit started it."

Sure enough, the kid grinned, like he was getting away with something.

Marcellus told him, "Stay put. You ain't goin' anywhere neither."

The kid looked like he might run, and catching him in all the chaos would be a mother, if he took off. But the look on Marcellus' face told the kid he'd find him sooner or later.

So he didn't flee. Just said, "That fat bastard 'bout pulled out half my hair."

If Marcellus could have simply sent them both on their separate ways, he would have. But their cars were stuck together. If he turned both of them loose and they got back into it when he turned his back, any resulting misfortune would land on him.

And he was not about to jeopardize his second pension, only five years away.

The postal inspector was trying to decide what to do next when the first motorcycle roared past on the nearby sidewalk. Big black bike and ... another one looking just like the first followed right behind. That made two and ... zoom, zoom, zoom, roar, roar, roar. Six more of them followed.

All eight of the motorcycles were black. Seemed to have some kind of Indian head design on the gas tanks. All the drivers had black helmets covering their faces. Each bike had saddle bags. The last of them to pass mustn't have had one of its bags fastened tight. It hit a bump in the sidewalk and a banded stack of cash flew out and landed on the sidewalk where Marcellus could see it.

The big guy and kid asked the same thing, "Who the hell was that?"

Marcellus said, "Only people in town goin' anywhere."

He told the kid, "Go bring me that money."

The kid looked at the postal inspector and the cash, weighing his options.

Marcellus knew what he was thinking.

He said, "You run with that money, you'll wish I let this guy hit you."

— CHAPTER 2 —

Montreal, Quebec

John Tall Wolf, a special agent with the United States Bureau of Indian Affairs, strolled along the rue de la Montagne with Sergeant Rebecca Bramley of the Royal Canadian Mounted Police. The two of them were on vacation. The morning air was clear and bright with a hint of fall in the breeze. They had two days of leisure time left together.

John had suggested they go to Paris.

Rebecca had said, "Montreal is Francophone, closer, less expensive and the exchange rate for the American dollar is better, too."

"Irresistibly romantic," John said. "How could I argue with that?"

"I'm saving you fourteen hours of flying time. I bet we could find better ways to put that time to use. How's that for romantic?"

"Makes me tingle all over." He wasn't kidding.

So they went to Montreal. Had a fine time in their executive suite at Le Crystal. The deep soaking bathtub held both of them, a combined twelve-and-a-half feet of international law enforcement. The separate shower stall was roomy enough for good clean fun, too. The bedroom and living room were furnished on the same scale.

Outside the hotel, they followed the tourist guide book. Visited La Citadelle, the largest military fortification in North

America. Built atop Cap Diamant with a commanding view of the city, it was constructed to defend Montreal against an invasion by the United States. Once that threat had passed it was used to put on military displays that entertained tourists.

They hiked the slopes of Parc du Mont-Royal, an urban oasis designed by Frederick Law Olmsted. Visited the Ile d'Orleans, where the French first arrived in 1535, and saw many of the six hundred heritage buildings that had been preserved there. They drove north to the Laurentian Mountains and saw First Nation relics that proved the native people had beat the French to the region by at least three millennia.

The night before they took their stroll, they'd gone to Le Piano Rouge to hear some music. John got far more of a show than he'd ever expected. The lead singer of the featured band said, "I'd like to perform a duet now, but I need some help. Is there a lady in the audience who knows 'I've Had the Time of My Life,' and would like to make her professional debut?"

With mischief in his eyes, he added, "I'll pick up the bar tab for two, if you get a round of applause."

John turned to see if there were any takers. By the time he looked back, Rebecca was on the stage. Tall, sleek and stunning in her cocktail dress, she got cheers before singing a note.

"You win, I surrender," the singer said, "but can you sing?"

She glanced at John before replying, "Let's find out."

The guy started the number with a spot-on knockoff of Bill Medley. John leaned forward, the better to hear if Rebecca could imitate Jennifer Warnes as closely. She didn't. Her voice was her own and pitch perfect. It blended as sweetly with the Medley voice as anyone could ask. Maybe a bit too well from where John sat. He felt sure he wasn't the only one in the club who felt he was seeing two people fall in love right in front of his eyes.

Rebecca not only got her round of applause, she got a standing ovation.

Under the cover of the audience's noisy approval, the lead singer whispered into Rebecca's ear, "You must be here with someone special, the way you sang."

She nodded and told him, "A great big American, in law enforcement."

Her message received and understood, the singer contented himself to buss her cheek.

Joined those clapping as she left the stage.

On the way back to Le Crystal that night, John said, "You were great."

Rebecca told him, "You haven't seen anything yet."

The following morning, they visited local art galleries and then ambled back to the hotel, their mood dampened by a sense of impending separation. They lived and worked in different countries. Their careers weren't the sole focus of their lives, but neither wanted to go looking for a new job anytime soon.

The circumstances that had brought them together, working a case, were the same ones that kept them apart. Most of the time. The days they spent together were wonderful, but that only made the nights they spent apart more difficult.

Phone calls helped. Skyping, though, made the distance more obvious.

They went back to their suite to … take a nap.

Rebecca told John hockey players did it all the time. John said toddlers did, too. A ringing phone woke them up two hours later.

Duty called for John.

There was trouble in New Orleans. A band of Indians had robbed a bank. Right after most of the town's electrical grid had gone down. Nobody thought that was a coincidence.

John needed to get down there. Right away.

He got out of bed, dressed and started to pack.

Rebecca said, "If you're going back to work, I might as well do the same."

John told her, "I'm hanging on to the two days of vacation time we didn't get to use."

She got out of bed, kissed him and said, "Right, me too, because this wasn't how I planned to end our naps."

— CHAPTER 3 —

New York City

In the time-honored tradition of government work, John's trip to Washington was a case of hurry up and wait. Not that John had been able to cover the 489 mile distance between Montreal and Washington quickly. The first direct flight that day didn't leave Canada until 7:30 p.m. By the time it landed and he got to the meeting to which he'd been summoned, it would be after nine at night. People might resent his lack of dispatch.

So he took a two p.m. flight to New York, figuring he could catch one of the many shuttle flights to the nation's capital and arrive at a more reasonable time. Soon enough, anyway, to be handed a summary sheet of what had been decided at the meeting, and maybe catch another flight down to New Orleans that evening. Things didn't work out quite so well.

John landed at JFK just ahead of a storm front roaring in from the Midwest. All flights into and out of New York were canceled and weren't expected to resume until that evening. John caught a cab to Penn Station. The high speed Acela trains ran hourly between Boston and DC. When there wasn't a power outage due to severe weather, that was.

John looked out at the downpour flooding the city and wondered if he should rent a car and drive to Washington. The cabbie who had driven him from the airport to the train station had told him the trip usually took a half-hour; their travel time had been three times that. John thought he might spend hours just getting out of the New York metro area, and who knew how long it would take to make the two hundred-plus mile trek to DC?

He decided to wait out the storm in Penn Station.

He left a voicemail message for his acting boss Nelda Freeland. Who, by no coincidence, was Marlene Flower Moon's niece.

Marlene was the director of the BIA's Office of Justice Services. John suspected she was really Coyote, the Trickster. The supernatural iteration of the flesh and blood animal that had tried to devour him when he was an infant.

John sat in the crowded station, a silent figure conveying no particular sense of menace, but he was nonetheless afforded an unusual amount of personal space. He wore a good suit, was closely shaved and recently barbered. He was also a bit over six-foot-four with wide shoulders and copper skin burnished to a red glow by the summer sun. Even on a day when no ray of sunshine was to be found, though, he wore his customary pair of Ray-Ban aviator sunglasses.

Not for affect. His eyes were sensitive to even artificial light.

His birth mother, a member of the Northern Apache tribe, had left him to die on a rickety platform she'd constructed in the foot-hills of the Sangre de Cristo mountains just outside of Santa Fe, New Mexico. John had been conceived out of wedlock, fathered by a young man who was probably Navajo not Apache. His mother had broken two social taboos — sexual promiscuity and tribal out-breeding — to keep her father from arranging a marriage for her. In that, she was successful.

Still, she thought the child she'd produced should be given unto the keeping of the Great Spirit. He would be better off that way. It was a convenient rationalization.

Until a large coyote came along and thought John would make a fine meal. The people who would become his adoptive parents, Haden Wolf and Serafina Wolf y Padilla happened upon the coyote trying to dislodge the infant from his platform and thwarted the plans of both John's birth mother and the beast. But not before the desert sun shining into the child's eyes left him with an inability to tolerate bright lights.

Doctor and Mrs. Wolf also defeated a lawsuit filed against them six years later by John's birth mother when she sought to reclaim custody of him. The idea that Coyote, the figure of mythic powers not the specific animal, might also try to retrieve John, was one that neither John's parents nor, later, he himself could dismiss.

As Coyote was a known shape-shifter, John always felt the need to be alert whenever he was among strangers. He was watchful even with people he knew. He was most suspicious of the woman who had recruited him for the BIA, Marlene Flower Moon.

John's thinking was to keep a nemesis within view. Marlene's idea was to use John's skills and talents to further her own ambitions. To consume him figuratively if not literally. Well, maybe she thought she'd dine on his remains eventually.

It was John's sense of relentless vigilance, combined with his size and his sunglasses, that kept crowds at a distance.

By the time the storm passed and the trains began to run again, John got to Washington just about when he would have if he'd taken the later flight from Montreal. Sometimes a draw was the best anyone could manage.

— CHAPTER 4 —

Washington, DC, Tuesday, August 20th

Just outside of the Eisenhower Executive Office Building, often thought of as the ugliest government structure in Washington, especially in contrast to the White House next door, John Tall Wolf met Acting Director Nelda Freeland of the Bureau of Indian Affairs' Office of Justice Services for the first time.

By way of introducing herself to John, she said, "Your absence forced Vice President Morrissey to delay the conclusion of our meeting."

"Exactly what I had in mind," John said.

Nelda's eye's narrowed and John was impressed by how much his nominal new boss resembled his nominal old boss, Marlene Flower Moon.

"May I see your teeth, please?" he asked.

"What?"

"Come on, humor me. If you do, I'll try to cut down on the wisecracks."

Nelda didn't find the offer irresistible.

She said, "I was warned about you."

"Of course, you were. Marlene told you as much as she thought you needed to know. Your resemblance to her has to make you family. She's never been married. So that would have to make you her niece ... or her illegitimate daughter."

Anger flashed in Nelda's eyes and her lips drew back to reveal perfectly aligned teeth.

Including four incisors that looked like they could make a meal of a bull moose. No cooking necessary. She was Marlene's kin all right.

Which she confirmed. "I'm Director Flower Moon's niece. Let's go. *I* don't want to keep the vice president waiting."

John held the door for Nelda and asked, "So has Marlene conquered Hollywood yet?"

She was working with movie icon Clay Steadman on his new film.

The one about a bigoted L.A. cop.

Nelda didn't answer, but John figured Marlene was doing well enough to let the new kid warm her chair for the time being.

John and Nelda beat the clock, got to the conference room attached to the vice president's ceremonial office before the appointed hour, but they were still the last to arrive. Vice President Jean Morrissey sat at the head of the table. To her immediate right were FBI Director Jeremiah Haskins and Deputy Director Byron DeWitt. To Morrissey's left were Director of National Intelligence Clement Archer and newly confirmed Director of Central Intelligence Robin Hannah.

Nelda Freeland sat next to Hannah.

John rounded the table and took the seat adjacent to DeWitt. He shook the hand the deputy director extended to him.

The vice president formally introduced John to the others. He nodded to each of his new acquaintances. Then he said, "A pleasure to meet you and everyone else, Madam Vice President. Sorry I was unable to be here yesterday, but I swam as fast as I could."

Nelda blushed, but the vice president chuckled and the others smiled.

"We'll have to increase your travel budget, Special Agent," the vice president said.

Everyone chuckled at that.

"Now that you've joined us, I'd like to recap our discussion of yesterday so we're all on the same page. If that's all right with everyone."

Nobody objected.

Louis Armstrong International Airport, New Orleans

The eight men sat in two facing rows of four seats in Concourse B. None of them was a Native American. Three were white; three were Latino; one was a lightly complected African American; one was Asian American. They were all young, relatively. They were all big, compared to most people. They were all dressed casually. Some with better taste than the others. None of them would make anyone look twice. The plane they would board had just pulled up to Gate 15, in a far corner of the concourse.

None of them fidgeted or exhibited a nervous tic. But neither did any of them read a magazine, play a video game or zone out to music coming through earbuds. They simply looked at the guys seated across from them and dwelled on their own thoughts. That and glanced at the one guy who was just a bit bigger, older and more wised up than the others.

His name was Corey Price. He ran the show. The operational end, anyway.

As the passengers on the arriving flight deplaned, Price's cell phone chimed to announce the receipt of a text message. All the others in the group heard the electronic signal. As an act of discipline, and following their instructions to the letter, none of them looked at Price as he took out his phone and read the one word message: Brock.

Price knew the code key by heart. Brock was Lou Brock. Hall of Fame baseball player. Former all-time leader in single season and career stolen bases. His glory years had come with the St.

Louis Cardinals. But for purposes of the code, Price recalled the uniform number Brock had used only during his largely forgotten first three years with the Chicago Cubs: 24.

Price leaned over to Reyes, the guy on his left and whispered, "Brock." All the others knew the code, too. And soon each of them had gotten the word and they were all smiling.

Why shouldn't they be? They'd learned that each of them would be getting twenty-four thousand dollars as his cut of the robbery of the Thibodeaux State Bank. Not a bad day's pay.

The gate agent announced that boarding for their flight to Las Vegas would begin in five minutes. Getting out of town soon would feel good, too. Everything was going according to plan.

Then Price's phone rang. He looked at the caller ID, stood and stepped away from the others before answering. "Yeah?"

The voice on the other end said, "I told you we'd do it, didn't I?"

"Really?" Price asked. "After all this time?"

"I'm like you," came the reply. "I don't give up."

"Christ." Perfect goddamn timing, Price thought.

Getting good news *after* you turn to a life of crime.

The boarding call came and Price headed off to Vegas.

EEOB, Washington, DC

Vice President Morrissey laid things out clearly. A cyberattack of alarming sophistication had taken out critical elements of a large American city's infrastructure yesterday. During the time that the greater part of New Orleans' electrical grid was down, a band of men who were either Native Americans or costumed to appear as such robbed the Thibodeaux State Bank on Rampart Street, making off with more than $200,000 in cash.

"We don't know if the robbery was motivated by anything more than money," the vice president said, "but there is a long and global history of terrorist groups that have committed such robberies to finance their activities. Political extremists from both the right and left have committed such crimes in Europe. Nationalist and religious zealots have used bank heists to fund themselves in Asia. And, of course, we've had groups and individuals ranging from the Symbionese Liberation Army in California to, more recently, a white supremacist in Utah rob banks to finance their aims."

John said, "Pardon me for interrupting, Madam Vice President, but that last guy, didn't he say he wanted the money so he could return the country to white people?"

Jean Morrissey said, "Yes, he did. Are you anticipating where I'm heading here, Special Agent?"

"That Native Americans are trying to show who really got here first?" John said.

Nelda Freeland closed her eyes and compressed her lips into a thin line.

No doubt committing each of John's words to memory.

To forward as soon as possible to Marlene Flower Moon.

The vice president smiled at John. She liked people with spunk. Was one herself.

"That's one possibility or an element of a larger plan, and the big picture is what concerns us most here. The fervent hope at the White House is that the event in New Orleans was strictly an exercise in criminality. If it wasn't, if the interruption of vital services in New Orleans traces back to a foreign power, then what happened was an act of war."

John said, "If I might ask, weren't there any other crimes committed in New Orleans, other than the bank robbery, ones that happened in the wake of the power failure? What makes the bank robbery stand out?"

The vice president nodded to Deputy Director DeWitt.

He turned to John and said, "There was a spike in crime across the board. Power wasn't restored until after dark. But most of the crimes reported by the NOPD were simply increases in the usual number of routine complaints. In terms of money lost, and sheer helpfulness to the criminals' efforts, nothing comes close to the robbery at the Thibodeaux State Bank."

John nodded and said, "Just wanted to check."

"It was a good question, Special Agent. Given the dimensions of the situation, the CIA and other federal agencies with responsibilities for gathering intelligence abroad will look for foreign actors: individuals, groups or sovereign states who might have had a hand in what happened. The FBI will look for domestic terrorists and organized crime elements. And you, Special Agent Tall Wolf, will …"

Vice President Morrissey gestured to him.

"Find the Indians," he said.

The meeting broke up, but before she left, Vice President Morrissey had a private word with John. She told him, "Clay Steadman recommended you. Said you did some good work in Goldstrike before he resigned as mayor there. That's why I asked for you."

John said, "I always try my hardest, ma'am."

She nodded. "Acting Director Freeland will give you a personal briefing."

John and Nelda left the building, walking side by side in silence.

The special agent thought the line between government and show business was all but disappearing. Mega-movie star Clay Steadman had become the mayor of the Sierra Nevada resort town of Goldstrike, California. John had helped with the investigation of a threat of eco-terrorism there. Then Steadman had resigned his office and gone back to making movies — taking John's boss, Marlene Flower Moon, with him as an executive producer.

Not that Marlene had left her government job, taking only a leave of absence to go to Hollywood. Then Steadman recommended John to the vice president to be involved in this case of bank-robbery-slash-cyberwarfare. Or was Marlene trying to manipulate him again, John wondered, using Steadman as her front man?

John and Nelda reached the private driveway adjacent to the EEOB and a gleaming black SUV pulled up in front of them: Nelda's ride. John looked at her and asked, "Any chance you ever wanted to be a movie star?"

"No," she said curtly.

"Me either. You might mention that to Marlene."

"She already knows everything about you."

Coyote, John thought.

Nelda handed him a thumb drive. "All the information we have for you about the bank robbery is on this drive."

"Who do I see first?" John asked.

She gave him the name of the New Orleans police captain, Edmee LaBelle, who'd be his liaison with that department.

"How about the FBI? Who's my contact with them?"

"I don't have a name yet. Deputy Director DeWitt should be in contact about that. If not, his phone number is on the drive. Give him a call."

"Right." Only if I need a feeb, John thought. "Any civilian witnesses I should start with?"

"Marcellus Darcy, but he's only sort of a civilian."

"Meaning?" John asked.

"He's a U.S. postal inspector but, really, what is it those people do?"

John said, "I'm sure he'll tell me. Anyone else?"

"A young guy who skipped out of the bank right after the robbers fled."

"An inside man?" John asked.

"That's for you to find out, but a bank employee identified him as a customer."

Well, John thought, at least he had something to start with, but he had one point to make clear to the new acting director.

He told Nelda, "Vice president or not, you need to understand, I still don't do reservations. If that's where these robbers are hiding out."

"Some Native American you are."

"I'm sure *you* know all about me, too," John said.

He still had the occasional nightmare about his biological mother trying to regain custody of him, take him away from the only home he'd known and bring him to the rez. Now, he directed a long look at Nelda.

"What?" she asked.

"Quite the resemblance between you and Marlene," he said.

Nelda smiled, her long, pointed incisors gleaming in the sun.

"What's the matter, Tall Wolf? You think I'm Coyote, too?"

She got in her car and left. Was she Coyote?

You never knew.

— CHAPTER 5 —

New Orleans, LA

John Tall Wolf made much better time getting to New Orleans than he had traveling to Washington. The weather was clear and he used his status as a federal officer to get priority seating on the first direct flight. As often happened when there was an empty seat in the business or first class section, he got bumped up from coach. It made airline employees feel patriotic.

He never argued the point with them. People his size needed their leg room.

It was after he arrived in the Big Easy that things started to get harder. Calling from the airport, he learned that Captain Edmee LaBelle, having worked a twenty-four-hour shift, had gone home to sleep. She'd check in for messages when she awoke. The cop asked where John was staying.

"What's a nice hotel?" he replied. "Maybe something a little different."

"Renaissance Arts Hotel, 700 Tchoupitoulas Street."

"Easy for you to say," John said.

"If you're taking a cab, just give the driver the name. He'll know."

"Someone in your family work there?" John asked.

"Head of housekeeping is my sister."

"They give federal employees a discount?"

"I wouldn't know about that, but if you tell the front desk

Buddy Brunelle sent you, you'll get the best deal in the French Quarter."

John said *merci* and found a taxi to take him into town.

He thought, for the moment, things were looking up.

But when he called the local office of the FBI they didn't know which of its agents would act as his liaison.

"*We* handle bank robberies, you know?" the agent who took his call said.

"You can have them. I'm the guy who handles Indians."

"Aren't you supposed to say Native Americans?"

"*You* are. I've got tribal license to say what I want."

The feeb knew he was being jerked around. He asked, "You want to stop by, we'll *try* to find someone to talk with you."

John said, "Never mind. I'll just call Deputy Director DeWitt. I've got his phone number right here."

The agent's demeanor changed in a hurry. "No, no need to do that. I'll speak to the —"

"Don't bother," John said. "This was just a courtesy call."

He hung up, having told the truth. He'd checked in with the FBI. Now, none of his colleagues in federal law enforcement would be able to accuse him of crashing their party.

He asked the cabbie, "You know where the Thibodeaux State Bank is?"

"Sure do. That where you want to go?"

"Yes, please."

The driver looked at John in his rear-view mirror.

"You an Indian?"

"I am." John saw the man's shoulders tense. He must've heard who had robbed the bank. "I have a license to take scalps, too."

He'd asked Marlene for one when he started work, but she'd yet to come through.

The driver relaxed when he saw John smile.

"You're funnin' me."

"I am. So what do you think of the Renaissance Arts Hotel?"

"I'll let you know, soon as I get tired of the Ritz-Carlton."

***

John's appearance — big, Native American, wearing sunglasses and carrying an overnight bag that could be used to make off with a large chunk of cash — caused some apprehension among the personnel at the Thibodeaux State Bank. Damn robbers were giving people with copper complexions a bad name. Having been raised in the Southwest in general and Santa Fe in particular, he hadn't often been the victim of unfavorable stereotyping.

His parents had taught him good manners. Made sure he was always clean, neat and well dressed. Years of good schooling had added polish. The few times he'd frightened people by simply being present, it had been because he was so big and wore sunglasses to protect his light-sensitive eyes.

Stepping into the bank, though, was a whole new feeling. He'd scared people specifically because he resembled, at least at a glance, the jerks who'd pointed guns at them only a day earlier. He felt a new degree of empathy with other minorities who were feared simply because of the way they looked.

That insight deepened when he saw a security guard start to reach for his sidearm.

Before things could get out of hand, John took his badge out of a pocket and said to the guard, "Federal officer. I'd like to see the bank manager, please."

The guard, whose face was badly bruised, looked closely at John's credentials.

Reading aloud, he said, "Special Agent John Tall Wolf, Bureau of Indian Affairs."

He looked at John, who nodded.

"You were hurt in the robbery?" John asked.

The guard bobbed his head, wincing as he did.

"Didn't you get any time off?"

"Didn't want it."

John nodded. Now, he could see what the man wanted, a chance to get even. But he'd chosen not to misdirect his anger at an innocent third party. Especially one who was a fed. He led John to the office of Arnaud Thibodeaux, the bank's president.

John introduced himself and asked if the guard might stay.

"Beau is needed outside," Thibodeaux said. "You never know. Someone might try to rob us again."

Thibodeaux was right, John thought. Banks, gas stations and convenience stores that had been robbed once with success became the favored targets of thugs with guns. Just as homes that had been burgled were often hit more than once. If you were victimized, you had to upgrade your defenses to make the bad guys look elsewhere.

John said, "I understand." He told the guard, "I'd like to speak with you after your shift, if you're feeling up to it."

The guard looked at Thibodeaux, who nodded.

He told John, "I get a break in fifteen minutes, if that'll do. Once I go home, I want to sleep."

"See you in fifteen," John said. As the guard left, he took the chair Thibodeaux offered him. "People are still pretty shook up?"

"We'll be having mental health counselors talk to all our people. I'm still trying to figure out what to do for the bank customers who were here at the time," Thibodeaux said.

John asked, "What about you?"

The bank president took a bottle of bourbon and a glass out of his desk. Remembering his manners, he reached for a second glass and held it up to John.

"Thanks for the offer, but no."

Thibodeaux filled his glass and took a sip.

"I was here in my office when the power went out. I waited a moment to see if the lights might come back on. Sometimes things work that way. When the bank stayed dark, I opened my door to ask my secretary to call the power company. Only I saw her lying on the floor with everyone else."

"So you came back in here," John said.

"To get the gun I keep in my desk." Thibodeaux tossed back his drink and poured another. "I had it in hand when I saw this picture."

He picked up a framed photo from his desk and turned it John's way.

A good-looking wife and two kids just about school age. After showing it to John, he took his own look. Carefully poured the bourbon from his glass back into the bottle and put it away.

"I stayed in my office with the door locked. I knelt behind my desk with my gun pointed at the door. What I'd decided, I wasn't going to bring a handgun to an automatic weapons fight, but if they tried to get me, I was going to shoot first."

"You did the right thing," John said.

Thibodeaux said, "Yeah, I got to go home to my family."

John could see that the man still had regrets.

As if he hadn't done the manly thing.

"Your family started this bank?" John asked.

"My grandfather. He brought it through the Great Depression."

The bank president was going to need some therapy, too, John saw.

He moved on to practical matters.

"When the power went out, did that take your security cameras down?"

"It did. The phones were out, too. I couldn't even use my cell phone."

John could sympathize with the man's frustration.

He said, "I was told a young man was the first customer to leave the bank after the robbers fled. Has anyone been able to iden-tify him?"

Thibodeaux nodded. "Marguerite Timkins, our consumer loan officer. The guy had an appointment to see her."

"May I speak with her?"

The bank president said, "She takes her break shortly, too."

John met with the bruised security guard, Beau Duplessis, and the loan officer, Marguerite Timkins, in a room filled with round tables and plastic chairs. But every table was graced by a real flower in a glass vase. Two curtained windows admitted natural light. Wicker baskets were filled with free apples and granola bars. A five-gallon bottle provided spring water.

Three vending machines offered coffee, tea, soda, candy and salty snacks.

Bank employees were allowed to pursue their own nutritional destinies.

A bulletin board was festooned with pictures of newborns, newlyweds and couples celebrating the anniversaries of durable marriages. Cars, furnishings and one Shetland pony were offered for sale. The standings of a banking community softball league showed Thibodeaux in second place, only a game out of first.

Appearances were sometimes deceiving, but John believed he was in one of those fortunate workplaces where people took care of one another, prospered together and formed an extended family. Beau Duplessis had certainly put himself at risk for his employer. The bruises he had on his face bespoke a genuine effort to cast himself as Horatius at the bridge.

John said, "I'm sorry to take up your free time like this. I imagine you've already given your statements to the New Orleans police."

Duplessis said, "They just asked for an outline, said we should save the details for the feds. I kinda thought we'd be seein' the FBI, though."

John told him, "They're working other aspects of the case. I'll copy them on my report. That might save you some time in the future."

"That'd be good," Duplessis said. "So what do you want to know?"

"Tell me how things went," John said.

"It was fast, at least for me. I tried to keep the bastards from entering the bank, but the automatic lock on the main entrance didn't respond and … two of them pushed me out of the way. Then I woke up in the hospital. The docs made me stay overnight for observation. This morning, they let me go. So, I went home, cleaned up and here I am."

"That's what you told the police?" John asked.

"Just what I told them."

"Is there anything you can add to your statement now?"

Duplessis took a deep breath and let it out slowly. It would have been reasonable for someone who had suffered a head trauma to say he couldn't remember, but he didn't take the easy way out.

"Their weapons," he said, "I got a good, close look at 'em while I was tryin' to keep those pricks from pushing the door open." He looked at his colleague. "Pardon my language, Marguerite."

"You say what you like, Beau. It won't be anything I haven't already thought."

The two of them shared a smile, reinforcing John's idea of a family atmosphere.

"Anyway," Beau said, "they had automatic weapons. Small ones. Almost no barrel. Pistol grip. Clips looked like they held about thirty rounds. When I went home, I looked online to see if I could find out what kind of weapons they were. And I think they were MP-5Ks. I think the K stands for small or something in German."

"Short," John said.

"There you go. Anyway, that's what I think they had."

"Anything else?"

Duplessis shook his head.

John said, "A moment ago, you were about to say something and you caught yourself. You want to tell me what you were thinking?"

The guard glanced at his co-worker, turned back to John and said, "No."

John turned to the loan officer. "Ms. Timkins, would you please go to your desk and write down the name, address and telephone number of that young man who left the bank right after the robbers did? If you have that information."

"I do," she said. She looked at Beau Duplessis. The guard gave her a nod.

"Very well." She left the break room.

"My guess is you were a cop," John told Duplessis. "It goes against your grain to speak ill of someone with whom you work. You don't want to be a rat. But now you have to weigh that against how you feel for all other people who work here."

"I love these people, that's how I feel."

"So make the choice that will be easier to live with."

Duplessis took a moment before nodding.

"There was another guard on duty yesterday, Harold Murtree. If he'd come to help me, we might've gotten the door locked manually. Kept those damn bastards out. Only he didn't help me. What I heard, and don't ask me who told, was Harold took off his uniform shirt *and* his gun and hid 'em so the robbers would think he was just another customer."

"You know where Harold lives?"

Duplessis' disgust with his colleague, probably another ex-cop, was plain now.

"Marguerite can get you that information, if the bastard hasn't run away. He didn't show up for work this morning."

"Thank you for your help," John said.

"Yeah, sure. I gotta get back to work."

— CHAPTER 6 —

Renaissance Arts Hotel

John caught another cab to the hotel. The first driver had been right; the name alone was enough to get him where he wanted to go. He felt good about what he'd learned at the Thibodeaux State Bank. He was reasonably sure that Beau Duplessis had it right about the type of weapons the bank robbers had brandished.

Tracking down a single MP-5K would be difficult, but if a shipment large enough to supply eight bank robbers had been hijacked or otherwise diverted from legal channels maybe that would be something that could provide a lead. He'd forward the information to the BATF. Let them make of it what they could.

The other path to follow was the one that led to Harold Murtree, the security guard who took the coward's way out. If John was right in thinking Murtree was once a cop, having the NOPD look for him would be the way to go; they would be able to find him faster than he could. Murtree might have been the inside man on the bank job or his hiring might have been an error in judgment made by the bank's human resources department.

When John presented himself at the front desk of the Renaissance Arts Hotel, he showed the smiling young woman his federal ID and asked, "Would you have a room for a weary public servant?"

"Of course, sir. Welcome to New Orleans." She took a second

glance at his badge. "By any chance, are you the gentleman Buddy Brunelle referred to us?"

"I am."

"In that case, we don't have a room."

For a heartbeat, John thought he'd been set up.

Suckered into going to a hotel where the Brunelle's name was mud.

Then the desk clerk gave him a wink and said, "Buddy said to have a little fun with you. What we've got for you, Special Agent Tall Wolf, is a suite at the cost of a room, with an appropriate discount for a government employee." She leaned forward and whispered. "It's one of our nicest suites, too. Buddy didn't say why you're visiting New Orleans, but with your being from the Bureau of Indian Affairs, it's not hard to guess. We hope you get those sonsa — son of a guns soon."

"I'll do my best," John promised.

The young woman beckoned and a bellman joined them.

"I see you have only the one small bag," she said, "but Antoine will show you around your suite and explain how the hotel might serve you."

"Thank you," John said.

The desk clerk handed him a message slip. "Captain Edmee LaBelle of the NOPD called. Her number is right there. She said you can call her at your convenience."

"I'll do that."

Before John called Captain LaBelle or anyone else, he decided to take Rebecca Bramley's advice of a day earlier. He'd lie down and take a nap. Wake up refreshed and … just the thought of indulging in a bit of rest inspired an idea. If no one else had already thought of it, he'd ask the NOPD to send a sketch artist to the Thibodeaux State Bank. Not that he thought the employees there would be able to provide meaningful likenesses of the robbers' faces.

Eyewitnesses who found themselves in stressful situations were notoriously unreliable. Any number of psychological studies had shown that. If someone stuck a gun in your face, the gun was what you remembered, even if it was never fired. In this case, though, there were unusual elements. The report Nelda Freeland had given him said the robbers had worn war paint, had long hair and some of them wore eagle feathers.

John thought about that. Would he know an eagle feather from that of a hawk? He doubted it. You might even sneak a turkey vulture feather past him. He'd just say a bird feather.

Ask if anyone at the bank could describe the pattern of the paint worn by any of the robbers. Ask how the feathers were placed in the hair of those who wore them. Maybe, if the robbers were accurate in their presentations, the sketches could lead to a specific tribe.

If that was the case, he'd turn the information over to a BIA agent who did work reservations. He made a note to himself to follow up on the idea. He set his smart phone to wake him up in an hour and lay down. Terrific bed and linens. He'd have to thank Buddy Brunelle.

Drifting off to sleep, another idea presented itself.

It'd be cool to hear Rebecca sing in a New Orleans club.

Galatoire's Restaurant

John walked down Bourbon Street, taking in his surroundings, processing what he saw: the narrow blacktopped street, the sidewalk of red paving stones set in a herringbone pattern, the wrought iron balconies, not all that far above his head, that overhung the people passing below. The French Quarter, his second cab driver had told him, was also known as Vieux Carré and was the oldest part of the city. The conjoined architecture of the buildings and hodgepodge nature of the businesses in them predated any idea of zoning codes. The meager width of the thoroughfare never anticipated the arrival of Cadillac Escalades. In short, there was a real feeling of age to the place.

After waking from his nap, John had called Captain LaBelle, introduced himself, gave her an encapsulated version of his visit to the Thibodeaux State Bank and ended with his suggestion that she send a sketch artist to the bank to work within the parameters he outlined.

Edmee LaBelle responded with a smoky contralto laugh.

"That's pretty good, Special Agent Tall Wolf. Draw the bad guys' make-up, hairstyles and the way they wear their feathers. Never heard that one in twenty-three years of being a cop."

"Always good to learn something new, Captain."

"Just what I tell my granddaughter. You like steak?"

"I've been known to partake."

She laughed again. "You talk so pretty. I like your name, too. Tall Wolf. You live up to it?"

"I'll introduce myself, Captain, and let you decide."

She said she'd get them a table at Galatoire's. They could arm-wrestle for who would pick up the check. John walked into the restaurant and was shown to the table where Captain LaBelle waited for him.

She stood and tilted her head back to look up at him.

"My, my. Truth in advertising."

John shook her hand and said, "I'll concede the wrestling match and pick up the tab."

They'd no sooner taken their seats than a gray-haired waiter in a tuxedo came by and smiled at Captain LaBelle, "A pleasure to see you again, Captain."

"You, too, Ciro."

"Are you and the gentleman ready to order, Ma'am: drinks, dinner and your check?"

Captain LaBelle told John, "Ciro knows sometimes cops have to skeedaddle. So I just tell him what I'd like and give him my credit card."

John did the honors, using a personal Visa account. He suspected dinner for two at Galatoires would exceed his per diem.

Ciro took it with a warm smile.

Then he turned to Captain LaBelle and asked, "The usual, ma'am?"

She nodded and let John in on what he'd be buying her. "A grilled vegetable platter, a petite filet mignon and a glass of old vine red. We can share the vegetable platter, if you like."

John agreed and asked Ciro, "You have a New York strip steak?"

"Yes, sir. How would like that cooked?"

"Medium."

"And to drink?"

"Mineral water, please. Sparkling, if you have it."

"We do. Dessert?"

"No, thank you."

He told the captain. "Your drinks will be right out. Dinner will follow shortly."

After Ciro departed, John said, "They must think highly of the police here or you tip very well."

"They think highly of me, and I do tip well. So will you. You could quibble when you see the bill, but you'd lose the staff's good-will and I'd have to make up the difference."

"Won't be a problem," John said.

Captain LaBelle smiled, as if he'd just passed a test.

Ciro was back quickly with their drinks, and departed without comment.

Captain LaBelle raised her glass. "Here's to showing the bad guys not to mess with us."

"Now or ever," John added. They touched glasses and drank.

The captain said, "I talked to one of the guys I know at Simon Boulevard."

"That the local FBI office?"

"Yeah. He said he thinks whoever the hacker was, the one working with the bank robbers, he isn't real hot stuff. If he was, my friend said, he wouldn't have needed anybody to actually go into the bank. He'd just have stolen credit card numbers, the way sophisticated hackers do. Then a bunch of working stiffs would hit ATMs around the world, like happened last spring."

By nature, John liked to work as closely as he could with local cops. They were more cooperative that way. It was also a way of building bridges for future assistance.

With the vice president of the United States, the FBI and all the spook shops in Washington involved in this case, though, John felt he had to be a bit more reticent.

He said, "Maybe money isn't the sole objective."

He'd been thinking about that since the briefing in Washington. The people in government were worried most about cyberwarfare, and he could understand that. But why use Native Americans as front men? He didn't have a handle on that yet.

Captain LaBelle said, "You think there's something, what, political going on? Like back in my daddy's days as a cop when people robbed banks to pretend they were starting a revolution?"

"Could be," John said.

Dinner arrived. Served with efficiency and a simple inquiry if anything else was desired.

Nothing was. Each of them sampled their entree and pronounced it wonderful.

Captain LaBelle understood that she wouldn't be getting a lot of information from John. Not that he was holding out on her just because he was a fed. She didn't get that feeling. She saw that he'd used a personal credit card. Dinner was on him not Washington. He hadn't flinched at the idea of giving Ciro a big tip either. Just took it in stride. No fuss at all.

That being the case, she'd give him all the help she could.

Not asking for anything back right now.

Maybe later when everything was all wrapped up she'd ask what was going on.

"The witness interviews," she said, "they all pretty much said the robbers were big dudes. Maybe not as tall as you, but fairly muscled up. Weight room guys. Maybe even a steroid muncher or two."

John said, "The way I heard it, they got in and out fast. So they moved pretty well, too."

"Must've known just where to go, too. Two of my officers have already stopped by Harold Murtree's apartment. He wasn't home. A guard, though, would surely know the bank's security procedures."

"The days and times when the tellers are cash heavy, too," John said. "Both of which would be helpful to robbers. I wonder if Murtree ever spoke of having Native American blood?"

Captain LaBelle grinned.

"What?" John asked. "You know something?"

"Not about this Murtree character. You just got me thinking about blood. Used to be down here, one *drop* of African blood made you black. Not that we didn't refine things with our quadroons, quintroons and octoroons. I never did the arithmetic to figure out who I am. But I remember reading about folks in Oklahoma who claim to be Cherokee because they have one sixty-fourth Indian blood."

John smiled. "It's funny how political power or a claim on casino profits can motivate people. But blood's just one measure to determine who might be a Native American. Some tribes require a level of fluency in native languages or time in residency on tribal lands. A few even require passing their own special civics test."

Captain LaBelle said, "My guess is we'll catch up with Mr. Murtree soon. When we do, we'll ask him who his grandma and grandpa were and where they lived."

John nodded. "Tomorrow, I'd like to speak with Marcellus Darcy, the postal inspector, and Louis Mercer, the young man who left the bank on the robbers' heels."

"I'm sure the NOPD can help you with that, Special Agent."

The two of them finished their dinners.

Captain LaBelle beckoned for the check. It came and John signed for the meal without a second glance. He held the captain's chair for her as she rose.

"What about you, Special Agent?" she asked. "How do you think of yourself?"

John said, "My mother is brown, my father is white and I'm red. I consider myself all-American."

The captain laughed. "Yeah, me, too."

She drove him back to his hotel.

Told him he could call her Edmee.

— CHAPTER 7 —

Rampart Street, New Orleans, Wednesday, August 21st

Marcellus Darcy, John saw, was maybe a couple of inches shorter than he was and broader at the shoulders by an equal measure. He shook John's hand with a smile and just enough strength to hint at how much more he had in reserve. Darcy's manner was polite, but John could see the question in his eyes. He'd encountered it often enough.

"You've never worked with someone from the BIA before, right?"

"Never have."

"I'm pretty much like any other fed, but I've been told I play better with others than some."

Darcy laughed. "I like that, playing well with others. You ever have any trouble with someone stealing your mail?"

"Never have."

"Ever beat up your mail carrier?"

"She's a sweet lady, a grandmother, I believe. I tip her at Christmas."

"So you've never had occasion to meet a postal inspector."

"No."

"So how come you're working a bank robbery? That's the FBI's job."

"The vice president asked for me," John said.

Darcy's eyebrows rose. "That pretty lady in Washington? Works with the president?"

John nodded. "That's her. So what's your background?"

"I served twenty years in the navy. Worked shore patrol for fifteen of them. Cooled out swabbies and jarheads who got too rambunctious on leave. Along the way, I picked up a degree in criminal justice. When I got discharged, I decided I was young enough to earn a second pension. Signed on with the postal service and here I am."

John nodded and asked, "So what was your first instinct when you saw those guys ride past on their motorcycles? You were standing right about here, weren't you?"

"Just out in the street a bit. Traffic wasn't going anywhere and I'd just broken up a fight. Force of habit, I guess. Those guys on the bikes? What I'd have liked to do was give 'em a taste of my old baton and clap 'em in the brig."

John found that to be reasonable, if only because they'd ridden their bikes on the sidewalk.

"You get an impression these guys were big, muscular even?"

Darcy thought about that. "They rode past pretty damn fast … but, yeah, thinking about it, I guess they were. Sort of a mix between you and me."

"What I heard," John said, "they were wearing helmets that covered their faces. So you couldn't have gotten any kind of look at their features."

"No, but I did see they all rode the same kind of bikes."

That was interesting, John thought. "Harleys?"

"Unh-uh. Was these black bikes. Looked expensive. Saddle bags and all, where they must've stuck the cash from the robbery."

"Did you see any kind of make or model insignia?" John asked.

"There was this design on each of their gas tanks. Found it real interesting after I heard about them being Indians. What the design was, it was a profile of an Indian's face. Wearing a full headdress of feathers. Like he was a chief, you know."

John had never owned a motorcycle, but growing up in Santa

Fe, he'd known plenty of guys who had a bike. Harleys were the favorites, but a lot of guys liked the superfast Japanese models. Then there were the riders who wanted something different. They rode Triumphs from England or BMWs from Germany — and for those who wanted an American ride with a difference, there were *Indian* motorcycles.

That would certainly be in keeping with the robbers' motif at the bank.

"You think you'd recognize the model of the bike if you saw a picture of it?" John asked.

"Sure," Darcy said.

John handed him his business card. "Let's stay in touch."

Darcy gave his card to John. "Glad to help. Tell the vice president I said hello."

John had just gotten in his rental car when his phone rang.

Edmee LaBelle was calling. "Thought you'd like to know. Somebody just put photos of your bank robbing Indians up on the Internet. You know, while they were busy grabbing the cash."

Easy Money Motel, Las Vegas, Nevada

Corey Price sat bolt upright in bed, still more asleep than awake, when someone began banging on his door. By reflex, his hand darted under his pillow for his gun, and his heart turned cold when it came out empty. Then he realized he wasn't at home. Whoever the hell it was at the door — and the bastard started banging again — it wasn't his ex-wife or a bill collector.

"What the fuck!" he yelled.

Loud enough to stop the banging and draw a laugh.

A raspy, old voice shouted back at him, "Skipper wants everyone at breakfast. Thirty minutes."

"Yeah, shit. You couldn't have used the phone?"

"My way's more fun." Another rusty-hinged laugh followed, and footsteps trailed off down the hallway.

"Crazy old bastard," Price muttered.

He put his head back on the pillow, and as if to mock him his cell phone sounded.

Not a call but a text. From his literary agent. The goddamn publisher in New York was offering only a five thousand dollar advance for his book. The agent said he was going to try for ten grand. Big damn whoop.

Price got out of bed and headed for the shower. Cheap little fiberglass stall barely big enough to hold him. Water dribbled out of the shower head like the plumbing had an enlarged prostate choking off the flow. Like the sonofabitch who'd just woken him up.

The water cut out entirely just when he had a headful of shampoo lather.

Price stepped out of the shower, fearing he might have to use the toilet tank to rinse.

But the water came back on, and full blast, too. He jumped back into the stall, and the water went ice cold and then scalding hot. He leaped out again. This time the bath mat shot across the room with him on it. He banged his right knee into the doorframe.

Christ, an injury was the last thing he could afford now.

Careful not to aggravate his back, he bent over and rubbed his knee.

It didn't seem too bad. Reassured on that point, his mind turned back to the parameters of his proposed book deal. Say his agent could get him ten grand up front. He'd take his fifteen percent off the top and the tax man would be right behind him. Price would be lucky if he saw six thousand dollars.

And wouldn't that go far?

He could maybe pay off the smallest of his credit card balances.

For just a moment, after first hearing from his agent, he'd thought maybe he wouldn't have to pull another job. Hell, he'd thought there'd be some *real* money involved. And enough public notice that he might land some kind of TV gig. Maybe back in his hometown. Make a couple hundred grand a year and live a decent life if not a flashy one.

He should have known better.

He had fifteen minutes to shave, get dressed and be on time for breakfast.

Runny scrambled eggs and microwaved waffles.

The prospect of which made him hope the next job would be a Carlton Fisk.

When Fisk was with the White Sox. Number 72.

J. Edgar Hoover Building, Washington, DC

Nelda Freeland walked into the conference room at FBI headquarters wondering how she might play Deputy Director Byron DeWitt. A blonde haired white guy, DeWitt should have been easy pickings. Ken and Barbie stereotypes aside, Nelda had found that the whiter the man, the ones who'd gone to college anyway, the more likely he was to be attracted to *exotic* women.

His type might be African American, Asian, Polynesian or … Native American.

Truth was, Nelda was just about any straight man's type.

The very image of what her aunt, Marlene Flower Moon, had looked like twenty years ago, she could have made her living posing for the covers of fashion magazines. Called herself Nelda Stone Fox. Which was a bit of a dated expression but had a nice Native American ring to it.

The only man she'd met since reaching puberty who showed no interest in her was that damn John Tall Wolf. She supposed that was understandable, if he thought she was Coyote, just as he also suspected Aunt Marlene of being the Trickster. If a man thought a supernatural being who could assume any guise it wished was pursuing you, and had tried to eat you when you were a baby, you'd have to be careful.

Still, a niggling doubt persisted in a corner of Nelda's mind.

Maybe Tall Wolf wouldn't find her attractive in any case.

That uncertainty put her off her game when it came to approaching Byron DeWitt. The file she'd read on the deputy director said he was more than just a handsome face. He was smart, subtle and behind his all-American façade, he might even be more than a little Chinese.

He spoke Mandarin. He'd been tutored by a mentor who'd fled China after the Tiananmen Square Massacre and he had a Warhol serigraph of Chairman Mao hanging on a wall in his office. Maybe Aunt Marlene would know how to win over such a man but —

Nelda needn't have worried. DeWitt wasn't in the room when she entered. Only one other person was present, a young man reading a file. He looked up when he heard her enter the room. He was considerably younger than the deputy director, pink cheeked and bright eyed. She could imagine him having received his Ivy League diploma only a few months earlier, and a commendation for finishing at the top of his training class at Quantico maybe last week. All of which would have made him eight or so years younger than her.

Not that she felt the least bit old.

Far from it. A woman in her prime, several jumps ahead of the young man in the bureaucratic hierarchy, she would manipulate him with ease.

He came to his feet and said, "Special Agent Christopher Panopoulos. May I help you, ma'am?"

"Acting Director Nelda Freeland, Office of Justice Services, Bureau of Indian Affairs."

She was sure that such a smart and attentive fellow had captured every word of her introduction, but it would be the first two that mattered most to him: acting director. The top of her particular pyramid. Not necessarily someone who could order him around but a woman whose position demanded respect.

"A pleasure, ma'am," He extended his hand.

She took it and let him feel how warm and smooth her skin was.

He was almost reluctant to let go, but he did so and told her, "I'm sorry, ma'am, but I don't have any news this morning from Special Agent Tall Wolf."

Nelda hadn't been expecting any from that maverick bastard.

Her brief from Aunt Marlene was to keep an overview of this case.

Forward anything to her that might prove useful in the future.

She asked the young FBI man, "How are we doing with the other possibilities? Organized crime and domestic terrorism?"

Panopoulos hesitated for just a second. Then he reseated himself and returned his gaze to the file he'd been reading. "We're looking at several possibilities in both areas."

He started to elaborate as Nelda looked on over his shoulder.

She read the file along with him and listened closely to his interpretation of the facts.

Still, she had to smile to herself when she put a hand lightly on his shoulder and felt a shiver run through him. There was no question in her mind that she'd found her source for staying plugged into the whole domestic side of the investigation. And if the spook shops working abroad shared what they learned with the FBI, she'd have that, too.

The only wild card might be that damn Tall Wolf.

— CHAPTER 8 —

715 S. Broad Street, New Orleans, LA

The GPS map in John's car showed him that police headquarters was not far from the New Orleans country club. He wondered if there was any significance to that. No honest cop could ever afford the initiation fee and the annual dues at such a place. Even the cost of a round of golf would strain a middle class family budget.

Maybe the idea was simply to have the cops close by.

In case someone started an Occupy Pontchartrain Boulevard movement.

Or, more likely, to assist in cases of overly slow play.

"Officers, those sonsabitches in the foursome ahead of us are taking a half-hour to complete a hole, and they won't let us play through. Arrest their asses."

What with the country's growing income inequality, maybe such discord would reach previously peaceful precincts. The super-rich would no longer tolerate being inconvenienced by mere millionaires. If somebody insisted on five-putting every green, have the cops haul him off and lock him away.

His brief mental foray into social satire amused John.

He'd never hit a golf ball in his life.

He'd worry about the country club set when caddies started packing MP-5Ks.

He presented his credentials to the female security officer at the entrance to police headquarters and said Captain LaBelle was expecting him. The officer studied the BIA identification, gave John a good long look and appeared intrigued by what she saw. She told him how to get to the captain's office and added, "She doesn't give you what you need, stop back here. I'll see what I can do."

A gesture of southern hospitality, nothing more, John was sure. "Thank you."

He found his way to Captain LaBelle's office. She was writing the old fashioned way, pen and paper. At a glance it seemed like more of personal task that a professional obligation. John didn't look too closely. Respecting people's privacy was another way to build a good relationship.

Edmee LaBelle looked up and said, "Didn't take you long to get here. You've been to New Orleans before?"

"First time," John said. "GPS."

"Oh, yeah. I forgot about that. Never use it myself."

"May I see what you've found?" he asked.

She hit the space bar on the keyboard of her computer and and swiveled the monitor so he'd be able to see it from the visitor's chair alongside her desk. John took the seat. He looked at a man's painted face. The shot was full color, well framed and had good resolution.

"Your people find out who posted this online, Edmee?" John asked.

"It's a new domain name: WarParty.com. The owner is soliciting bids from media outlets. Claims the stills were taken from a video he shot of the robbery with his cell phone. So this war party thing, is that an Indian term?"

Edmee hadn't answered his question but John kept things friendly.

He said, "War parties were also known as raiding parties. The raiders might be the warriors of one Native American village or several working together toward a common goal. They'd scout an enemy settlement or military position at night and then attack just before dawn."

"Huh," Edmee said. "I picture something like that, it comes out like a movie."

John had the same feeling the first time he'd heard of war parties. Working for the BIA, though, and trying to stay a step ahead of Marlene Flower Moon, he'd done his homework. Over the years, he'd completed an informal survey course in Native American studies.

Edmee said, "So these people in the war parties, the old-time ones I mean, they were serious about their work?"

"Entirely. Intertribal rifts were resolved, alliances were formed, pre-raid feasts were held, war songs and dances were performed. In short, the troops were rallied for war."

"So you think it's possible these guys who hit the Thibodeaux State Bank might have cut loose with their automatic weapons?"

John hadn't thought of that before now, but he nodded.

"Yes. If they felt threatened or trapped, I think they would."

"Good thing for all us cops to keep in mind," Edmee said.

More details from his reading came to John's mind. "There were times when war parties went out to avenge slain members of a tribe. On other occasions, the purpose was to gain personal war honors."

"How about to make off with something the other guy has?" Edmee asked.

"That, too," John said, "including women and children who'd be adopted into the tribe."

"But not the menfolk?" Edmee asked.

John shook his head. "The fortunate ones were killed in the fighting. Some tribes, like the Iroquois, took male captives but only so they could torture them."

"Damn," Edmee said. "Let's hope these new boys don't get up to that."

"You mind telling me who posted the pictures of our bank robbers?" John asked.

"Be happy to, but why don't you look at the rest of the pictures first?"

John nodded. The photographer, working covertly with only a cell phone, had done a great job. He'd gotten all six Indians who'd come into the bank, both head shots and full length images. He'd tried to shoot the two who remained outside guarding the motor-cycles, too, but the sunlight on the bank door washed out their likenesses.

Finishing the photo gallery, John said, "All this was done by the guy who ran out of the bank right after the robbers did, right?"

Edmee said, "That's our thought. He couldn't wait to get home and see what he had. Now he's trying to sell his pictures."

"License them, if he's smart," John said.

"He just might be. We got his name from his Internet service provider. He's a teaching assistant at Tulane."

"And his name is?"

"Louis Mercer," Edmee said.

Bingo, John thought.

Louis Mercer was the name Marguerite Timkins, the loan officer at the bank, had given to John. Maybe she was supposed to keep her head down and not see Louis run out the door. Most of the people in the bank had probably stayed turtled up. Not calling the least bit of attention to themselves.

Even if the end had been near, they wouldn't have wanted to see it coming.

John felt talking with Louis would be a fine idea. The sooner the better.

But Captain LaBelle labored under the misapprehension that John had backup he could call on. He shook his head and told her, "Sorry, there's just me."

"Well hell," Edmee said, "I knew all those damn federal cutbacks would come to no good. Can't you call the FBI or somebody?"

"I could but I'd rather not."

"I know how you feel. Problem is all my cops are tied up

right now. We've got our own budget and manpower problems."

"Be a shame to let the bank robbers get away because we couldn't muster enough troops," John told her.

Edmee sent the photos of the robbers to her printer and pulled up a duty roster on her computer. She read it top to bottom, shaking her head all the while. When she finished, she let out a sigh.

"I just can't pull anybody off what they're doing for the rest of this shift. I'll have to put in a request for overtime money, too, and, honey, that ain't easy."

An idea occurred to John and he said, "You think it was just a happy accident this Mercer guy got all those good pictures?"

"What else would it —" The light dawned for Edmee LaBelle.

And John vocalized the notion. "Maybe Louis is one of the gang. He's looking to make money off the robbery, isn't he? Think how cool that would be for the bad guys. They steal money and make their video to show the world what slick bastards they are. Plus, they make *more* money from it. Next thing, they might start selling popcorn."

"Sonofabitch," Edmee said. "The assholes ever get that smart, we're all in for a world of trouble." She took a moment to extend her thinking. "Or you're the smart one. Coming up with that idea to get me to divert my people to working for you."

"Okay," John said. "Let me ask you this, Edmee. Your patrol people have been talking to their counterparts on the state police, right? To check if any group of eight guys on black motorcycles went roaring down the interstate right after the bank got hit."

"Yeah, we did that."

"And?"

"State police didn't see anything like that."

"And your cops around town checked with their street snitches to see if they spotted those same motorcycles roaring through town?"

"We covered that, too. Didn't get anything there either."

"That suggests the bad guys might still be in town, doesn't it?" John said.

"Maybe," Edmee allowed. "You think they could be hiding at Louis Mercer's house?"

"I think it would be worth checking."

"Let me see your eyes," Edmee told John.

He lowered his Ray-Bans to the tip of his nose.

His pupils and irises were all but indistinguishable shades of dark brown.

The sclera was an unblemished white.

"I can't tell, damnit. You could be lying to me and I'd never know."

John put his sunglasses back in place and said, "I'm not lying. I don't know that I'm right. I'm just making a guess, but maybe it's a good one."

He stood up and told Edmee, "I'm going over to Louis' place."

"By yourself? It's going to take me at least an hour before I can send some cops over there."

"I'll put in a call to another federal officer."

"But not from the FBI?"

"No. The United States Postal Service."

Toulouse Street, Midcity New Orleans

John drove past the down-at-the-heels apartment building in the middle of the block. He didn't stop to take a close look. Just cruised by doing the speed limit, taking in the structure as he approached and with his peripheral vision as he went past it. Three stories high in need of maintenance and yardwork. A sign proclaiming FOR RENT was attached to the front door. The windows of the first and second floors were unadorned by curtains and shades, giving an impression the flats were not only vacant but unfurnished.

The third floor had the curtains drawn even though the morning was sunny with a breeze moderating the day's heat. For most people, the conditions were right to embrace nature not shut it out. Unless, of course, you didn't want people to see what was going on inside your walls.

John turned right at the corner of the block, made a three-point turn and parked at the curb near the intersection with Toulouse Street. He had an oblique view of the apartment building. He called Edmee LaBelle to give her his position and a description of the building. She said he'd have four plainclothes cops in two unmarked cars for company within thirty minutes.

"If you spot the bad guys," she added, "don't try going all John Wayne on them. Wait for the cavalry."

John laughed. "I'm BIA, remember. Cowboys and cavalry fought my ancestors."

"As long as you understand what I'm saying, we're good."

"Don't be a hero?"

"Right."

"I'll try to restrain myself."

"You think the robbers might be in that building?"

"It's a possibility."

"I'll get my people to step it up. Be there soon as they can."

John said goodbye. Then he put in a call to Marcellus Darcy.

— CHAPTER 9 —

White House — Washington, DC

Vice President Jean Morrissey's working office was in the West Wing, just down the hall from the Oval Office. As soon as the former governor of Minnesota had been chosen to replace Vice President Mather Wyman as the first person in the line of succession to President Patricia Darden Grant, the chattering classes began to talk of how Patti Grant, as part of her legacy, wanted to see another woman in the Oval Office.

As a reply, the president said, "I chose the best *person* I could find to succeed Vice President Wyman. Likewise, I want to see the best person succeed me."

In private, she told her husband, James J. McGill, "Damn right I want to see another woman follow me, as long as she's Jean Morrissey. The old boys network has run the country long enough."

"And not all that well of late," McGill replied. "The question I wonder about is not whether the country would elect another woman, but will the voters elect a *single* woman?"

"You're right. I might have to do something about that."

McGill made a note to himself to steer clear of helping with that chore.

In the meantime, Jean Morrissey found herself getting one important assignment after another. The vice president conferred with the president on the possible foreign cyberattack on New Orleans, but the second in command was running the show. When the time came for the party to choose a new presidential nominee, both women intended that the vice president have a record of accomplishment no one else could match.

The same strategy would apply to the general election.

With the added twist of accusing the Republicans of not having the nerve or the smarts to nominate a woman. The Democrats' fondest hope was to have a GOP female as one of the two final Republican primary candidates. When the male candidate inevitably won and showed the Republicans still had their glass ceiling firmly in place, millions of disaffected, moderately conservative women would cast their votes for Jean Morrissey.

That was the plan, anyway.

At the moment, FBI Deputy Director Byron DeWitt stopped by to bring a report to the vice president. She asked him, "News from New Orleans?"

"Yes, ma'am. I just heard from Captain LaBelle. Special Agent Tall Wolf is staking out the building where the young man who made a video recording of the bank robbery lives. He's waiting for back up from the NOPD and the U. S. Postal Service."

That last tidbit drew a broad smile from the vice president.

"The Postal Service?"

DeWitt explained the presence of Marcellus Darcy, as relayed by Captain LaBelle.

"So Tall Wolf is resourceful. I like that."

"So do I."

"The Bureau isn't annoyed I brought the BIA in?" Jean Morrissey asked.

"Director Haskins is withholding judgment; others never want to yield an inch of turf. I like it, myself."

"You're a maverick, DeWitt. You don't see yourself ever becoming director or even retiring with an FBI pension, do you?"

"Can't imagine either of those things."

"Why did you join the Bureau in the first place?"

"I thought with my background in Chinese culture and language I might be of help to our country."

The vice president nodded in agreement. "And, of course, you could always continue to do the same job as a private contractor and make a lot more money."

"When I'm not teaching or surfing," DeWitt said.

Jean Morrissey smiled again. Then she pushed her personal feelings aside.

"So, Mr. Deputy Director, do you see Chinese involvement in this case?"

"It will be carefully disguised and distanced, but yes."

"And Tall Wolf will give us a good start on finding a way to deal with it?"

"I can't think of anyone who'd have a better chance."

"Let's talk again later today. Maybe things will start breaking our way."

DeWitt got to his feet. "Yes, ma'am."

"One more thing. Will Tall Wolf be able to outmaneuver Marlene Flower Moon as well as catch the bank robbers?"

"I've taken steps on that front, ma'am."

That brought forth Jean Morrissey's warmest smile yet.

But only after DeWitt had left.

The vice president had learned of Marlene Flower Moon's presidential ambitions from White House Chief of Staff Galia Mindel.

It was never too soon to start thwarting potential rivals.

If any woman was to come out of this affair with the lion's share of the credit, it was going to be her. After yielding due deference to the president, of course. Leaving little if anything for the woman who was out in L.A. making a movie with Clay Steadman.

— CHAPTER 10 —

Toulouse Street, Midcity New Orleans

Marcellus Darcy parked his government sedan behind John Tall Wolf's rental car. He joined John in his vehicle, taking the shotgun seat. Followed John's gaze to the building given as Louis Mercer's home address.

"Glad you could make it," John said.

The NOPD cops had yet to arrive.

To be fair, Marcellus had gotten there quickly.

"You were on your rounds nearby?" John asked.

"About a mile away." The postal inspector pointed his chin at the building the two of them were watching. "First two floors look empty. Top floor has all the windows shaded. You know what that makes me think?"

John said, "If the bad guys are in there, maybe they're hiding in the basement."

Marcellus looked at John. "You're one of those guys, huh?"

"What guys?"

"The two or three who're just as smart as me."

John smiled. "You have any trouble persuading your boss to join me?"

"Only that he'd never heard of the BIA before. Had to look it up on his computer."

"And once he did?"

"I told him the bank robbers and whoever turned off all the lights for them had interfered with the orderly delivery of the U.S. mail. It's my responsibility to see it doesn't happen again."

"Perfect rationale," John said.

"Plus, I told him it'd look good for both of us if we got some of the credit for bringing these dudes in."

"Enlightened self-interest. How could he refuse?"

"He couldn't, being my brother-in-law on top of everything else."

John laughed. A moment later Captain Edmee LaBelle slipped into the car's back seat.

"NOPD has the block surrounded. Anybody tries to run, they won't get far."

John introduced Marcellus and Edmee. Then he asked the captain, "Everybody's ready if the bad guys come out shooting full auto?"

She said, "We don't overlook little things like that. I even brought body armor for you two. The biggest sizes I could find. Hope they fit."

"We'll let the pros go in first," John said. Turning to Marcellus, he added. "If that's all right with you."

"I was Shore Patrol, not a SEAL. I can wait."

Edmee LaBelle smiled. "I like a sensible man. Problem is, I can't keep my people out here for a long spell. The city doesn't have that kind of money."

John said, "Let's see if we can do this on the cheap."

He took out his cell phone and called Louis Mercer's phone number.

The NOPD SWAT team entered the building and met no resistance. They cleared the basement, first and second floors within minutes and found Louis Mercer lying face down with his hands clasped behind his head in the open doorway of his third floor apartment, as John had instructed him to do. Louis was home alone.

Once it was determined he was unarmed and no weapon more deadly than a baseball bat and a steak knife could be located in his dwelling, the SWAT commander allowed Louis to sit in an armchair. After Captain LaBelle appeared with John and Marcellus, command of the scene was turned over to her.

She sat on the love seat opposite the armchair and said, "Louis, Louis, Louis. What am I going to do with you?"

John and Marcellus stayed on their feet, flanking Edmee. Staring at Louis.

Louis Mercer wore a thick, well-barbered goatee, but looked like he could still be an undergraduate, not a teaching assistant and a Ph.D candidate. Wearing sneakers, cut-off jeans and a sleeveless Tulane sweatshirt, he dressed like a kid, too.

"I don't believe I did anything wrong," he said. "Not in terms of breaking any law."

The room was filled with bookcases. End tables and a coffee table were piled high with academic magazines and copies of the *New York Times,* the *Washington Post* and *Le Monde.* Neither of the federal cops nor the local police captain took Louis as a mope they'd be able to BS. Not for long anyway.

Which wasn't to say they couldn't put him off balance.

Edmee looked at John, silently inviting him to take the lead.

After all, he had the primary responsibility for the case. And the federal government was scarier than the NOPD. Then there was the fact that John was a very big guy who never took his sunglasses off.

He sat on the love seat next to Edmee and leaned forward.

Marcellus moved behind Louis' armchair.

Giving him one more thing to think about.

"You know any of those guys who robbed the bank, Louis?" John asked.

The teaching assistant's eyes got big. "The Indians? No way."

"You left the bank with them," John said.

"Unh-uh. I left right *after* them."

"How *soon* after them?" John asked.

Louis sat back in his chair, folded his arms and crossed his legs.

"Pretty soon, I'll admit."

"Soon enough that it doesn't look good for you," John said.

"I was scared, all right? How could I know some of them wouldn't come back and kill everyone there? I ran while I had the chance."

The flush of embarrassment on Louis' face buttressed his claim of cowardice.

Or good sense, if you wanted to be charitable.

At the moment, John didn't. He asked, "How could you be so fearful once the robbers had left, but you were brave enough to shoot a video of the robbery in progress?"

For a moment, Louis looked confounded. As if he'd never thought of that contradiction. He started to speak twice, couldn't find the words he wanted and finally spat out, "That was different."

"How?" John asked.

Louis gritted his teeth. "I'm a teacher, all right? In the Communications Department. The media and technology section. Having the opportunity to shoot a video of a bank robbery in progress, with robbers dressed up like Indians and carrying automatic weapons: That was a once in a lifetime opportunity. My first thought was, I'll put this on YouTube. It'll go way beyond viral. It'll be a global pandemic. I didn't have time to think about being scared."

"But then, being a teacher who knows something about media, you thought of something better than YouTube," John said.

Louis lowered his eyes and muttered, "I thought I could make a fortune selling limited rights."

"Television, websites, newspapers, magazines," John said. "Home and abroad."

"Yeah."

John said, "Or that could be your cover story."

Louis dropped his defensive posture and said, "What?"

Fearing he was in a bad spot now, he looked like he might jump out of the chair, until Marcellus dropped a heavy hand on one of his shoulders. Louis looked up and decided to sit back. Seek a measure of composure.

"I don't know what you mean," he said.

John told him, "What I mean is, you could be a part of the gang or at least working for them. You shoot the video at no risk, bug out right after them. Sell the video rights for whatever the market will bear. You get to keep all the glory and maybe a cut of the earnings but kick back most of the money to the robbers."

Louis' jaw dropped. Then he smiled.

"Man," he said to John, "you are one cool thinker. You were in my class, that idea would get an 'A.'" Louis laughed and said once more, "That is way cool. Only I didn't do that."

John looked at Marcellus and glanced at Edmee for their reactions.

They didn't seem to feel Louis was lying.

Playing along with that, John said, "You know what you would have done if you were really an honest guy, Louis? I mean, once you'd cashed in."

Saving himself from a lot of trouble, Louis saw right where John was going. He tried to get up once again, unsuccessfully. He looked at Marcellus and said, "Hey, man, I was just —"

"Tell us where you want to go, Louis," John said.

"My bedroom, second door down the hall. Move the bureau out from the wall. Pull the carpet up. There's a compartment cut out of the floor. You'll find what you want there."

Edmee got up and said, "I'll go look."

She came back within minutes, holding a small metal box held shut by an unsecured clasp. She sat next to John and handed it to him, saying, "I used my phone's camera to document where it was hidden."

"Open it up," Louis said. "But, hey, the money's mine."

The money was three hundred and twenty-six dollars in old bills.

Hardly the stuff of a bank heist.

"Emergency money," Louis said. "In case another big storm comes and I have to leave town in a hurry."

John said, "So if we check this against what the bank lost ..."

"Long as I get the same count back, go right ahead."

Louis was sounding cocky now.

He added, "What you really want is right in there, too."

The box held three flash drives. One of them was labeled in what looked to be Wite-Out, saying NOPD.

"See. I was planning to share with the cops all along. Once I made my commercial deals."

John looked at Edmee and Marcellus. They both shrugged.

If John had wanted to be a hardass, he could have referred Louis' situation to a U.S. attorney. An obstruction of justice charge might be considered. Concealing physical evidence of a crime, even if under no compulsion to produce such evidence, was a no-no. Punishable by up to five years in prison.

But that wasn't the way John operated.

If he thought of something he wanted to ask Louis down the road, the guy would be more likely to cooperate if he caught a break now. John made plain to Louis that this was in fact his lucky day. He would get off with just a warning.

Then John asked his final question, "You went to the bank to see about getting a loan. What was the purpose of that loan?"

Louis said, "I wanted to see if I could refinance my motorcycle."

After watching the flash drive copy of the robbery of the Thibodeaux State Bank on Louis Mercer's laptop — thus assuring themselves that Louis wasn't trying to chump them — John, Marcellus and Edmee left Louis' apartment. John also had with him a complete list of the media outlets to which Louis had sold limited licenses to present his work of daring to the public.

Louis said he was also talking to a literary agent about a possible book deal.

He allowed that work on his doctoral dissertation might get pushed back.

Stepping out onto Toulouse Street, Edmee asked John, "You'll send me a copy of that video?"

"Right away," John said. "To your personal attention."

Edmee smiled. "You aren't careful, Special Agent Tall Wolf, you'll give the federal government a good name."

Captain LaBelle told Marcellus Darcy it was a pleasure to meet him.

He said he felt the same way. The two men watched her go.

"Fine looking woman," Marcellus said.

"Absolutely."

The postal inspector looked at John and asked, "You got someone special?"

"I do."

Relieved that there was no threat of competition, Marcellus told John, "You let me know if there's anything else I can help with. Your job's a lot more interesting than mine."

John nodded and watched him go.

Then he walked across the street to handle a task that was his alone.

He got into the back of the town car with the tinted windows that hadn't been on the street when he'd entered Louis' building. He was half-expecting to see Marlene Flower Moon, but Nelda Freeland greeted him, if the bleak look she directed at him could be characterized that way. The partition between the driver and the rear seat was up.

"How did you know this was my car?" she asked him.

"It wasn't here when I went into the building. But there were still cops out here not that long ago. So the vehicle had to belong to someone who wouldn't get chased away."

"You might have just poked your nose into an FBI car."

John shook his head. "A town car for DeWitt? Unh-uh."

Nelda couldn't argue that, much as she wanted to.

"I did think it might be your auntie," John allowed.

Nelda frowned. John could see the lines she'd have on her face as an old woman.

Barring a Botox counterattack.

Nelda told him, "I've had it with your impertinence, Tall Wolf."

"You're going to resign?" he asked.

"You bastard."

"Or you could put my resignation into effect."

John had give Marlene Flower Moon his signed resignation on the day he started work at the BIA. All it needed was a date and and a shove in the direction of the appropriate paper shufflers and he was gone. That was the way he wanted it.

He wasn't going to let Coyote, or Coyote Junior, send him into a trap.

By pushing Nelda now, he'd learned that Marlene wouldn't allow her niece to fire him.

Not for the moment anyway.

"You have anything helpful to say," John asked, "or are you just snooping?"

"Get out," Nelda told him.

John made no move to leave the car. "Just snooping then. That's all right. As long as you're here, you can do something for me."

"I don't work for you," Nelda said with a note of glottal fry.

Sounded just like a low growl. She was Marlene's niece, all right.

He said, "All right. I'll go to the FBI. It'll take longer that way. And with Vice President Morrissey watching this case closely she might wonder why I needed to go outside the BIA. But, hey, you're the boss."

Nelda called John a bastard again. He didn't bother to criticize her use of repetition.

"What do you want?" Nelda asked.

"I'd thought of using a sketch artist to recreate the patterns of warpaint the bank robbers used. Then they could be checked against historical markings. Give us an idea of whether we're dealing with a particular tribe. Now that we've got actual video that should be a lot easier to do."

Nelda said, "That's not something you could do, either from personal knowledge or searching reference material?"

"I don't have the personal knowledge, and time spent doing research is time away from the investigation."

"Some Indian you are."

"Native American," John told her. "But I can tell you one thing."

"What?"

"The face-paint designs I saw? Looked kind of Hollywood to me."

— CHAPTER 11 —

French Quarter — New Orleans

John Tall Wolf spent the afternoon checking the alleys of the four square block area surrounding the Thibodeaux State Bank. He'd thought he might take the easy way out and use Google Earth's street view, but to his surprise the nearly omniscient behemoth had yet to get around to photographing the world's alleys. Or at least those in New Orleans.

That meant there was nothing else for him to do but walk. Well, he could have driven, but you missed half of what there was to see that way. If you had the windows up and the A/C on, you smelled almost nothing. Which in several instances that day would have been a blessing. Especially when he found a type of dead animal he'd never seen before.

At first, he thought it was a baby kangaroo. An animal control officer named Aggie Bing, sent his way by Edmee LaBelle, corrected his misimpression. She said, "It's a young wallaby. That's a macropod, a pouched animal, like a kangaroo. Comes from Australia, too. I'm pretty sure the Aussies don't allow their export, at least not to private owners. You may have stumbled on some illegal animal trading here, Special Agent."

"Glad I could help," John told her.

"So what's a BIA man doing in a New Orleans alley?"

"Looking for a garage where eight Indian motorcycles might

be stashed."

"The bank robbery?"

John nodded.

"You find any possibilities?"

John shook his head.

"Tell you what," the animal control officer said. "You helped me out — I hate illegal animal traders — so I'll help you. I'll round up some police cadets. We'll check all the alleys for, say, a square mile around here. Look for any more exotic critters some asshole might have dumped. While we're at it, we'll check for places those motorcycles might be hid, too. How's that?"

"That'd be great," John said.

He handed over a business card and they shook hands.

The animal control officer said, "Cool shades you've got there, Special Agent."

Renaissance Arts Hotel, New Orleans

John was just about to enter the hotel when a Mercedes pulled up to the curb opposite him. The passenger side window slid down. John's hand brushed back the hem of his suit coat and went to his duty weapon. He relaxed when he saw Deputy Director Byron DeWitt.

"Buy you dinner?" he asked.

That was a first, John thought. An FBI poobah offering him hospitality.

"Sure. Can you give me thirty minutes? I need a shower and a change of clothes."

"Meet you in the lobby," DeWitt said.

John nodded and went up to his suite. He shed the suit he'd worn that day, put on a terrycloth robe and called a bellman to take his garments to be dry-cleaned. He even sent his shoes out to be polished. That poor wallaby had left an odor that lingered.

The shower stall had a ceiling mounted immersion head. A

comfort for a tall man. John turned the water on hot. He relaxed and let his mind roam. He had been less than completely honest with Nelda Freeland.

He knew a few things about Native American war paint. The pigments used derived from colored clays, berries and flowers. Different colors had different meanings. Red stood for war, blood, strength and power. Black might mean a powerful warrior who had proven himself in battle. Yellow could indicate a warrior who was heroic and would fight to the death.

Exactly the opposite of the way the newcomers regarded the color.

There were also symbols. An open palm, fingers and thumb represented a warrior who was successful in hand-to-hand combat. A zig-zag line across the forehead symbolized lightning and implicitly a combatant who possessed the same power and speed. There were other icons peculiar to specific tribes, and there were lots of tribes.

That was why John didn't mind shifting the burden to Nelda and others who were far more in touch with Native American culture. Then again, he'd also wanted to see how far he could push the new boss. And let her know she couldn't push him at all.

He got out of the shower and, while drying off, another tidbit of Indian folkways came to mind. It was a small thing. Might be significant, though.

He dressed casually and went downstairs to meet DeWitt.

— CHAPTER 12 —

Mr. B's Bistro, New Orleans

At DeWitt's suggestion, they went to the place at the corner of Royal and Iberville. DeWitt had the barbecued shrimp; John went with the wood grilled fish. The deputy director had reserved a semi-circular booth that both afforded them privacy and let them cover the front and back doors should any villains make a surprise appearance.

John asked DeWitt, "The vice president send you?"

DeWitt laughed and shook his head. "Interesting question, but no. I just like to get out of DC and see things for myself."

"Not very managerial of you."

Unless you were Marlene Flower Moon, he thought.

She snooped on him relentlessly.

"I'm something of an outlier," DeWitt said. "You can ask James J. McGill, if you'd like to confirm that."

Didn't sound to John like the guy was just dropping a name. That made him uneasy. The vice president, the husband of the president and a deputy director of the FBI didn't usually figure into any of his cases. Not even by casual mention. There had to be a lot more at stake here than a bank robbery. The spooks had to be finding some disturbing intel, and DeWitt had to know more of what was going on than he did.

"I'll take your word for it, Mr. DeWitt. What can I do for you?"

"I thought I'd give you the early take on things. Get your opinion."

The deputy director repeated the opinion held by the local FBI office, according to what John had heard. The hackers working with the bank robbers weren't top notch. Otherwise, they'd have stolen credit card numbers off the Internet and either use them to loot ATMs or sell them to third parties.

"What do you think about that?" DeWitt asked.

John told him, "I think you've got a different opinion and you're wondering if I might feel the same way."

"I'm *not* looking for a yes man."

"No, just a kindred spirit, someone on the same wavelength."

"So?" DeWitt said.

John replied, "I don't think there's any lack of technical proficiency."

"Neither do I."

"I think the robbers went into the bank because it made them feel good."

"My thought was they felt it was their last chance to do something big," DeWitt said.

That tweaked John's thinking. "You see it as the end of something, not the beginning?"

DeWitt nodded. "For the planners, if not the guys with the guns."

John said, "So you do think the robbers are going to hit again."

"I do. Using the same idea. Tie people up in knots. Divert the cops."

John moved the conversation in another direction.

"If I get this thing worked out, will you have any problem with the BIA getting the credit?"

"No, not at all. Though I don't think you're looking for personal glory."

John smiled. "Not hardly. I'm a maverick, too. So I don't mind sharing a couple of other thoughts."

"For instance?"

"Have you seen the video of the robbery yet?"

"Yes," DeWitt said.

"Three of the robbers wore feathers in their hair, eagle feathers, I think."

"You're right about that."

"Okay, so I checked that out. Native American warriors got to wear them only *after* they'd proven themselves in battle. The feather was the equivalent of a modern military medal. Say a bronze or silver star."

DeWitt saw where John was heading. "If the feathers were legitimate, those guys in the bank would have had to do something on a par with the robbery. There'd be a record of such a crime, even if there wasn't an arrest yet."

"Right," John said. "The FBI should be able to check whether any Indians have been on the warpath anywhere in the country the past ten or twenty years. See if there's anything that might connect the past to the present."

John concluded, "If there isn't … well, you can figure out what I'm thinking."

"Some white boys with guns are playing dress up?"

"Uh-huh."

"Okay, that's one thing," DeWitt said. "What's your other thought."

"The war paint those guys wore, it looks to me like it's more informed by Game Boy culture than Native American."

DeWitt nodded. "So you're saying there are no Indians involved?"

John said, "Only the eight motorcycles."

Renaissance Arts Hotel, New Orleans

The man stepped in front of John a heartbeat after DeWitt dropped him off at the hotel. The deputy director must have caught the stranger's approach in the passenger side mirror because he stopped the Mercedes and got out with his gun drawn and aimed.

The man gaped at him. Turning to face John, he saw another gun pointed his way.

He raised his hands and with a nervous grin said, "I come in peace. I'm an Anderson School MBA."

"UCLA?" DeWitt asked.

"Yeah." Then he said the magic words. "Marlene Flower Moon sent me."

Putting away his gun, John asked, "You have a card?"

Aware that the other guy still had a bead on him, the man used only his thumb and index finger to withdraw a business card from a pocket in his suit coat. He handed it to John.

"Nahotabi Ambrose," John read.

"I'm a Choctaw," Ambrose said. "On my mom's side."

John nodded to DeWitt and said he'd be in touch.

The deputy director holstered his weapon, got back in his car and drove off.

Ambrose asked John, "Is it all right if I buy you a drink?"

Cochon, New Orleans

The restaurant was just down the street from John's hotel. The special agent and the L.A.-educated MBA had the far end of the bar to themselves. Ambrose had a glass of Piper Heidsick Brut to celebrate not being gunned down by federal agents. John went with a bottle of Perrier sparkling mineral water to keep his head clear.

Ambrose made note of John's choice of libation.

"No alcohol for you?"

"No."

"I watch it, too. Never more than one glass per day. Most days, I go without."

"What did Marlene have to say to you?" John asked.

"She asked that our people check their sources to see if any Native Americans were involved in the bank robbery here in New Orleans. We were already on it, and I told her so. She said we should get in touch with you as soon as we found out anything."

"And the results of your investigation were?" John asked.

"If there were any Native Americans involved in the robbery, it was purely coincidental. No way was the crime organized or carried out exclusively by Native Americans. There are bad guys in our communities just like any other. But organized crime or thugs carrying out thefts to finance radical agendas, that's not happening. Not in Louisiana anyway."

"No? So how are the local Choctaw people occupying themselves these days?"

"We just opened a new casino upstate this past spring. We observe all the gaming laws and run a clean operation. A friend of mine who graduated from the Northwestern University School of Law monitors compliance with all the rules and regs; I handle all our marketing efforts. We're already ahead of revenue projections. The tribe is making money and our employees earn living wages. The last thing we'd want to do is mess up a good thing."

"What about any other bands or tribes in the Southeast?" John asked.

Native Americans no longer made war on one another, but there was competition, and it was not always friendly. Just like any other ethnic group.

But Ambrose shook his head.

"Things are peaceful, Special Agent. Some people have their gripes, but nothing that rises above filing a lawsuit or two."

Nahotabi Ambrose was one slick Indian, John thought.

He called to the bartender for his own bottle of Perrier, even though he'd taken only a sip off the top of his glass of champagne.

John thought it was a good sign that Native American businesses were expanding the employment of homegrown professionals. Not that he'd ordinarily be inclined to take the word of either a lawyer or a marketing man regardless of their heritage. But what Ambrose had to say only reinforced John's idea that the bank robbers had to be make-believe Indians.

Carrying on a tradition of blame shifting that went back at

least to the Boston Tea Party.

Ambrose raised his bottle to John and said with a smile, "To honest Injuns."

John said, "And higher education."

They clinked their bottles.

Both of them pleased to point the finger of blame elsewhere.

Renaissance Arts Hotel, New Orleans

John received a text message from Nelda Freeland just before he turned off the lights for the night. It read: *No sign of robbers hiding out in any rez in Southern U.S.*

That still left a lot of country to cover, he thought.

He tried to remain positive, though.

Told Nelda: *Thanks for info. Say hi to Auntie for me.*

Sometimes he couldn't stop himself from taunting Coyote.

Of course, Coyote paid him back immediately. He no longer felt like going straight to sleep. He thought there must be something else he could do to move the investigation forward. He plugged the flash drive Louis Mercer had given him into his laptop.

He'd watched the video four times by now.

Maybe the fifth time would be … the charm.

John paused the video to look at the robber covering the customers lying on the bank floor. Like all his accomplices, he was wearing black latex gloves to avoid leaving any finger prints. He was also practicing good firearm discipline: off target, off trigger.

That meant if you didn't have a target lined up that you were going to shoot in the next breath you kept your finger off the trigger to prevent an accidental discharge.

The robber John had spotted had his finger extended above the trigger guard, and he'd cut off the index finger of his black glove. John could only guess that was for a better trigger feel. In any event, it showed that the man's finger was white. Not the copper color of his face in the areas that weren't covered by war paint.

Now, John had proof at least one of the robbers wasn't Native American.

He wished he could ask the other robbers for a show of hands.

He'd have to share his discovery with Byron DeWitt in the morning. The FBI had the technology to determine whether what he was seeing was some sort of photographic glitch that distorted color values.

But first he decided to call his mother and father.

Email them a copy of the video.

He'd thought of a way they might be able to help him, too.

After speaking with his parents, John was able to get to sleep.

— CHAPTER 13 —

Renaissance Arts Hotel
New Orleans, Thursday, August 22nd

John woke up at 6:30 a.m. and his first thought was he should have called Rebecca before he'd turned in last night. It wasn't that they'd made any promises to stay in touch on a daily basis, and she hadn't called him. Still, it would have been thoughtful.

Good to hear her voice and maybe share a laugh.

He could call now, but she was probably back in Calgary and the time there was … It took him a moment to remember the time zone. Five-thirty. Too early. She was still on vacation, unless she went back to work before her scheduled return.

Thinking of Rebecca, he remembered how he'd gone for his gun twice yesterday. The first time when Byron DeWitt had pulled alongside him in his car; the second when Nahotabi Ambrose had approached him on foot. John was usually anything but tightly wound. Then again it had been quite a while since he'd had a special woman in his life. Now, there was one and … maybe he wanted to be just a bit more careful?

He made a mental note to call Rebecca sometime that day.

He got up, stepped into the shower and reviewed the conversation he'd had with his parents. They'd looked at the video file he'd sent them. Neither his father, a doctor, nor his mother, an anthropologist, thought the white finger was the result of vitiligo.

They couldn't come up with any reasonable explanation.

Other than to say the color of the man's face was a product of makeup.

His mother told him she could compare the robbers' facial structures to Native American archetypes. She said she'd get back to John once she had the results. Dad said he'd look on over Mom's shoulder as she worked. Make sure she wasn't comparing the bad guys to Polynesians.

Mom rebuked him in a language that John didn't recognize.

But she made Dad laugh.

John thought that was cool, his parents having their little joke, probably talking dirty, right in front of the kid, not worrying that he'd ever know what had been said. Maybe he and Rebecca would have to learn Aramaic or something.

He'd said goodbye to his parents, pleased he'd also thought the robbers had used makeup on their faces.

Only now, having allowed his subconscious several hours to consider the color discrepancy, he thought maybe the gang of robbers might be really clever. Could be only one of them was a white guy, and they deliberately had him expose that trigger finger.

Then if some sharp-eyed investigator spotted the anomaly he might think *all* the robbers were white men. That would be a great diversion if the others were, in truth, Native American. If the bad guys were really diabolical they might have intentionally fudged their use of war paint and eagle feathers, too.

If all that was the case, and he was looking for the gang among the general population of the country, hiding out on a rez would be just the thing to do. Or not. Plenty of Native Americans lived off-rez. He'd bet Nahotabi Ambrose did.

John got out of the shower, dried off and got dressed.

He emailed Byron DeWitt.

Told him about the white trigger finger and his two lines of speculation.

He'd see what the FBI made of things.

Café du Monde, New Orleans

John got a table under the building's green and white striped awning before seven-thirty. The café was open twenty-four/seven, three hundred and sixty-five days a year, almost. On Christmas Day and the six hours preceding and following the Nativity, the place was closed. There had been a momentary lull when John arrived. The table he'd chosen had a buffer of open space around it.

His order of three beignets and fresh orange juice sat before him.

Louis Mercer arrived a minute after he did, not bothered by what he said was normally an early hour for him. The moment Louis sat down, he made an announcement. "A local TV is going to air my video today."

Realizing he'd made a mistake that made him want to kick himself, all John could say was, "What?"

"I gave you a list, remember?" Louis looked at his watch. "They recorded an interview with me right before I came here. It should be airing, along with the video, in a couple minutes. I was going home to watch it, but when you called, I set my DVR."

John sighed. "I thought you might have waited. Synced the television broadcast with the other media exposure you mentioned. The newspapers and the magazines."

"Nope, all at once doesn't work as a modern media strategy. For the Internet, TV and even radio, a story's value declines as it loses freshness. On the other hand, laying a foundation with 'immediate' media …" Louis made air-quotes around immediate. "That piques interest and lays the foundation for *comprehensive* media like magazines, books and films."

Louis emphasized comprehensive by inflection.

He used a hand this time to point at a beignet.

"You mind if I have one of those?"

"Go ahead," John said.

As Louis bit into the pastry with a smile, John thought he'd have to suggest to the faculty of the Federal Law Enforcement Training Center that they should add a class on the impact of modern media on the investigative process to their curriculum.

He certainly hadn't had a clue about it. He ate a beignet.

Louis told John, "I was up all night writing, but I'm still jazzed. *Wired* and *The New York Times Magazine* are bidding on my story. The *Times* has a prestige factor but *Wired* published the Iranian hostage rescue story that became the movie "Argo." You know, the one that won this year's best picture Oscar."

John had seen the film. "Yeah, that was good."

Louis swallowed the last of his beignet and was eyeing the one that remained on the plate.

John gave him a nod and he grabbed it. Scarfed it. Smiled and looked at John's orange juice. John shook his head and picked up the glass.

Louis muffled a belch with a hand and asked, "Did you ask me here to talk about media?"

"I wanted to ask you how long I had before you went public with the pictures of the bank robbers," he said. "Maybe ask you to hold off for a while. I never thought ..."

John sighed. He'd even been prepared to threaten Louis with the power of the federal government to make his life miserable. Invoke the vice president by name, if necessary. He certainly wasn't going to mention any of that now.

His words would only wind up in another news story.

Wouldn't look good at all.

Yet another thing federal cops needed to know.

"Didn't mean to mess you up, man," Louis said. "Just striking while the old iron was hot."

John couldn't find it in himself to be angry. Having Louis' images of the criminals was helpful. Might be more so, if his mother's analysis of facial structure comparisons proved to be definitive.

"Not a problem," John said.

Then he had an idea, maybe a bit of a reach, but Louis would be —

"What're you thinking?" Louis asked. "You just cocked your head, and I bet if you weren't wearing sunglasses I'd see a gleam in your eye."

John said, "You're telling the story of a bank robbery from your point of view, right?"

"Uh-huh."

"What if one of the bad guys is planning to do the same thing?"

Louis sat back in his seat, crossed his arms over his chest.

Looking as if someone were trying to steal his winning lottery ticket.

He said, "They can't do that. Crooks can't profit from their crimes."

John knew about that; Louis had it right. But maybe there was another way.

For bad guys to make good.

John said, "You're correct about *domestic law*. But the Internet is global. Maybe there's a foreign online magazine similar to *Wired*. Say one of the robbers submitted his story anonymously. Set up a way to get paid that couldn't be traced."

Louis wasn't happy to hear John's speculation.

"That would be *the* inside story of the crime, wouldn't it?" John said.

"Shit," Louis said.

Now, he appeared tired as well as disgruntled.

"Wasn't there some guy who wrote a novel about a presidential campaign without giving his name?" John asked.

"Primary Colors," Louis said. "Book cover listed the author as Anonymous. Turned out to be Joe Klein, a reporter and columnist. He was uncovered but only because he had a lot of other published writing to use as comparisons."

John said, "Hmm. Probably unlikely a bank robber is broadly published. So you couldn't catch him that way. But if he's looking to make a splash on his first try …you think you could use your media contacts to see if anyone is peddling such a story, here or abroad?"

Deep in a funk now, thinking his thunder might be stolen, Louis asked, "What good would that do me?"

John leaned forward, slid his glass of orange juice over to Louis.

"Well, if you can help me find these guys, and I can lock them up before they do any deals, you're covered. There aren't any TV or publishing opportunities inside a federal prison."

Louis brightened. His fatigue fell away. He guzzled the juice.

"Now, you're talking." He got to his feet. "Man, I'm all over this."

Louis left without saying goodbye.

John didn't seriously think the bank robbers would do a story on their own. But who knew? He'd never have thought Louis would reap a fortune from trying to refinance a motorcycle either.

He'd made the best retrieval from his mistake that he could.

In that spirit, he ordered more beignets and orange juice.

The White House, Washington DC

Vice President Jean Morrissey's video conference with the mayors of the five largest cities in the United States — New York, Los Angeles, Chicago, Houston and Philadelphia — went live at nine a.m. She could have done the conference from her office in the Eisenhower Executive Office Building, but she chose to use her White House office.

Nothing commanded attention like a message straight from 1600 Pennsylvania Avenue.

Jean Morrissey paid careful attention to how Patricia Darden Grant went about her job. You not only had to outthink the other guy, you had to look good doing it. Stagecraft was a large, indispensable part of a successful presidency.

She was coming to think that a happy, solid marriage was part of it, too. The president earned her own standing with the voters, but her position was buttressed by James J. McGill. He was a roaring success as the first presidential husband. He'd shown he could crack a joke or bust a nose with equal panache.

Finding a good man, eliminating the need to look for a date at state dinners, would be smart politics. It would be good for her, too. Her most recent boyfriend, the headmaster of a prestigious Washington school, had succumbed to the rigors of dating the vice president after the corpse of a street person, made to look like his beloved sister, had been left in the trunk of his car.

She could hardly blame him for that.

Still, it left her without a man in her life.

Finding a more stalwart replacement wouldn't be easy. For one thing, any man she chose would inevitably be compared to Jim McGill. That was just the way the popular press worked these days. She'd need to find someone who was smart, charming, handsome and tough as nails. Every girl's dream. Unfortunately, that kind of guy —

Just knocked on her door and asked, "Madam Vice President, may I come in?"

Deputy Director Byron DeWitt. He'd come to apprise her of Special Agent Tall Wolf's latest report from New Orleans. She heard and remembered every word. And never stopped thinking: What about him?

Would they make *too* cute a couple?

If that was the only drawback, she could live with it.

She could already see he was interested in at least a physical way.

The vice president decided to explore if there were other levels of compatibility.

She'd start after she got on with the video conference. She told the five mayors, "Good morning and thank you for setting aside this time for me. I'm speaking to you on the president's behalf. She wants me to inform you that our country's foreign intelligence community is working overtime to determine whether the recent bank robbery in New Orleans was a cover to test a cyberattack on America's critical infrastructure.

"Our initial reading is that a foreign power was involved in taking down New Orleans' power grid and causing all the traffic signals to show green at the same time. We also think there will be another attack. Every resource we have will be deployed to prevent such an attack from happening, but we can't be sure that we'll succeed.

"If there is another attack, our intelligence community thinks it will be directed at a larger population center. Most likely, it would come against one of your cities. So that's where we'll be deploying the most personnel and resources."

— CHAPTER 14 —

Easy Money Motel, Las Vegas, Nevada

For all its glitz and illusions of glamour, the gambling capital of the United States was only the country's thirty-first largest city. The president had former careers in modeling and acting, but on the advice of her agents, she'd avoided the neon gaming Mecca in the desert. The vice president had a far more personal reason to give the place a miss. Her late father had been a gambling addict.

After Mom finally gave up trying to rehabilitate him and filed for divorce, as Jean Morrissey was entering high school, Dad left Minnesota and moved to Las Vegas.

He somehow got a job as a card dealer. Sent his kids postcards two or three times a year. When Jean was a senior in high school, he didn't show up for his shift at work one night, and nobody ever heard from him again. His girlfriend called Mom to say he'd been murdered.

She never said why she suspected foul play, and then she disappeared, too.

The best guess was they both got title to six feet of desert outside of town.

Experts who studied foreign terrorist organizations often mentioned Las Vegas as a high probability target. If nothing else, its gaudy infidel decadence called out for a strike. But the town wasn't on the radar for either of the two women at the top of the federal government.

***

Corey Price was once again awakened by an urgent knock on his motel room door.

Having had a reason to celebrate the night before, he woke up with a hangover. He held his head in both hands and said, "Jesus Christ, what now?"

In response, a voice said, "It's me."

No further identification was needed. Tut Warren was the most imperturbable guy in the gang. He rarely spoke, but when he did his Alabama drawl was unmistakable. Price got out of bed and let him into the room.

He looked up and down the hallway, didn't see anyone else up and about yet.

He closed and locked the door behind Tut.

"What's going on?" Price asked.

Never a man to waste words, Tut just turned on the room's television. An older model, it took a moment to bring up a fuzzy picture. Tut tuned it to a channel with a news program and —

Holy shit, Price thought. There they were. Robbing the damn bank in New Orleans. It was a video clip lasting maybe twenty seconds. Showed all six of them inside the place. Then it replayed in a loop.

Price said, "How the hell —"

Tut held up a hand. "Watch."

With the loop running in a little box in the top right corner of the screen, another shot was stacked under it. The face of some guy with a beard Price had never —

"Oh, hell," he said. "I remember that guy. He was one of the people in the bank when we charged into it."

Tut nodded. On the left side of the screen were two TV news people, a man and a woman.

A name appeared under the bearded guy's chin: Louis Mercer.

"Bastard," Price said.

Under Louis' name were the words: Recorded earlier today.

Louis said, "I just happened to be in the bank. Like everyone else in the world, I always have my phone with me. So I decided to use it. I thought it might be helpful."

The loop of the robbery filled the whole screen again.

Price and Tut shook their heads.

Tut turned off the television.

Price said, "I never saw that asshole taking pictures. How could we have missed him?"

"First time robbin' a bank for all of us."

"There's always goddamn something."

"I wasn't watchin' TV this mornin', we wouldn't know about this."

"We thought we were cool when we knocked out the bank's cameras," Price said.

"Always something to fuck you up."

That pretty well summed up the life stories for the whole gang.

"So now what?" Tut asked. "We quit?"

Another thing about the gang: They were all diehards.

Price said, "I had fun in New Orleans. How about you?"

"It was better'n most a the sex I had the past five years."

"If we keep going," Price said, "it'll have to be all of us. One guy's out, we all gotta quit."

A guy left the gang, he'd be the first one the cops would flip.

Give all the rest of them up for a light sentence.

"True," Tut said.

"Talk to the others and let me know. One more thing: We do another job, we take everyone's cell phone."

Tut nodded and left.

No sooner was Price alone again than his phone rang.

Half-expecting a cop to be on the line, he said, "Yeah?"

"Didn't wake you, did I?" It was his literary agent.

"No."

"Good. Listen, I could hear it in your voice yesterday. You were disappointed by the advance you were offered for your book. So I want to give you something more hopeful to think about."

"What's that?"

"I talked to a movie producer last night. We went to dinner and I told him about your book deal. He said he liked your story. Wants to read the book. So I told the publisher about that at breakfast this morning. He said if the producer options your book, he'll double your advance."

"That's good," Price said.

"Yeah, and if a movie goes into production, we're looking at big league money."

"Christ."

"You're happy, right?" the agent asked.

"Yeah, yeah, I'm happy."

"Good. Here's the only other thing for you to think about. The producer says you have to finish your year big to help him find financing for the movie. You still have that in you?"

Price told him what he'd done last night.

The agent said, "Just what we want. That's beautiful."

"Yeah," Price said.

Now if he could only do it again. Under pressure.

— CHAPTER 15 —

Woldenberg Park, French Quarter, New Orleans

John sat on a park bench looking out at the Mississippi River. He had his laptop resting on his thighs. He expected Marcellus Darcy to join him shortly. Before the postal inspector arrived, his phone rang.

"Special Agent Tall Wolf?"

"Yes."

"This is Aggie Bing."

It took him a moment to remember the name. She was the animal control officer he'd met while looking for a garage that might have hidden eight Indian motorcycles. He asked, "You have any news for me, Officer Bing?"

"Only the second best kind, and you can call me Aggie."

"Okay, Aggie, what's second best mean?"

"Means the police cadets and me have eliminated any garage space in the French Quarter big enough to hide eight motorcycles. So at least you know where the bikes you're lookin' for aren't."

That was something, John thought. "Thank you, Aggie, that helps a little."

"Worked out better for me. We found the creeps that dumped that poor little wallaby. They had all sorts of illegal snakes, lizards and other critters. One of the snakes bit the wallaby. That's what killed it."

"You got your bad guys cold?"

Aggie laughed. "Colder than my former mother-in-law's frown. You done me a solid, Special Agent. Don't suppose you'd let a girl buy you a drink?"

"I'm still working my case."

After a moment's silence, Aggie said, "Bet you have someone special, too."

"I do."

"You got a brother?"

The question stopped John cold. He knew his biological mother had died, but it had never occurred to him to ask if she'd given birth again before she passed away. If she had —

"You still there, Special Agent?"

"I don't really know if I have a brother. I was adopted as an infant."

"Oh. Sorry. Listen, I'll just say thanks for the help. You made me look good."

"My pleasure," John said. "If you don't mind my asking, how'd your bad guys get the restricted animals into the country?"

"Cargo ship out of Indonesia. Paid people over there and over here to look the other way."

John said goodbye ... and wondered if he might have a sibling. Brother or sister. If so, where might that person live? And would he care to meet him or her?

Marcellus Darcy settled on the bench next to him. He'd brought his laptop, too.

He said, "Looking out at that river is a good way to start thinking about all sorts of stuff."

John nodded and asked, "Your boss going to let you keep helping me?"

"He says I can work with you as long as you're here in town. Says he doesn't have a travel budget."

John nodded. "Not everyone gets to work for a glamour agency like the BIA."

Marcellus grinned. "I've always thought that's something,

Indians having their own lands and their own cops."

"Would've been nicer if we got to keep Manhattan and Disney World."

Marcellus booted up his computer. He Googled the ten most popular makes of motorcycles in the USA. Found the bikes he saw the bank robbers on within minutes. Gave John the URL.

John went to the site and read aloud the information he saw there.

"Indian motorcycles. Made by Polaris Industries. Medina, Minnesota."

"They have your kind of Indians up there?" Marcellus asked.

John said, "There are Native Americans in Minnesota: Chippewa, Ojibwe and Sioux. My biological mother was Northern Apache. My biological father was maybe Navajo. I never met him."

Marcellus laughed. "Welcome to the club. Anyway, the bikes I saw had that Indian guy in the headdress on the gas tanks."

"The Chief Dark Horse model. This gang has a motif going, that's for sure. But a motorcycle that starts at $28,000? That's more than most people pay for their cars."

"Maybe they used the loot from some other jobs to pay for their bikes," Marcellus said.

John tapped his keyboard to send an email. "I'll ask the FBI to see about other banks being robbed by guys on motorcycles. Ask them to check on stolen Chief Dark Horse bikes, too."

"They'll do that for you?"

"Sure, I'm their favorite Indian. They like that I keep them in the loop."

Marcellus asked, "You won't mind if they catch these guys?"

"I focus on the work. That's what matters to me."

"You don't care about getting famous, huh? You must be rich."

"I pay my bills. Have enough left over to go my own way."

"Must be a comfort. Them motorcycles I saw looked good, but they might have had a few years on them. If they were legal rides, maybe they were bought used."

John thought about that and nodded. "Lots of people are

poorer these days than they were a few years back. Maybe the robbers bought bikes from sellers who had to readjust their life-styles. Got their fancy rides at discount prices."

Marcellus said, "I can see that."

"Let's move on to the robbers' helmets," John said.

Marcellus Googled motorcycle helmets. That search took a bit longer. Then he found what he wanted. "This is it, I think. They all had the same one, I'm pretty sure. Covered up their faces, not just their heads. Looked expensive. Had lettering on them. Couldn't read the word 'cause they were going too fast. But the *look* of it was like this."

He showed the photo to John.

He brought up the web page on his computer.

"Shoei Air-GT Wanderers. Six hundred bucks a pop. Multiply by eight robbers, add sales tax and you're talking five grand or so."

Marcellus whistled. "These boys do like to travel in style."

"Yeah," John said. "So we've got eight guys roaring along on expensive bikes wearing flashy helmets. Question is, where'd they go? Captain LaBelle told me that NOPD and the state police neither saw nor received reports of conspicuous bikers racing down any local street or interstate highway."

Marcellus laughed. "In this town, there could be ghost riders in the sky and nobody'd look twice. Or maybe they just hid out somewhere close to the bank."

John shared the information he'd received from Aggie Bing.

Then he said, "Sitting here, looking out at the Mississippi River, I wondered if they didn't get their bikes out the same way some people sneak things in, on the water. And then there's one more thing to think about."

Marcellus knew right where John was headed. "The ninth guy in the gang. I've been thinking about him."

"Yeah," John said. "The Indian who turned out the bank's lights and clogged the streets. How do we find him?"

Hard & Fast Fitness, North Las Vegas, Nevada

Corey Price sat in an ice bath in a quiet corner of the men's locker room. He'd been immersed in the frigid water, ice cubes bobbing all around him, for ten minutes. That was long enough for most hard core athletes, young guys who went in for extreme sports. Nobody was supposed to extend exposure beyond twenty minutes. Price sometimes wondered if he should try lasting twenty-one minutes just to see what happened.

Standing outside the tub, Lamar Dekker peered down at Price. "Your wienie tucked up between your lungs yet?"

"Haven't felt it since I got in," Price said.

"You might want to thaw it out and use it again someday. Maybe just to make frozen margaritas."

Price laughed. "Bad as this is," he said, "it beats pulling a hamstring. Be embarrassing to limp out of a bank I just robbed."

"Yeah, that'd be the shits, especially if you couldn't swing your leg high enough to get on your bike."

"You see the news about this Louis Mercer asshole?" Price asked.

Dekker nodded. "We should've thought about cell phones. You bend over these days, someone will show you a picture of your hemorrhoids."

"We still gonna do the next job?"

"You tell me," Dekker said.

"The guys are all up for it; so am I. What about you?"

"Yeah, me too. I'm having fun."

"No worries?"

Dekker grinned. "Other than going to jail for the rest of my life? No. You and the others, you're the guys who could get shot."

Price nodded. He'd thought about getting killed. Told himself it'd never happen.

Seemed more likely when someone else said it out loud.

Then Dekker added, "I'd miss you and the boys, something bad happened."

He showed his sincerity by offering a sad smile.

The sight of which raised a question in Price's mind. Where'd Dekker get his new movie-star set of teeth? His old ones had been gray and snaggled. The new ones must've cost plenty. But the plan was, none of the stolen money got spent until after they did their last job. Then they'd count it out and divide it up with everybody watching. Nobody would complain he'd been shorted.

Price asked, "Who fixed your teeth? Who paid the bill?"

"Found a dentist that gives credit."

Yeah, right, Price thought. He thought maybe he should jump out of the tub and hold Dekker's head under until he got a straight answer. Only, cold as all his joints were, he wouldn't be moving too fast, and right now Dekker was the only one who knew where the money from the New Orleans job was.

Wouldn't be a good idea to scare the guy off.

Price said, "You know how this cold therapy stuff works?"

"Makes you too cold to feel any other pain?"

"No, it's a combination of what they call vasoconstriction and reflexive vasodilation. Squeezes the lactic acid out of your muscles and then brings in more highly oxygenated blood."

"That was going to be my next guess," Dekker said.

Back when Dekker had first brought Price the idea of robbing banks, Price had asked Dekker how he would manage pulling off all the diversions he'd mentioned. Taking down a power grid while turning all the traffic lights green. Seemed like something you'd see in a movie.

Dekker had said, "I went back to school the past few years."

"On top of your trucking business?"

"Yeah."

"Huh."

Waiting to hit the bank in New Orleans, Price and all the other guys had to clamp down on their bladders not to pee their pants. They'd put their faith in Dekker, but only up to a point. He hadn't delivered on screwing up a whole city, they wouldn't have gone into the bank.

Sonofabitch came through, though, and it *was* just like a movie. Traffic jammed up all over the place. Crashes and fistfights everywhere. Cops couldn't get anywhere except on foot. Maybe in the air, too. But with all the chaos on the ground some guys riding motorcycles wouldn't draw any special attention.

Fact was, they hadn't been the only ones riding bikes up on the sidewalks. Inside the bank, even with that one guard trying to be a hero, everything had gone as slick as the path to hell. It'd been a real ass-tickler, being the dudes to pull off a heist like that. None of them had touched a drop to drink for a whole day before the job but they were all stoked on adrenaline for hours afterward.

Couldn't stop laughing.

Looking back on it all now, Price wondered exactly *how* Dek had pulled off his end.

What kind of school taught you how to take down a city?

Even if there was one, would Lamar Dekker be up to mastering the lessons?

Fucking guy didn't even know about vasoconstriction.

"So we're all good for the next job?" Dekker asked.

"Yeah," Price said.

"You're turning blue, man. I was you, I'd get out of there."

Price did, but he needed Dekker's help.

Still, he'd made twenty-one minutes.

Port of New Orleans

"Don't let no one drop a shipping container on you," Lieutenant Gaston Rule told John.

"You're going to let me wander around by myself?"

"While you were in the men's room, I called my chief."

He meant the chief of the Harbor Police, the department that provided security for the port.

"And?" John asked.

"And you got some juice, brother. Chief called Homeland

Security in Washington, and guess who they called."

"The vice president?"

Rule looked like John had spoiled his story. "That's right. Her chief of staff said to render all possible assistance."

John returned to his original point. "So you intend to let me roam free?"

"If you want, I'll escort you anywhere you want to go. My only other experience with federal agents, though, they like to go their own ways."

John decided he would, too. He'd just watch out for heavy lift cranes hoisting shipping containers. That and any number of motorized vehicles racing about the motorways of the port. To provide at least a token of safety, Rule lent John a hardhat.

Before John left the lieutenant's office, he asked, "Were you hit by the power blackout here?"

Rule nodded. "I was in the first Gulf War. You remember that, Operation Desert Storm? I was with the 22nd Support Command. Man, we moved everything you could think of, personnel and machinery. I thought that was the toughest job I'd ever have. But when the power went out here the other day I about soiled my drawers. Because I knew if things stayed dark long all sorts of hell was going to roll out across the whole country."

The lieutenant backed up his fears with relevant facts. The port handled the largest volume of cargo in the country. Three hundred and eighty thousand jobs, nationally, were dependent on cargo handled at the port. Goods arriving in New Orleans were shipped coast to coast by rail, trucks and barges.

Stepping out of port police headquarters, John made sure to walk only where he saw workers walking, and kept his eyes open and his ears cocked. The port was a living thing, a vast monster, twenty million square feet of cargo handling area. Over three million square feet of covered storage area. Almost two million more square feet dedicated to leisure cruises and parking areas.

Every corner of the port was filled with the workers and the machinery needed to keep it running smoothly. Inside of ten minutes, John knew he'd never be able to find the eight Indian motorcycles used in the bank robbery. They might already be at the site of another intended bank robbery or headed to the far side of the world.

It would be just as unlikely that a computer search of the cargo passing through the port would turn up the bikes. If someone in the shipping chain had been paid off and had entered the bikes as something innocuous with the equivalent weight, say tractor parts, they would never be found.

Now, he could only hope the motorcycles hadn't left New Orleans as cargo on a ship.

Underlying his personal task was the growing realization of how damaging cyberwar could be. If the Port of New Orleans could be brought to a screeching halt, so could any other port in the country. He imagined the air traffic control system could be taken down, too. And if the power grid in general was vulnerable …

Life in the United States would become pre-electric.

Modern society would be unable to cohere or even to communicate.

For a moment, John wondered if some Native American mad genius wasn't behind the robbery after all. There were those among tribal peoples who believed the white man's dominance was no more than a passing thing. Eventually, things would return to the way they'd been before the arrival of the first ships from Europe.

Native Americans would resume their traditional roles.

Reverence for the earth, water and sky would be restored.

Buffalo would return by the millions.

To be honest, given a country without electrical power on demand, John liked the chances of Native Americans better than those of any other ethnic group.

Only that scenario assumed the rest of the world would be in the same fix.

Any sizable country that was able to defend its modern infrastructure while all the others succumbed would hold dominion over the world. They would call the tune. Everyone else would dance to it.

Returning his hard hat to Lieutenant Rule, John had a new understanding of the dimensions of the case he was working.

— CHAPTER 16 —

Renaissance Arts Hotel, New Orleans

John called Deputy Director Byron DeWitt from his suite.

He asked, "How all-seeing is the NSA these days?"

"It's more like all-hearing, and I don't know. Couldn't tell you, if I did."

John told DeWitt about his conversation that morning with Marcellus Darcy about the bank robbers. "What I'd like is to have your FBI people look into any thefts of Chief Dark Horse motorcycles. That's what Marcellus saw them riding."

"We already checked on your earlier request," DeWitt said. "Guys on bikes robbing banks. There were lots of individual guys using single motorcycles. One loving couple, male and female, both drug dependent, tried to get away on the same bike. She was too stoned to hang on and fell off, scattering their take. He helped her up, after he collected as much of the cash as he could, and that's when the cops grabbed them."

"Proving flawed chivalry doesn't pay?" John asked.

"Not after pulling a bank job anyway. We have one instance of three guys robbing a bank, each trying to get away on his own bike. Might've made it, too, except a guy driving a catering truck barreled out of an alley, late for a charity luncheon, not worrying about whom or what he might hit."

"He nailed the robbers?" John asked.

"They ran into the side of his truck. Killed two of them. Third one's serving twenty years in prison and life in a wheelchair."

"And the truck driver?"

"With any other victims, he'd have been locked up, too. But he got his charge knocked down to reckless driving. Interesting thing? The luncheon was for the police benevolent league."

John laughed. "Instant karma."

The deputy director said, "You want anything else besides theft reports on Chief Dark Horse bikes? They could have bought them, you know."

"Marcellus said the same thing. If the Thibodeaux State Bank was their first job, I'd agree. If they have a history of stealing things —"

"Point taken."

"Even if they didn't steal the motorcycles, there's the question of how they came by their fancy riding helmets. Maybe they bought all of them at the same time."

"Or the helmets might have fallen off a truck," DeWitt said.

"Might have, but hijacking a truck would have been an unnecessary risk, and how could they make sure they got sizes that fit right? Buying from a fence would be taking a chance, too."

DeWitt said, "Good points."

"That's why I was wondering: Does Washington have the computing and snooping power to track down a single purchase of eight motorcycle helmets from the same manufacturer and retailer?"

"Interesting question. I don't know. Maybe if I ask politely I can find out. Of course, if hijacking didn't appeal to the robbers, maybe they bought their helmets separately from different stores and paid cash."

"I asked myself about that," John said. "If they bought them through bricks and mortar retail stores, unless they used surrogates, which would be another risk, they would be showing their faces to store security cameras. On the other hand, nothing is easier than buying online. Shop for the best price on the helmets and pay only one shipping charge. Watching their money might have been a consideration before they hit the bank."

DeWitt chuckled.

"What?" John asked.

"I like the way you think, that's all. I'll see what I can find out."

"Good."

The two feds ended the call.

With John thinking this was the second case in a row he was working well with the FBI.

He wondered what the world was coming to.

Of course, if cyberwarfare was the answer, cooperation was a good thing.

Yo Mama's Bar & Grill, French Quarter

John ate alone that evening and decided to dine within the bounds of his per diem. Just to show Marlene Flower Moon that he wasn't solely responsible for the federal budget deficit. He had a burger, the specialty of the house. His waitperson asked if he'd care to try one of the establishment's eighty-nine varieties of tequila. He went with a ginger ale.

Told the waitperson it was a religious thing.

She said, "*Cher,* New Orleans is where people come to *break* a commandment or two."

"I know." John said. He showed her his badge. "You know anyone who rides an Indian Chief Dark Horse motorcycle?"

"As a matter of fact, yeah. My ex. We fought over who'd get what, the house or the bike. He won. Headed off to L.A. Thought he would get into the movies, but five years later I ain't seen him onscreen at the cineplex. I just keep having this nightmare. That he had to sell that beautiful ride for a song because he ran through all his money. The bastard."

The waitperson's story made John think the robbers *might* have bought their motorcycles used. He said, "If you don't mind my asking, what did your ex do for a living?"

"He was a weekend sports guy for a TV channel in town, but

his real claim to fame was he used to be a second-team All-America tailback at LSU."

"Did he buy his bike new?"

"He didn't buy it at all. It was a gift from a booster. Honest booster, though. He gave the bike to my ex *after* his college football eligibility was used up. Of course, back then we all thought his pro football days would be right around the corner, but that never happened either."

"Why not?"

"Dumbass went zip lining. Line snapped. He broke both legs. Worked like hell at his rehab but he never got his old speed back."

"He didn't sue?" John asked.

"He tried. Company that put up the line went bankrupt. Tough luck, dude." The woman shook her head and said, "Damn, now I need a tequila."

John laid out the cash for a drink. Told her to keep it off his bill.

Then he added some more money for a taxi.

"Get home safe," he told her.

Mississippi Riverfront, New Orleans

The burger at Yo Mama's tasted great but it sat heavily on John's stomach. He decided to go for a walk along the riverfront. Aid his digestion and burn some calories. The night was pleasantly cool for August in the Big Easy, but John had little company on the footpaths he chose.

He didn't know the city, wasn't sure if he was walking through areas where the more knowledgeable feared to tread. Places where a tourist might get mugged. He had no illusions of immortality, but he knew he was big, fit, armed and a federal officer. He'd use his gun if the need arose. Use of his weapon, if that was what happened, would be backed up by the BIA.

The federal government had a long history of standing by its agents in the matter of "justifiable shootings." The FBI, in fact, was batting 1.000, going back as far as John knew. Other agencies did their best to keep up.

John set his own standards. He would have no qualms about protecting himself. But he would also make sure his actions were defensible to a jury more objective than other people on the same payroll he was.

Unmolested, he stopped to look out at shipping on the Big River. He saw barges headed upstream and cargo ships moving out to sea. It was another way of looking at the activity he'd seen at the Port of New Orleans. Without having the benefit of any evidence, he felt that the motorcycles used in the robbery of the Thibodeaux State Bank hadn't left town by water.

Making use of marine shipping would have involved too many other people, both on departure from one port and arrival at the next. Any criminal with a three-digit IQ — though that was far from all of them — would want to limit the number of people with knowledge of their crimes. The fools, on the other hand, boasted to their friends and sometimes perfect strangers about what they'd done.

They were the easy ones to catch.

The guys who robbed the bank hadn't shown any sign of being morons.

Catching them was going to take a sustained effort.

Still, their disappearance after the robbery continued to suggest they'd shipped their bikes out of town by some means. A new insight hit John. The helmets Marcellus Darcy had seen the robbers wear? They'd have been packed off with the motorcycles.

So would the stolen cash. The "Indian" hair styles? Wigs, extensions and feathers? Put them in the traveling kit, too. Wipe off the warpaint and makeup and …

These guys weren't fools by any means.

They could have left town by any legitimate means of travel.

No one would have paid them any special attention.

John turned his back on the river and looked at the city. The robbers might still be in town. They could be watching to see how the feds chasing them were conducting their investigation. Learning whatever they could and making their plans accordingly.

John was sure they intended to hit again.

Somewhere else probably.

Following a timetable that made sense to them.

John's phone vibrated in his pocket. He thought it might be Byron DeWitt calling. Or Nelda Freeland. Maybe Marcellus Darcy or Edmee LaBelle. Even Marlene Flower Moon.

He was wrong on all counts.

He made the connection and heard Rebecca Bramley's voice.

"So have you solved the case?" she asked.

John laughed, glad to hear her voice. "Not yet. Might be a while."

"Then I'm going back to work tomorrow. I'll bank the unused vacation day."

"That's what I'm doing with my time."

"Can you tell me where you are or is that a secret?"

"I'm in New Orleans."

"Hey, cool. I've never been there, but I always thought I'd like to go. Mardi Gras and all."

"This is my first time, and I've thought it would be a great place to see with you. What do you say the next time we can scrounge even four days off, I bring you here?"

"*Merveilleux.*" Marvelous.

Like many Canadians, Rebecca was bilingual.

John had learned French in college.

Rebecca said, "I can't wait, but once I get back to work, I won't be so needy."

"This is the first time in three days that you've called me."

"For a Mountie sergeant, that's practically hysterics."

"Well," John said, "at the risk of making you swoon, may I ask a favor?"

"What?"

"I don't have a picture of you. Will you email one to my phone?"

There was a moment of silence.

"Rebecca?"

Her voice was choked with emotion when she first tried to speak.

Clearing that impediment, she asked, "Would you like one where I'm clothed or nude?"

"Well ... to quote Randy Newman, you can leave your hat on."

Rebecca laughed. "My dress uniform hat, of course. I'll call a photographer."

"Can't wait," John said.

Renaissance Arts Hotel, New Orleans

The living room window in John's suite faced north. He looked out, pivoting his point of view to the west by the number of degrees he estimated would put his gaze in line with Calgary. The curvature of the earth and the limitations of the human eye kept him from seeing Rebecca's house, but neither his imagination nor his spirit was so constrained.

Instructed in the Lutheran faith of his father and the Catholicism of his mother, John had also learned the mystical beliefs of people around the world. That was what happened when your mom taught cultural anthropology and both of your parents believed they could travel in planes of existence beyond the physical.

John had yet to experience anything like that for himself.

But he knew of his parents' expeditions into domestic and foreign wilderness areas.

Each time they came back they were both familiar and new to him.

As if they'd seen such things as he couldn't begin to guess at.

Right now, he was attempting something that would never be proven in a laboratory. Trying to let Rebecca know his spirit was with her. That she might not always be at his side or even at the front of his mind, but she was always at the center of his heart.

With luck, he'd dwell in her heart as well.

He finally turned from the window and got back to work. He sat with his laptop in front of him and felt an impulse to review Louis Mercer's video of the bank robbery. He did his best to block the memories of what he'd seen before. He tried to see it as if it was his first time.

To a degree, he succeeded. Last time, the first things he'd noticed were the automatic weapons the robbers brandished. That was a conditioned reflex. He was a cop who carried his own firearm. The quick, accurate use of his gun might be the difference between life and death.

Now, though, the first thing that registered was how the robbers communicated.

Both with the bank customers and staff and among themselves.

The large flash cards they directed at the civilians were easy to read and used very basic English. They were unlikely to be subject to forensic linguistic analysis. They just got the job done. Even if there had been people in the bank who couldn't read English, it would have been completely natural for a foreign visitor to imitate the actions of everyone else.

No subtitles necessary.

Again, a sign of intelligent planning.

Among themselves, the robbers communicated with hand signals. No, not quite. There was only one of them who gave the signals; the others just followed his directions. They'd been well trained, and they all had the eyesight not to misinterpret any of the signs.

None of them wasted so much as a step that John could see.

The man directing the others stood near the entrance to the bank. He was just a bit taller than his accomplices. John pegged the man as nearly of a height with him. He was a bit broader and deeper in the chest than John. His forearms stretched his shirtsleeves as if they were knotted with dense muscle that been developed to generate great power.

John reversed the video and reviewed the signs the man gave

to see if he might decipher them. There *was* something familiar about them, but he couldn't pinpoint what it was. He didn't try to force it; his subconscious didn't like to be hurried.

He closed the video and checked for messages on his computer. He found an email from Deputy Director DeWitt: a further roster of bank robbers who had used motorcycles in the commission of their crimes. The list was lengthier than John had suspected. He appreciated the fact that DeWitt had been so thorough in completing the task.

His eyes were heavy with fatigue by the time he reached the last item.

A criminal named Carl Gugasian had developed a highly successful technique for robbing banks. He entered a bank five minutes before it closed. He wore a mask from a horror movie and carried a gun. He jumped the teller counter and took everything he could from the cash drawers. He exited the bank less than two minutes after he'd entered it.

He used a dirt-bike to make his getaway.

But he traveled only a short distance on the motorcycle.

Then he hid it inside a windowless van and drove off.

John sat back in his chair, thinking you'd need more than a delivery van to hold eight large motorcycles. You'd need … He looked up the weight of a Chief Dark Horse: 746 pounds. Multiply by eight and you had almost six thousand pounds, three tons. That'd take a pretty big truck. Big enough to …

John made an intuitive leap. Smart robbers like these guys wouldn't want a truck that was just big enough. They'd want extra room. So they could hide the bikes, helmets, cash and everything else behind a wall of other goods. In other words, a fifty-three foot trailer pulled by a powerful rig.

Something that would blend in with all the other long-haul brutes on the road.

He returned to reading about Carl Gugasian. Damn, the guy was an Ivy League graduate, had a master's degree in systems analysis from Penn. After each robbery, he cached his stolen loot, his guns and masks — all of which bore his fingerprints — so they wouldn't be found in his possession if his van was pulled over by the police.

He didn't worry about hiding the dirt-bike. It hadn't had any plates on it when he made his escape, but he put the tags on once the bike was tucked into the van. The title he held on the bike was legal. The thing was even insured.

All that meticulous planning didn't matter in the end. Bad luck brought Carl down. Two kids playing in the woods not only found one of his caches, they told their parents, and the grownups called the cops. Neither the kids nor their mother and father had been seduced by the prospect of easy money.

The police were waiting when Carl came to collect his bundle.

He was convicted of five bank robberies.

But only after he'd gotten away with forty-five others.

An advanced degree paid off, John thought, but it went only so far.

Which brought another half-formed thought to mind.

He was too tired to grasp it, though, or do anything but go to sleep.

Hoping to dream of Rebecca.

— CHAPTER 17 —

Tulane University, New Orleans, Friday, August 23rd

The fall semester had yet to begin, but when John called to ask Louis Mercer to join him for breakfast, Louis said they could get together, but only if John came to campus. They met at the Bruff Commons Dining Room. Louis had a black coffee and a glazed donut with sprinkles. John started his day with a bowl of whole grain cereal, a container of Greek yogurt and a glass of fresh orange juice.

Louis had kept John waiting, but only for a minute or two. That had been time enough for John to develop one of the two fragmentary ideas he'd had the night before. The story of Carl Gugasian, the Ivy League bank robber, had prompted the first notion. There might not only be a ninth Indian — the one who drove the truck with the motorcycles inside — but a tenth Indian.

A really smart guy.

A computer hacker par excellence.

Maybe someone from MIT or Caltech. Someone who'd long ago noodled the notion of turning all the traffic lights in a big city green at the same time. High-end techies loved their practical jokes. Played them on each other all the time. Coming up with something that topped your peers was a badge of honor.

And if you could walk away with bags of cash, too, why not?

Just because you were a whiz at writing code, though, didn't mean you knew how to start a business. Or — John liked this idea a lot — maybe some number crunching savant had started a business and a sly bastard had come along and stolen it right out from under him. Suckered the book smart kid but good, gotten his signature on legally binding contracts that left the guy with the bright idea with only a pittance from a digital gold mine.

Someone like that would be seriously pissed, wouldn't have any trouble rationalizing the theft of someone else's money. Then Louis arrived and they sat down to eat and talk. John wanted help with the element of the bank robbery that was still inches beyond his grasp.

How the robbers communicated with each other during the robbery.

"The bank robbers," John said, "did you notice how they moved?"

"What do you mean?"

"Did they seem to know what they were doing? Were they … efficient?"

"Yeah, seemed like …" Louis caught up with John. "They knew right where to go."

That dovetailed perfectly with John's thought about the gang having one smart cookie at the top of the pyramid. Somebody had to scout the bank, let the guys doing the heavy lifting know what the layout of the crime scene would be. That might have implied an eleventh Indian, but John didn't think so.

The more links in the chain there were, the better the chance one of them might break. Made more sense to think the smart guy had two tasks, the scouting and the hacking. Visiting the scene of the crime would also be a thrill for the mastermind, give him a greater sense of participation. Of ownership.

Louis filled John's silence, "You think the robbery was an inside job?"

"No. From what I saw, the people who work at the bank are a close-knit group. The next thing to a happy family."

The sole exception, of course, was Harold Murtree, the chicken-hearted guard who'd ditched his uniform shirt and gun, and hadn't shown up for work the next day. The NOPD hadn't been able to find him at home. Maybe it was time the FBI started looking for the guy.

"Anything else you want to know?" Louis asked.

The wait-person at Yo Mama's popped into John's head.

She'd said her ex, the one who'd been a football star, had a Chief Black Horse.

John said, "Besides being efficient, did you notice anything else about how the robbers moved?"

"How?"

"Yeah. You're a writer. Characterize the way they moved for me."

Louis peered into his memory. Something that caused him to squint.

"They moved like they work out. Strong and sure. A couple of them almost glided. The ones that jumped the teller counter had some real hops, too. That good enough for you?"

John thought of a word to sum up such movement: athletic.

"One more thing. There was a robber by the door giving hand signals to the others. I'm sure that was part of the reason they were so efficient. What did you think of that?"

Louis gave John a blank look. "Never noticed."

"You shot it. It's on your video."

"I wasn't looking at what I shot. Just pointed my phone. Trying to be real careful nobody saw what I was doing and shot me."

That was a point, John thought. But he still had a question.

"You didn't notice it when you looked at what you shot?"

Louis shook his head.

"Go back and look for it, will you? Tell me what you think."

"Okay. Is that it?"

"You find out if anyone else is trying to sell a book about the robbery?" John asked.

Louis slumped a bit in his chair, a posture of relief. "Nobody is, not that I've been able to find. I've still got people looking, though."

"All right. Just keep this in mind, if you help me crack this case, it'll add to your story's value."

"Yeah, I'll remember that," Louis said.

Decatur Street, French Quarter, New Orleans

John met Marcellus Darcy outside a small bakery. The postal inspector hadn't had his breakfast yet, so he'd bought a bag of pastries and offered John one. He took an apple turnover and thanked his new colleague. Marcellus started his daily nourishment with an eclair.

John told Marcellus the story of Carl Gugasian, the Ivy League bank robber.

"Wait a minute," Marcellus said, "the man went to one of the fanciest colleges in the country, got himself a master's degree that could have landed him a real good job, and he still went out and robbed banks?"

"Must've been what he *liked* to do," John said.

"Wonder what his mama and daddy thought about that."

"The FBI report didn't cover that."

Marcellus grinned. "That's another thing. Never heard a the feebs bein' so cozy with anyone outside their own shop."

"Must be my winning personality," John said. "That and the fact that I play nice."

John had sent off a long email to DeWitt, outlining his thinking and asking what he and his people might make of the bank robber's hand signals.

"So right now, it's your idea the robbers hid their bikes in a truck, right?" Marcellus asked.

John nodded. "I thought they might've put them on a boat at first."

"They did that, it could limit where they might hit next. Somewhere near another port city. You do think they've got more than New Orleans in mind, don't you?"

"Yeah," John said. "Problem is, I don't have any idea where. But

I don't think it'll be a long time in coming. Something like what these guys do, they'll want to grab everything they can and disappear before all us federal heroes catch up to them."

Marcellus bobbed his head. "Believe you're right about that."

"So here's what I'd like you to do while I'm probably off chasing them somewhere else."

The postal inspector listened and frowned.

He said, "I know how dumb some criminals can be, bragging to their friends how they broke the law and got away from the cops, but I don't think these guys'll be like that."

"I don't think they blurted out any public confessions," John said. "What I'm looking for is somebody in a club, bar or restaurant who remembers a party of eight large guys in a very good mood who maybe left exceptionally big tips."

Marcellus brightened. "Yeah, I can see that. Dudes who maybe went so far as to tell some sweetie bringing their drinks that they just closed a real big business deal. Laughing to themselves about their little joke."

"I could see that," John said. "If you find someone who served a party like that, maybe the place has security cameras and we can get some pictures of what these guys really look like."

Marcellus offered a fist and John bumped it with his own.

"I like the way you think, Special Agent."

"Mostly, I just try to figure out ways people can mess up their own plans."

"And we all surely do that, don't we?"

John brought up the idea that the bank robbers probably had someone scout the premises for them. "I'm going to have the local FBI office look at the bank's security videos for the preceding two weeks. If you don't mind, I'd like to have you watch them, too. See if you can spot someone trying to act casual but studying everything he can about the place."

"You think the bank will let me do that?" Marcellus asked.

"I already put a call in to Arnaud Thibodeaux, the bank president. He's good with it."

Marcellus smiled. "Sure, I'll see what I can see. I find someone who looks wrong to me, who do I call first?"

"Me," John said. "I'll pass the word. Mention your name."

"Okay."

"You spot someone, we'll see if he has any connection to the trucking business."

"Yeah, I like that. You know, I think you're gonna bag these suckers."

"Let's hope one of us does. Would it be all right if I ask you a personal favor?"

Marcellus said, "I give you a pastry, you're the next thing to family."

John smiled. "I have a friend. She'd like to visit New Orleans with me. Will you give us some recommendations? Places the tourists usually miss."

"Man, I'll give you a list long as a bull 'gator."

And Marcellus started citing examples.

NOPD Headquarters

John went to see Captain Edmee LaBelle at her office.

He told her he'd be moving on later that day.

"You're leaving our fair city so soon? Maybe you got a new lead you're following somewhere else?"

John shook his head. "Hate to say it, but for the moment, I've about run out of ideas about how to catch the bank robbers."

"Huh, I hate it when that happens to me. Gives me an uneasy feeling I'm not as smart as I like to think I am. Even worse, I'm not as smart as some damn criminal."

"Doesn't do a lot for a cop's self-regard," John admitted.

"Then again, you said you're *about* out of ideas. Means maybe you've got one or two left."

John told her about Marcellus Darcy looking at the bank's security videos to see if he could spot whoever it was that scouted the premises for the robbers.

"The local FBI office will probably be doing the same thing, but even with a push from Washington, they might find a way to procrastinate. You know, thinking they're too good to follow the lead of some BIA guy. I asked Marcellus to look into anyone he finds suspicious. See if that person has any connection to the trucking business."

It took Edmee just a moment to see the connection.

"You think those motorcycles got trucked out of town."

John told her the story of Carl Gugasian.

Edmee shook her head and gave a mirthless laugh.

"Good Lord, that's —" She brought herself up short. Looked closely at John. "Is that where you're going? Pennsylvania? To see if maybe the Thibodeaux State Bank robbers had some connection to that Gugasian fellow? That university up there?"

"I thought a trip to Philadelphia might be in order. Ask a few questions. See if one unlikely criminal had any protégés who wanted to expand on his methods. Failing that, I thought I might talk to the vice president, see if she knows any ways to track down library records of people who took out materials on Gaugasian."

Edmee's eyes got big. "You think the government can do *that*?"

John said, "I've heard there are some people on the rez back home who think the feds are tapping their smoke signals."

He had Edmee going for a moment. Then she laughed.

"You can get away saying shit like that, can't you? Being an Indian and all."

"Only when there are no Native Americans in the room."

"Listen," Edmee told him, "you tell Mr. Marcellus Darcy to bring his video over here and we'll watch it together. Maybe I'll see something he doesn't. And if the FBI drags its feet, I'll see what NOPD can do to look for a trucking connection."

Exactly what John had hoped for. Better being offered by Edmee than asked for by him.

"Thank you, Edmee. I'll do that."

John was about to say goodbye when a cop poked his head into the office.

"Boss, turn on your TV. News about the bank robbery."

Edmee took a remote control out of a desk drawer and pointed it at her office television. A picture came up quickly and the set was tuned to a news channel. A local anchorwoman was speaking above a crawl that said, *Responsibility Claimed for Bank Robbery.*

The news anchor told them, "To repeat the news that came into our studio just moments ago, a previously unknown militant Native American group has claimed responsibility for the robbery of the Thibodeaux State Bank. They said the money will be used to finance what they call the 'reclamation of our land.' The statement said more banks will be robbed, but did not specify whether those banks will be located in New Orleans or elsewhere."

John and Edmee looked at each other.

They turned back to the television in time to hear the anchorwoman say, "The group calls itself Red Nation Rising."

— CHAPTER 18 —

Las Vegas, Nevada

The city and adjacent unincorporated areas hosted one hundred and twenty-two casinos. Fifteen of the twenty-five largest hotels in the world, each of them featuring a lavish gambling emporium, called The Strip, Las Vegas Boulevard South, home. Downtown on Fremont Street, traditionally known as the place where the locals gambled, there were still more hotels and casinos.

Beyond those two wagering fantasylands were any number of other registered gaming establishments, many of them closer to mom-and-pop bars than pleasure palaces. When the cascade of alarms flooded police headquarters, reporting robbery attempts or other interruptions of the orderly separation of money from the the suckers who so eagerly brought it to town, they came from the high-end properties.

All of them.

The big casinos had their own well trained and heavily armed security forces, of course. Still, the cops were expected to haul off the miscreants to the Clark County Detention Center. In the un-likely event that a number of wily criminals, thinking they were Clooney or Pitt, managed to slip their own firearms past security, the cops, their SWAT teams and maybe even the National Guard would reinforce their private sector counterparts in large numbers.

Gambling revenue was the lifeblood of the city.

It wasn't to be trifled with, much less pillaged.

So when the blizzard of alarms lit up metropolitan police headquarters — conveniently located near The Strip — like a casino marquee, the sheriff himself became immediately involved. The metropolitan police had devised plans to deal with any imaginable assault on a casino. What had never occurred to anyone was the idea that all the major casinos in town would be ripped off simultaneously.

Metaphorically speaking, there were more fires to put out than men and women to do the job. The sheriff, wisely, got on the phone to the governor's office immediately to request that troops be mustered. Only the governor was on vacation, out of the country, that fine August day. The lieutenant governor was in Hawaii.

The head of the department of public safety was on the job and promised to send all available Highway Patrol units immediately.

To add to the confusion, and the idea of fires needing to be doused, the Clark County Fire Department experienced alarms in every district it covered. The department's chief knew immediately that someone was fucking with him. False alarms were a fact of life for any fire department. It was just one way some morons got their giggles.

The only way all the alarms could be legitimate would be if the North Koreans had napalmed the whole city.

Still, there could be real fires or other life-threatening emergencies among the false alarms. With no immediate way of separating the wheat from the chaff, the chief had to prioritize. The places that provided the most tax money to the county and kept his people employed would get the first looks. That meant The Strip and Fremont Street.

Within minutes, every piece of equipment he had was rolling toward those locations.

Sirens blaring.

Just like those of the cops.

All of them headed for the same places.

Leaving the rest of the city unprotected.

Desert Mountain National Bank, Summerlin, Nevada

The Las Vegas bank the eight Indians hit was in Summerlin, a master-planned community developed by the Howard Hughes Corporation. It lay in the northwest quadrant of Las Vegas. Compared to the town at large, it had weathered the economic crash better than most of its neighbors. Where many parts of the city had suffered from droves of people simply abandoning their homes and the state, Summerlin had the second highest population growth rate in Nevada.

Golf courses and country clubs abounded there.

So did people who could afford memberships and greens fees.

Desert Mountain National Bank on West Charleston Boulevard catered to the financial needs of a highly solvent depositor base. To keep the customers caffeinated, there was a Starbucks next door. If they needed investment advice, there was a well appointed office on the other side of the grande lattes bearing the name Rothschild Wealth Management.

If a sports fan needed financial guidance, a storefront just beyond RWM traded in rare and authentic baseball cards.

All of this conspicuous capitalism lay unguarded by the public forces of law and order when the bank's electricity went out. Once again, operating with precision timing, the gang burst into the target premises before the bank's security personnel could bar the doors. This time, though, a relatively younger guard, age fifty-four, got his hand on his sidearm and looked as if he meant to use it.

Corey Price closed the distance between himself and the would-be hero quickly, feeling a tug in his right hamstring as he went. Ignoring the small jolt of pain and telling himself that it wouldn't get worse, he slammed the butt of his MP 5K into the man's jaw.

The robbers had come prepared for such an eventuality. Tut Warren, who held the flash cards instructing the customers what to do held up one that announced a dire warning.

Next hero gets shot.

Everyone seemed to take the words of caution to heart. In moments, following further communiqués, every customer and staffer was prone on the floor. The seriousness of the situation was reinforced when a burst of automatic gunfire was heard from outside the bank. Now, people began to whimper and cry.

Price saw one of the two guys outside watching the bikes flash him an okay sign.

They'd discussed the possibility of people trying to leave one of the other adjoining commercial establishments. To prevent that, it was decided a brief hail of bullets would convince everyone to stay inside. Customers might try to make their escape through rear doors, but that was all right because they would have to flee on foot.

Patrons of the businesses and the people who worked in them all parked out front. They wouldn't get to their cars. They wouldn't be able to block the gang's getaway by using their motor vehicles. The robbers also collected the cell phones of everyone in the bank and turned them off so they couldn't be tracked.

The one eventuality for which they were unprepared was the size of their haul.

They couldn't fit all the available cash into their canvas bags.

They had to leave money on the table.

Well, in the teller drawers anyway.

Once again, they were out of the bank in less than two minutes.

Only one guy had been hurt. Nobody had been shot. Another short fusillade the robbers fired after stepping out of the bank persuaded everyone inside to keep their heads down. Customers in the other nearby businesses exercised the same precaution, but many of them were trying to call 911 on their cell phones. Nobody got through.

All the circuits were jammed.

Within fifteen minutes, all the robbers were off their motorcycles and back into their everyday clothes. The cash, the motorcycles and the Native American accoutrement were in a sixteen-wheeler on I-15 heading to Los Angeles. Lamar Dekker was driving.

Corey Price was the only member of the gang with a complaint. His leg was getting worse not better.

— CHAPTER 19 —

Louis Armstrong Int'l Airport, New Orleans

John Tall Wolf sat outside a gate waiting to board a flight to Philadelphia, home of the University of Pennsylvania, alma mater of master bank robber Carl Gugasian, when he got a call from Nelda Freeland.

He was surprised that it had been more than forty-eight hours since he'd last had any contact with her. Marlene Flower Moon liked to keep a much closer watch on him. Maybe the younger generation just wasn't as attentive as the old guard.

Or, in terms of being Coyote, maybe Nelda was only a pup.

"On my way to Pennsylvania," John said. "I've done everything I could in New Orleans."

Nelda told him, "You're coming back to Washington. On an FBI plane. The gang just robbed another bank in Las Vegas."

John took that in, thought about it.

"So how come I'm not heading there?"

"Just do as you're told."

"Do I get a meal service?"

The acting director hung up on him.

John had to interpret what that meant. He could go to Las Vegas after all? He'd received his instructions and he'd better not screw around? Nelda only wanted to see him because she was going to accept his resignation?

That last notion, if true, would mean Marlene was giving him the axe.

Using the excuse that he hadn't caught the robbers within the first few days of his investigation. That wouldn't look reasonable to an unbiased observer. Unless the FBI or one of the spook shops had dropped a net over the bad guys in Las Vegas.

No need to go there in that case.

Taking things a step farther, losing his BIA job wouldn't be all bad.

He'd have more time to spend with Rebecca. Time to think about other career opportunities. Maybe the vice president could come up something for him to do. She'd seemed to like him.

The FBI, he was sure, flew out of the general aviation section of the airport. He got directions from an airline flight crew passing through the corridor. He hadn't gone far when he got a phone call from his mother.

Serafina Wolf y Padilla told him, "Your bank-robbing Indians are Caucasian, African-American, Latino and Asian."

"All of God's children."

"Just about."

"Television news said they claim to be Native American, Red Nation Rising."

His mother laughed. "Who are you going to believe, me or Brian Williams?"

"You, every time."

"You're a good boy, John."

"Can you provide me with images of what they look like without their warpaint?"

"Check your email."

"You're the best, Mom."

"So your father also tells me. *Vaya con Dios, mijo.*"

John was about to use his phone to look at the images his mother had sent when he saw Byron DeWitt standing at the entrance to the jetway leading to the FBI plane. Waiting for him? With further news? They'd have to catch each other up on the flight to D.C.

En Route to Washington, DC

A couple of special agents out of the FBI office in New Orleans traveled with DeWitt and John, but they sat at the back of the cabin. The rushing sound of the plane's jet engines was quieter than on most commercial flights, but with the deputy director and John keeping their voices at a conversational level neither their fellow passengers nor the flight crew behind its closed cockpit door would be able to hear what they said.

John saw the aircraft for what it was, DeWitt's private ride.

That perk made it clear to him just how high up the FBI food chain the deputy director was. His status belied the impression he gave of being just a regular guy. Not that he fit the button-down collar model of the Bureau. DeWitt came off as an easy-going surfer who'd given his long blonde hair a marginal trim and had added to his persona the polish that came with an elite education.

John kept his thoughts on the matter to himself.

It was DeWitt who broached the subject of personal appearance.

"You ever wear your hair long?"

John shook his head. "That was never my thing."

"You were thoroughly assimilated into the post-'60s mainstream culture?"

Hesitating only a moment, John told DeWitt of the circumstances of his birth. Single, teenaged mother ashamed of her pregnancy. Leaving him as an infant on a sepulture to die. Coyote trying to make a meal of him. The rescue by his adoptive parents.

He didn't mention that his biological mother had tried to reclaim him after her domineering father had died. She'd wanted to bring him back to the rez to live with her. Mom and Dad had fought that in court and won. John had always had a relatively short hair cut. His dad had told him if he ever got into a fight he wouldn't want to give the other guy anything to grab.

John took that to heart.

He also wanted to make sure Mom and Dad knew he loved

them.

Never regretted for a moment that they'd adopted him.

As a boy, his haircut, much like Dad's, symbolized being an inseparable part of his family.

As a man, he still held fast to the idea.

DeWitt told John that he had a second family, too. A scholar and his family who'd fled China after the massacre at Tiananmen Square came to America and lived with the DeWitts in California. The deputy director had come to love them as an extension of his own flesh and blood. He'd acquired a working fluency in their language and some knowledge of their culture. Enough of both for the FBI to recruit him after he'd graduated from law school.

Enough to rise quickly in the Bureau's hierarchy.

Enough to get his own jet and an exemption from a regulation haircut.

It was amazing, the things people revealed to each other during air travel, John thought. Getting back to business, he told DeWitt about having Marcellus Darcy and Edmee LaBelle check the bank video to see if they could spot someone scoping the layout of the place for the robbers.

"Now, we can crosscheck to see if the gang used the same scout in Las Vegas," John said. "Assuming the bad guys haven't already been caught."

DeWitt shook his head. "They haven't. But they might have had someone inside each of the banks."

"That wasn't the feeling I got at Thibodeaux State Bank."

"It is more of a reach. Subverting people in two different banks."

John said, "It becomes a diminishing possibility with each new bank they hit."

The deputy director smiled. "Makes me wonder if someone in DC has started a pool. How many banks do these guys knock off before we catch them."

"Wouldn't want my name attached to that kind of wagering," John said.

"Me either. But I think you're right. The more people you involve in a criminal enterprise, in this case bank insiders, the greater the chance somebody screws up."

John said, "From what I've seen, these guys are cohesive and function efficiently."

"Almost like they rehearse the jobs."

"That's possible, I suppose," John said. "If their scout has a good eye for detail, a retentive memory and basic drawing skills, he could create floor plans."

DeWitt nodded. "The scout might even pace off the bank's dimensions. If the gang has a secluded hideout with a bit of room, they could do full-scale mockups."

The two of them were just spitballing. Could be they weren't even close to how the robbers worked. Still, they both liked the way they could play off each other's thinking. Because, who knew, they might have things exactly right.

And if not this time, maybe the next.

John told DeWitt about his mother's conclusion that the robbers, despite the claim to the contrary, were not Native American.

"How did she arrive at that?" DeWitt asked.

"Let's take a look."

John brought out his phone and pulled up the file his mother had emailed him. It began with Serafina explaining that two social scientists in Scotland had developed software that allowed them to *average* the features shown in the photos of thousands of people from several countries around the world, creating an archetype for each nationality.

Then Serafina had outlined, pixel by pixel, and lifted out the warpaint areas worn by each of the robbers. Next step was to do side-by-side comparisons: the faces of the robbers and those of male archetypes from around the world. The robbers' closest matches were to Caucasian, African-American, Latino and Asian individuals.

Under those generalized archetypal headings, Serafina refined the identities to specific subgroups of nationalities. At each step she measured how well the robbers' warpaint fit the features, like a mask being tailored for an individual.

Then she showed how poorly each of the warpaint patterns looked on the archetype of a Native American male.

At the conclusion of the presentation, DeWitt gave Serafina's work a round of applause.

"Brilliant," he said.

"Yeah, but knowing my mom, she's not done yet," John said.

It took just a moment for DeWitt to see what John meant.

"Your mother is going to show us what the robbers look like without their makeup?"

"Yeah, she'll get close to their true skin color."

"That's wonderful. The government has to compensate her somehow."

"She'd probably go along with that, but she won't want money."

"What then?" DeWitt asked.

"Probably license to conduct research the government might ordinarily frown upon."

The deputy director thought about that. He bobbed his head.

"Anything I can push for in good conscience."

"That's reasonable," John said. "Now how about you tell me why we're going to Washington?"

DeWitt said, "The spooks think they found a foreign connection to the robbers."

Tulane University, New Orleans

Louis Mercer sat in his cubbyhole of an office going over his teaching assignments for the coming term. The professor for whom he labored was a really decent guy. He did his own stints in the classroom, something a person with his seniority and publishing history didn't have to bother with anymore. He gave credit to his research assistants, including Louis, when it came to including names on his scholarly papers. He even threw two or three memorable parties during the course of the school year.

All in all, he was as accommodating a boss and mentor as a grad student could want.

Being a bit of a greedy prick, though, Louis wanted more. He wanted fame and fortune. In the words of the late Jim Morrison, he wanted the world and he wanted it now. His decision to risk his precious backside had brought him an unexpected measure of approbation among the faculty and administration.

Most academics experienced the world at a safe distance, their feet firmly planted in libraries and laboratories. Interaction with the larger world did occur, but most disciplines didn't require venturing near the brink of mortal risk. Those who did put their skin in the game were the ones whose books found large general audiences with the sales advanced by appearances on morning news programs.

Louis had already made his major media debut. Had been congratulated by people he was sure hadn't known his name a week ago. He'd even detected hints of envy from his peers. Being a celebrity academic was one thing; achieving the status of a famous grad student was unheard of.

Perhaps best of all, he'd learned that both sections of the class he taught had reached their maximum number of students and both had a waiting list in case someone dropped the course. More than two-thirds of the students enrolled in each class were girls. He'd had a bit of undergrad fawning from coeds in the past — he wasn't a bad-looking guy — but now he could imagine … all sorts of things.

Louis Mercer groupies. Wouldn't that be wonderful?

Then, not twenty minutes ago, his agent had called.

Told him the damn Indians had robbed another bank, this one in Las Vegas.

"Are you sure it's the same people?" Louis asked.

There was a moment of silence, then his agent said, "You know, that's a good question. But even if they're not, it's still a problem. You had a great story, being a witness to an extraordinary robbery, but now it seems like you were just the guy who saw the opening act. The real story will be told by the guy who's there for the finale."

John Tall Wolf immediately popped into Louis' mind.

That sonofabitch.

Hey, now, wait a minute, he thought. Could a working federal agent profit from doing his job? Hardly seemed fair. It'd be like double dipping.

It took barely a second for Louis to answer his own question.

Still, if the payday was big, a fed would have to be stupid to keep his job.

He'd quit and take the money while he could.

"I'm sorry about the way things worked out," the agent said, "but, hey, you did make out in a small way, didn't you? The *Wired* story, if they decide to run it, and the TV appearance."

It had never occurred to Louis that *Wired* would spike his story.

As for being on TV, he wanted that to be a regular thing.

"What if I help catch these assholes?" He said it without realizing where the idea came from.

After another pause, the agent asked, "What do you mean?"

"I mean …" It took him a moment to figure it out. "I mean, what if I come up with the information that gives the feds a way to arrest the robbers."

"How would you do that?" the agent asked.

"Well … just about every asshole in the world uses social media these days. Terrorists sure do. They have their own websites. They tweet. They use email. So why not these guys, too?"

"That would be …"

Louis thought the agent was going to say absurd.

Then the guy thought about it, saw the possibilities.

"Your tracking them down would be something I could get a bidding war going on in a heartbeat. Can you really do that?"

"I'm writing my dissertation on social media's real world effects."

"All right, no skin off my wienie. Go for it."

That was when Louis had an insight. Maybe the robbers were

old school. If they wanted to publicize their activities and ambitions, they might focus on traditional outlets for notoriety. The idea dovetailed with a question he had for the agent.

"Did you ever check, like I asked you, to see if anyone else submitted a book proposal on the bank robbery here in New Orleans?"

"It was on my calendar, but this news about the robbery in Las Vegas happened, and —"

"You didn't. Thanks a lot."

"Hey, you want to work with me or not?"

Louis said, "I want a list of every nonfiction book proposal in New York."

"Are you crazy? There are hundreds, if not thousands, of proposals all the time."

"That's okay. I know how to sift through large amounts of data to find what I want. The nugget of gold. But if you're not interested, I'll ask someone else."

"Wait a minute. Just a damn minute. You … you actually think these robbers might try to peddle their own book?"

The idea was originally John Tall Wolf's, but Louis didn't have to tell the agent that.

Besides, the fed had been thinking more a magazine story than a book.

Louis said, "Why not? These days, even assholes want their moment of fame."

The agent said, "You got that right. I'll send you every nonfiction book proposal I can find. I'll keep my fingers crossed you find that golden nugget. But if you don't … I hope you go blind."

"A pleasure doing business with you," Louis said, ending the call.

Turning his thoughts to finding some way to ingratiate himself with Tall Wolf, he remembered the big fed asking him if he'd noticed the way the robbers had communicated. Hand signals or something like that. He hadn't noticed, but he'd said he'd review the video.

He'd do that now. Hope it led to something.

— CHAPTER 20 —

Eisenhower Executive Office Building, Washington, DC

Vice President Jean Morrissey told the group assembled in her conference room, "The CIA has received word from an outside asset that the bank robberies in New Orleans and now Las Vegas have been used as covers to test our country's abilities to protect its critical infrastructure. The asset is less clear on who is behind this probe. The suspects include the Chinese, the Russians, the Iranians, other Middle Eastern factions or a Balkan crime family acting as a front for one of the aforementioned sovereign nations.

"All these possibilities are being investigated, but that raises its own concern."

DeWitt said, "Maybe the asset has been turned, if he was a real friend in the first place, and we'll be spreading our resources too thin to be successful."

Seated opposite from the FBI deputy director, John had thought the same thing.

Only he'd decided to wait to be asked for his opinion before he spoke.

As it was, DeWitt's interjection had drawn everyone's attention.

"That's exactly right, Mr. Deputy Director. Given that the Chinese are your particular area of expertise, do you think they are behind these attacks?"

"I do, Madam Vice President. The approach used in these robberies is to build a step-by-step sense of insecurity. A strange crime happens in New Orleans? Well, it's a strange place and everyone knows about its infrastructure problems. It's a local concern. But now, in another part of the country, the strange crime is repeated. Again, Las Vegas isn't your typical city, but now there's a much broader awareness among the American people that something is going badly wrong. Of more concern, if something scary can happen twice, there's no reason it can't happen a third time. Maybe in some town that looks closer to home to most Americans. If the robbers do that, people might start to panic.

"They might worry about the air traffic system being sabotaged with planes crashing in midair; they might fear that natural gas pipelines will explode; people who trade stocks and commodities might fear to make deals because the markets might be sabotaged by false buy or sell orders. Any of these things by itself could cause the economy to stall; in combination they might cause a full-blown crash.

"At the same time, the overt purpose of these cyberattacks is to facilitate bank robberies, domestic crimes, of which there were more than five thousand last year. Any foreign actor we might accuse could simply point their fingers back at us. Say that if we can't cope with our own thugs, don't blame them.

"That would be a hugely appreciated strategy in China, winning on several levels: learn how prepared or unprepared we are; deflect blame from themselves; intimidate or at least embarrass us; have a good laugh in the bargain."

"Quite chilling, Mr. Deputy Director," the vice president said, "but couldn't the Russians or others be just as devious?"

"The Russians wouldn't be as deft; the others wouldn't be as able."

John saw the vice president was impressed by DeWitt's insights.

So was he. Then, as if she was reading John's mind, Jean Morrissey looked at him and said, "It would be very helpful if we had more than a shrewd analysis to pin on the Chinese. What we need to do is catch these bank robbers and see what we can learn from them. Special Agent Tall Wolf, you've heard the claim that the robbers are part of a radical movement called Red Nation Rising?"

"Yes, ma'am."

"And what is your opinion? Are they Native Americans?"

"No, ma'am."

"Why not?"

"My mother told me so."

The laughter in the room broke the tension for a minute.

John went on to explain Serafina's facial modeling analysis.

Told the VP that the robbers were white, black, brown and yellow.

None of them was red.

"Then why the pretense?" the vice president asked.

"Goes back to the Boston Tea Party, doesn't it?" John said. "You do something that'll get you in big trouble, pretend to be an Indian."

The vice president grunted but said, "Point taken."

DeWitt jumped back in. "That particular deception, using Native Americans, might also score propaganda points. It allows our adversaries to say this country treats its original inhabitants so poorly they have to rebel against us. That argument might be used to deflect an accusation by our side against a foreign malefactor or it could be made proactively."

"A fine mess indeed," the vice president said. "Special Agent Tall Wolf, will your mother's analysis that the robbers are not Native American hold up against contradictory opinions? I hope she won't mind if we have her findings independently confirmed."

"No, ma'am, she won't mind at all. My mother's a very self-confident woman."

"Good."

DeWitt said, "But we shouldn't give away what we know until —"

The VP held up a hand and said, "Until you or Special Agent Tall Wolf catch these bastards. I trust you won't keep everyone waiting long."

She looked at both of them.

John felt a sense of pressure Marlene Flower Moon had never been able to produce.

When she turned her challenging look to DeWitt, though, John thought the vice president was asking for something more than professional results. Her challenge to him contained a personal element, too. John didn't understand that but he thought he'd have to factor it into his own work. Be careful he didn't step on anyone's toes.

Both men told the vice president, "Yes, ma'am."

— CHAPTER 21 —

EEOB, Washington, DC

Nelda Freeland, who hadn't been present in the meeting with Vice President Morrissey, buttonholed John the moment he stepped out of the conference room. She had something to say, but couldn't do so just then because Deputy Director DeWitt was right on John's heels. He nodded to Nelda and said to John, "I'll need just a moment after you're done speaking with Acting Director Freeland."

He then moved to the end of the corridor and looked out a window at the White House.

Nelda gestured John to the opposite end of the hallway and waited for incidental foot traffic to clear before she spoke.

In a heated whisper, she told John, "*I* should have been in that meeting."

He said, "From what I could see, every seat was taken."

"Then I should have been in the one you filled, damnit!"

"Can't blame me, Nelda. I wasn't the party planner."

"You call me Director Freeland, Special Agent."

"*Acting* director, remember? Deputy Director DeWitt got that right."

Nelda tried to continue her snit, but John held up a hand.

A traffic cop ordering a car to halt.

"If you'd like, I'd be happy to go back inside. Ask if the vice president might spare me a moment. Express to her your displeasure at being excluded. Is that what you want?"

Nelda ground her teeth a minute. Then she said, "I want two things from you. I want respect and I want a summary of what was said in that meeting by the end of the day."

John took a step toward Nelda and looked down at her to emphasize their difference in height. He spoke softly so as not to allow himself to be accused of bullying the woman who was his nominal superior.

"Firstly, Nelda, true respect is earned not demanded. Secondly, my agreement with your aunt is I work cases my own way. Check with her, if you don't believe me. Thirdly, if I thought I had to work with you on a regular basis, I'd resign immediately. Only, in this case, I don't think the vice president would allow me to quit or you to fire me."

Nelda took a step back, possibly to relieve the strain on her neck.

John told her, "So we're stuck with each other for a little while, but we're stuck on *my* terms. Tell Marlene to give me a call, if she wants to know what's happening."

The acting director did an impressive about face and stalked off toward the elevator bank.

DeWitt passed her without a word as he walked over to John.

The deputy director's manners were too good to comment on someone else's private conversation. He handed John his business card, "If it's not too much to ask, will you have your mother send me copies of all the images of the robbers she produces, including the ones with their natural skin tones when she has them. Also, if she could write up a summary of her analysis of who these guys really are, that would be great."

"Speed is of the essence?" John asked.

"I think that's what the vice president was hinting at."

One of the things anyway, John thought.

He was tempted to ask DeWitt if there was anything else he should know about, e.g. was there something personal going on between high government officials? But he didn't know the deputy director that well. He also wasn't sure he really wanted to know.

"I'll talk to my mother on the way to the airport," John said.

"Good. Take my car. My plane, too. That'll be the fastest way to Las Vegas."

John nodded and shook DeWitt's hand.

Enjoying the deputy director's good manners.

And the perks of having a friend in a high place.

En route to Las Vegas

Serafina Wolf y Padilla talked to her son by phone. He'd just told her he was flying west in DeWitt's Gulfstream. "I thought federal agencies jealously guarded their jurisdictions and prerogatives,".

Every FBI agent John had met that day had been the soul of graciousness.

Didn't treat the BIA guy like a poor relation.

Showed, at a minimum, they knew how to follow the boss's orders.

"It can work that way," John said. "Actually *does* happen like that far too often. But you can meet good people wherever you go."

That nugget of wisdom was one his parents had taught him early.

He could almost see his mother's smile.

John told Serafina that the deputy director had said the government would like to reward her for her assistance. "I told him you probably wouldn't ask for money. More likely official consent to do research would be her recompense."

"You think you know me that well, *mijo?*" Serafina asked.

"Only the secrets you and Dad have shared with me."

"Your father talks to you about me?"

"Did I say that? Must have been a slip of the tongue."

Serafina laughed. "We've taught you several things, but your charm is your own. I'll be happy to share my humble gleanings with your friend. Will you be busy with your investigation for very long?"

Or: When is the next time you'll be coming home?

She hadn't gotten around to asking if she'd ever become a grandmother, yet.

"The powers that be are urging me to waste no time."

"I won't pester you with any other questions then. Be well, *mijo*."

"Always, Mom."

Five minutes after talking with his mother, he called DeWitt to tell him to check his email.

The deputy director was quiet for a moment, before he laughed.

"Something funny?" John asked.

"You mother sent me the requested material, copying me on what she just sent you. Says she's still working on getting the robbers' skin tones right. She should have that before too long."

"None of that's funny," John said.

"She also asked if I know any nice girls who might be right for you. If so, please send her some pictures. She'll let me know which ones she prefers."

John groaned.

He'd told Mom about Rebecca, but not in detail.

Only that she lived and worked in Canada.

Maybe made things sound too casual.

"I think it's cute," DeWitt said with a chuckle.

John told him, "It's my mother's none-too-subtle way of telling me she wants to know about the woman who's already a big part of my life."

"Bravo, Mom."

"You don't mind, let's get back to business for a minute."

"Sure."

"I forgot to mention it before, but take another look at Louis Mercer's video of the New Orleans robbery. See if there's something familiar to you about the hand gestures the robber near the door uses to direct the guys who went into the tellers' cash drawers."

"I saw that he was giving directions, but I didn't connect it with anything else. I'll take another look."

John said thanks and goodbye.

He wanted to call Rebecca with a question, but she'd said she was going back to work today. Her job was more structured than his; you put on a uniform that was how it went. Her career also meant more to her than his did. Not that he didn't love doing investigations; he just wasn't at all interested in climbing the bureaucratic ladder.

Rebecca, on the other hand, was proud that she soon expected to be made a staff sergeant and would be earning over $100,000 per year. John had been surprised when he'd learned how well the RCMP paid. He could see how a strong woman doing an important job that paid a very good salary would become quite attached to it.

The RCMP saw things the same way. If you wanted to retire after twenty years, you could, but not at full benefits. For that, you had to put in twenty-five years. For a maximum pension, you had to do thirty-five years.

The thought of Rebecca sticking things out that long chilled John.

He was attached to the U.S. as deeply as Rebecca was to Canada.

That made it difficult to see how things could work out for the long term.

He decided to wait to call her until after working hours.

The thought had no sooner entered his mind than she called him.

"You didn't go back to work?" John asked.

"I did. That's why I'm calling. One of my constables just pulled me over to get a peek at a TV news story. A band of Indians just robbed a bank in Las Vegas. This happened after another bank robbery by Indians in New Orleans. I missed that one because I never pay attention to the news when I'm on holiday."

John could attest to that.

"My constable," Rebecca said, "asked me if I wasn't seeing a handsome fellow from the U.S. Bureau of Indian Affairs."

"Nice to know people think well of your looks," John said.

"I didn't have any trouble figuring out what you're working on. Are you in Las Vegas?"

"On my way. Have you ever been there?"

"A couple of times."

Rebecca's tone was less than enthusiastic.

"So you don't think much of the place?"

"I'd give it another try, if it was with you."

"But you say you'd like to see New Orleans?" John asked.

She perked right up. "Yes."

"We'll have to do something about that."

"Set a date when you catch your bad guys?"

"Find a time that works for both of us."

"Good." Her tone turned businesslike. "One more thing. You know I'm related to certain mildly influential muckety-mucks up here, right?"

"I believe you've mentioned that."

Rebecca was far from the first member of her family to join the RCMP.

"Well, after I heard the news about the bank robberies, I sent word upstream that I know the investigator working the case."

"Mighty sure of yourself."

"Yes, I am. Word came back and that's the official reason for this call."

"And that word is?"

"If you should need us again, the Mounties stand ready."

"Always a comforting thought," John said.

Off the phone and alone with his thoughts, John reclined his seat. He asked himself what, if anything, New Orleans and Las Vegas had in common. Other than being tourist destinations.

They were both party towns.

Providing *illicit* fun, if that was what you wanted. He asked himself if organized crime might be involved in the bank jobs. He spent several minutes poking at that idea. He didn't think the mob in any ethnic or regional permutation had a hand in the situation.

They'd be smart enough to foresee the kind of response that had been provoked.

They also liked the odds to be on their side.

In this case, the entire weight of the federal government would be landing on somebody.

He went back to his original question: What did the two towns have in common? He asked his smart phone's "personal assistant."

The reply in a synthesized female voice was: "Both are major American cities."

Looking for a more specific answer, John decided he'd ask the FBI for help.

After he woke up from a nap.

Rebecca had gotten him into the habit, taking his rest when it was convenient.

— CHAPTER 22 —

McCarran International Airport, Las Vegas, Nevada

As John Tall Wolf's flight from Washington, DC made its final approach to the airport, Corey Price, along with the other seven bank-robbing Indians and the other members of his traveling party, waited at a departure gate for the announcement that they could board their flight out of town.

Price got a two-word phone call, "Frank Thomas."

He needed a moment to work out the code. Frank Thomas. The Big Hurt. Hall of Fame player with the Chicago White Sox. Number … thirty-five. Price smiled. He and his friends had each made thirty-five thousand dollars from the Las Vegas bank job.

Better than they'd done in New Orleans by nearly fifty percent.

Put the two robberies together, they were up almost sixty grand per man.

He passed the good news along to the guys. Each of them was happy, too.

That was when Price started to feel uneasy. Guys like them weren't supposed to make out. Not big time. Certainly not tens of thousands of dollars in a matter of a few days. That kind of money was a solid year's take-home pay. If they ever got ahead of themselves, started thinking they could play better than their scouting reports, reality was bound to smack them upside the head.

Price started to feel a throb in his right hamstring. That one damn muscle had kept him from fame and a legitimate fortune.

Achilles had his heel; Price had his damn hammie. He hadn't been expecting the guard at the Vegas bank to go for his gun. What kind of lunatic was he? Reaching for a handgun when eight guys with automatic weapons could have shredded him.

He didn't have any choice but to rush the guy and clock him before the shooting started. Tweaking his leg in the process. That had been bad enough. Then, afterward, two of the guys told him they'd just about blown him to pieces, too. Had just managed to hold their fire as they saw Price clobber the guard. They'd almost killed him.

Wouldn't that have been a grand fuckup?

If the cops had a chance to identify his tattered remains, catching the other guys wouldn't be hard. Right now, they all looked happy. Getting a Frank Thomas for less than an hour of putting their asses on the line.

If banks started beefing up their security, though, things might not go so well. Price didn't think it would look good for banks to have guards carrying their own machine guns at the ready. That might look like they were eager to have a firefight, collateral damage be damned. Holding on to the bank's cash was all that mattered.

Might encourage a whole lot more online transactions.

So what else could the banks do to upgrade their security? A chill running down his spine, Price thought: snipers. The banks could put guys with rifles somewhere up high in concealed positions. Maybe place them so they could get a crossfire going. Take out Price and his guys before they knew what hit them.

That happened and they all might get a Don Baylor.

Number: 00.

They'd talked about using that code if they ever decided to call off a job.

Never occurred to them coming up empty might happen in a far worse way.

A hand fell on Price's right leg, startling him. He looked over and saw the skipper had taken the seat next to him. All the other guys had already boarded the plane.

"How's the leg?" the old man said.

"Good, Skip. Real good."

"You did good, too, last night, Corey. Didn't know you could still motor like that."

"I got only one gear. That's always been my problem."

"Yeah, well, you've been setting the tone these past few days. All the other guys have been following your lead. It'll be nice if we can go out with a bang."

The skipper wasn't talking about bank jobs.

But he'd done a good job of pushing Price's concerns away. Made him feel almost young again. "Thanks, Skip."

"You are gonna get on the plane with us, right?"

"Sure thing." Price stood up. Still felt his hammie, but it wasn't too bad now.

He let the skipper board the flight ahead of him.

His mind returned to the Las Vegas bank job. Getting back to the motel afterward, he'd seen the TV news. How all the casino and fire alarms had been triggered to keep the forces of law and order busy while they were doing the robbery.

Lamar Dekker had told Price he'd gone back to college after starting his trucking company, and the guy always did have a kind of low cunning. But pulling shit like he said he'd done — like had happened — in New Orleans and Las Vegas, Price couldn't help but wonder if there was someone a lot smarter than Dekker standing in the shadows.

Someone pulling all the strings.

Meaning he and the boys were nothing more than somebody's puppets.

That made him more uneasy than the idea of banks using snipers.

McCarran Airport had a VIP lounge for people who came and went in private planes. It was used by the big-time gamblers who were known as whales. Them and the entertainers whose names appeared on the marquees outside The Strip hotels. John Tall Wolf joined that gilded number, though he didn't recognize anyone else in the lounge.

It was, however, the first time he could remember sharing a room in which everyone else was also wearing sunglasses. He found a quiet corner and called Deputy Director DeWitt. While the call was going through, it struck him as funny that these days he was talking to the FBI far more regularly than he ever did with Marlene Flower Moon.

"Special Agent Tall Wolf," DeWitt said. "How may I be of assistance?"

The greeting was a good example of why John maintained a dialogue with DeWitt.

He believed the man was sincere, not playing some devious game.

They both put closing the case first, not caring who got the credit.

John said, "I forgot to mention something back in Washington."

He asked if the FBI might look into whether anyone at the University of Pennsylvania was known to be a fan of the prolific bank robber and Penn alumnus, Carl Gugasian. Someone there might have studied Carl's methods as part of a scholarly pursuit, gotten intrigued, thought of how the robber's methods might have been technologically upgraded and then decided to give them a try.

"You are a free thinker," DeWitt told John. "I'll have someone make inquiries. But it wouldn't necessarily have to be limited to Penn. True scholarship knows no boundaries. Might be any U.S. college or even somewhere abroad."

"You're right," John told him. "I should have thought of that. But I'd still start at Penn."

"Me, too," DeWitt said.

The West Wing, The White House

Vice President Jean Morrissey, being a relatively recent addition to the Patricia Darden Grant Administration, decided early on to show the president's chief of staff, Galia Mindel, due deference. Unless the vice president was directly summoned to the Oval Office, she always went through the chief of staff if she wanted to speak with the president.

Galia had recognized immediately that Jean Morrissey was as much of a hard charger as she herself was. She appreciated that it took a conscious effort for the vice president to be so courteous to her. At first, she thought Morrissey might want her to stay on as chief of staff, should she move up the ladder to the presidency.

Then Galia came to understand that whoever nominally filled that post, the vice president's brother and longtime advisor, Frank, would be running the day-to-day workings of the executive branch in a Morrissey presidency. Galia approved. Every president should have his or her most trusted confidante.

At the moment, though, the two women, meeting in Galia's office, were working on more immediate plans, making sure the vice president faced no significant or distracting primary challengers. It was always better to let the other side's people throw mud at each other while your candidate remained above the fray.

The vice president asked Galia, "Have you heard how well Marlene Flower Moon's new career in Hollywood is coming along?"

"She's charming people or scaring the hell out of them, as appropriate."

Jean Morrissey laughed. "The two necessary attributes of being a movie mogul."

"Apparently. Word is, she's also the main reason Clay Steadman still has the ability to focus on directing his film. She won't let anyone distract him with any crap. She's also making sure he eats right and gets enough rest."

"I won't ask what other comforts she might be providing," the vice president said.

"Best left unspoken," Galia agreed.

"I was wondering, though, if Marlene's absence from her government job might not be a disservice to the Office of Justice Services at the BIA. Her niece, Ms. Freeland, doesn't strike me as anything more than a snoop and a conduit to Marlene."

"What about the BIA special agent working the bank robberies? This Tall Wolf fellow?"

"Funny you should mention him," the vice president said. "I was thinking he might take Ms. Flower Moon's place."

"Assuming she prefers to stay on in the movie business?" Galia asked.

"The president might give Marlene a choice, but I'd suggest not giving her an undue amount of time to make it."

The chief of staff said, "That sounds reasonable. I'll discuss it with the president. It would look better, of course, if Tall Wolf could help end these particular bank robberies."

"Yes, it would," Jean Morrissey said.

VIP Lounge, McCarran Airport

After speaking with DeWitt, John was about to leave the airport when he saw Marlene Flower Moon's face on television. The device featured a huge high definition screen. He'd read that many of the people who appeared on camera hated the advance in broadcast technology because the stunning resolution showed every flaw and blemish on their faces.

He couldn't find any imperfections on Marlene. She'd gone Hollywood with her hair, makeup and wardrobe. No more buttoned-down DC striver. She was casually, exotically gorgeous. The Great Spirit hadn't stinted at all when making her.

Then again, if she was Coyote, as John suspected, she was a supernatural being, too.

No reason for her ever to age, wrinkle or sag.

The only public figure John could think of who compared to her was the president, Patti Grant. Remembering that Marlene's ambition, other than making a meal of him, was to also sit in the Oval Office, a shiver passed through John.

Coyote as president. Marlene at the summit of power.

The thought was truly frightening.

As if she knew just what John was thinking, he heard her mention his name.

"Special Agent John Tall Wolf of the Bureau of Indian Affairs is assisting other federal agencies in the pursuit of the bank robbers who are portraying themselves as Native Americans."

A lean woman with an intense face was interviewing Marlene. A superimposition on the screen gave her name as Ellie Booker, doing a special report for WorldWide News.

Booker asked Marlene, "So you think the robbers are not Native Americans?"

"I don't know," Marlene said. "What's important is the idea that they *might* be is in any way credible. That speaks volumes about the amount of help indigenous peoples still need from Washington."

John thought Marlene was about to launch into a political speech and he started to move on. He stopped when Ellie Booker steered the conversation in another direction.

"If you're on leave from your duties at the BIA, Ms. Flower Moon, how is it you know about Special Agent Tall Wolf's involvement in this case?"

Marlene smiled. John saw Coyote in her eyes much more clearly now.

"I may be on leave," she said, "but I'm never out of touch."

Confirming to John that Nelda Freeland was ratting out his every move.

And that he'd never truly escape Coyote.

— CHAPTER 23 —

I-15 Northbound, Las Vegas, Nevada

John took a taxi from the airport to the Las Vegas Metropolitan Police Department on South Martin Luther King Boulevard. On the way his phone beeped. He'd received a text message from his mother.

She said she'd finished the first color correction of the bank robbery crew.

The only African-American, she said. John clicked on the link. The face he saw looked to be late 20s to early 30s in age. Still young and vital but with ... what in his eyes? Not exactly fear, despite the fact he was in the act of committing a crime that might end in a lengthy prison sentence or death. What John thought he saw was disappointment.

As if the guy thought his life never should have come to that point.

Interesting. A bank robber who thought he deserved better.

John texted his mother, asking her to send DeWitt a copy of the face.

A moment later, he received his reply: *Done.*

Then Mom added: *Fee for my services from you?*

John wrote: *Dinner for you and Dad with, and courtesy of, your devoted son?*

On impulse, he added: *With someone special I'd like you to meet.*

Mom said: *Wonderful.*

John took it one step farther: *In New Orleans?*

Mom replied: *Magnifico!*

Now, he'd have to see how Rebecca would feel about meeting his parents.

Ellie Booker got to John before he could get to the front door of LVMPD headquarters.

"Special Agent Tall Wolf?"

John recognized her and said, "What gave me away?"

Ellie smiled. "Just a lucky guess. I'm Ellie Booker, working a special —"

"I know. I saw you on TV."

John saw her recalculating her estimation of him.

"Let me ask you then," she said, "is it true you just came from a meeting with Vice President Morrissey?"

Wasn't hard to connect the dots between Nelda Freeland and Ellie Booker, John thought. Marlene had dropped tidbits off-camera and pointed Ms. Booker at him. Coyote wanted to see if he could do his job while she put hurdles in his way.

"I can't comment on any details of an active case. I'm sure you know that, Ms. Booker."

She turned to the guy trailing her with the videocam and drew a line across her throat. He killed his camera and stepped back a few paces. John decided not to be misled.

"You happen to have an audio recorder running, Ms. Booker?"

She took one out of a pocket and turned it off. Dropped it back into the pocket.

"If you're trying to establish trust with me ..." John let it hang there.

She gave him a look for a count of three. Exhibited, deactivated and replaced another recorder. Gave the video guy a thumb. He went back to their car, reclined his seat and appeared to start a snooze.

Ellie said, "I can be helpful. I'm looking into these robberies myself. I might spot something before the local cops do or I might tell you something they hold back."

"The assistance of concerned citizens is always welcome," John told her.

She gave him a cynical smile. "Yeah, I bet it is. We concerned citizens don't mind getting a little help ourselves."

"Such as?"

"The jump on a good story."

"Professional advantage."

"You bet, but only in fair trade."

"An example being?"

"Don't know if the cops will tell you this, but one difference in the robbery here? The robbers took everyone's cell phone. These guys learn as they go. Do we have a deal?"

John thought about it and asked, "Do you know if anyone covering this story has a last name that begins with the letter A?"

Ellie was puzzled, but considered the question. "No, I don't think so."

"In that case, any talking I do with the press might well be in alphabetical order."

Ellie Booker laughed. "Yeah, okay. I can live with that. If I learn anything else, how can I get in touch with you?"

With some reluctance, wondering if this woman was really working for Marlene, John gave her his business card.

Ellie returned the favor, handing him her card.

LVMPD Headquarters

Once inside the building, John was directed to the office of Captain Eric Grunwald of the Robbery/Homicide Bureau and the department's liaison with federal law enforcement agencies. He got to his feet to shake hands with John and stood tall enough to look John in the eye. Had John not been wearing his Ray-Ban sunglasses, as usual.

Unlike many people, Grunwald didn't assume John was just trying to be cool.

"Your eyes sensitive to light?" the Metro cop asked, gesturing John to a chair and taking his own.

"They are, even high lumen bulbs or fluorescents bother me."

"My wife's the same way. Lucky for me, I think she looks great in shades, and we enjoy a lot of candlelit dinners at home.

"Make the best of any situation," John said, "that's the way to go."

Grunwald sighed. "Yeah, well, that's exactly what those asshole bank robbers did. They had just about every first responder in town running around in circles when they hit."

"Distraction seems to be their thing," John said.

"They're pretty good at pissing people off, too. Every cop in town would love to plug those bastards. The firefighters, I hear, would prefer to use their axes." Grunwald took a breath. "Is the BIA here because the bad guys are Indians?"

"They're not, actually," John said. He took out his phone and brought up the image his mother had sent him. Showed it to Grunwald. "That's one of them without his makeup."

"He's black. Well, sort of. He's not really too dark. Where'd you get this?"

John offered a concise explanation.

Grunwald smiled. "Your mother? That's great. She does fine work. Please tell her I said so."

John nodded and sent a copy of the robber's image to Grunwald's computer.

He said, "You can distribute that to your patrol people. I doubt this crew is still in town but, who knows, maybe we'll get lucky."

Grunwald checked to make sure his computer got a clear rendering of pixels.

"Doesn't look like my machine lost any definition. I'll get this out right away." He looked at John. "You've run this through NCIC, right?"

The National Crime Information Center. The database held records of tens of thousands of criminal histories, including mug shots. There were also files on fugitives, stolen property and missing persons. The NCIC was operated by the FBI, and was available to federal, state and local law enforcement agencies. The database was accessible around the clock and every day of the year ... barring computer failure.

Even with his sunglasses on, Grunwald could see that John had just thought of something disturbing. He asked, "What is it?"

John said, "I sent a copy of that image to a deputy director of the FBI. I assumed he'd run it through the NCIC."

"Sure he would. So what's the problem?"

"Somebody connected to these robbers is screwing with bedrock infrastructure. Here in Las Vegas and in New Orleans. What's to say these hackers couldn't crash the NCIC, too?"

"Holy shit. Would that be possible? Aren't there people guarding against that?"

John said, "I have to think so, but are they as good as the bad guys?"

"Let's see." Grunwald logged on to the NCIC. "The system's up and responding."

The Metro police captain attached the image John had sent to his computer to his request for a match in the system. There didn't appear to be any problems as the software did its search, but the result was negative. Nobody in the database matched the image of the robber.

Both John and Grunwald thought about that and came to the same conclusion.

The captain said, "You bring the whole system down, everyone's gonna notice."

"But if you delete a handful of files and cover your tracks," John said, "who'd ever know the difference?"

"Damn. This is getting scary."

"All the more reason to catch these guys fast. Did your people collect the names and addresses of people in the bank that was robbed for me to interview?"

"Yes, we called the FBI first, of course, but they told us you'd be flying in from Washington. Thought it was because of the Indian angle. You still going to be kept on?"

John thought about that. "Yeah … I'm pretty sure."

Grunwald read between the lines. "In case somebody needs to catch the heat."

"Maybe. But there are people who know I do good work, too."

"Glad to hear it. Anything you need besides the witness information?"

"Have you read any of their statements?"

The captain shook his head. "I've been swamped by meetings with casino security chiefs and people from the fire department regarding their false alarms."

"So you haven't heard the bank robbers stole everyone's cell phones?"

Grunwald frowned. "No."

"Well, they did."

That led John to think there might be value in having Ellie Booker help him.

Grunwald said, "But taking the phones is smart, after that dude in New Orleans got those shots of them."

John told Grunwald about the idea of a truck carting off the motorcycles.

"That'd be slick, too," the captain said.

A new idea occurred to John. "If the robbers were camera shy in the bank, maybe the guy with the truck was, too."

"What do you mean?"

"Does Las Vegas have a lot of security cameras looking at your streets, the way a lot of big cities do these days?"

"We've got 'em everywhere you can imagine. Probably some places you can't."

"Okay," John said. "So let's suppose the guy driving the truck doesn't want to be seen picking up the motorcycles. He knows his accomplices have already had their pictures taken at the bank in

New Orleans. How does he avoid the cameras?"

Grunwald told John, "Only one way, shut down the electricity. Hell, with everything else going on today, are you saying there was a power failure, too?"

"I don't know for sure," John said. "Why don't you check with your power company? Look for something localized within a mile or so of the bank. You wouldn't need to black out the whole town. Wouldn't need to keep the lights off a long time either. You'd want something that started just before the general frenzy began and ended maybe a half-hour after the robbers left the bank."

Grunwald bobbed his head. "Say that you're right. What we'd have to do then is go to the affected area and search for witnesses who saw a truck that was just sitting around for a while."

"A truck big enough to hold eight motorcycles," John said. "Don't let the news get out that we're not looking for Native Americans. We don't want to give that away."

"Right. I'll just tell the troops to look for the truck."

"That's enough for now. We find either the truck driver or the one robber whose face we know, we'll get the others."

— CHAPTER 24 —

J. W. Marriott Resort & Spa, Las Vegas, Nevada

Captain Grunwald detailed a patrol car to take John to the Desert Mountain National Bank. They were en route when a radio call reached the officer behind the wheel. The lieutenant in charge of the crime scene had chosen to release the customers and bank staff; they'd all gone home. The lieutenant insisted he'd done what was best for the investigation.

"Half the people were crying, the other half were screaming. They all wanted out. Nobody was in a mood to talk to the feds. Give 'em a little time, they'll all play nice," the lieutenant said.

John didn't offer any criticism.

If things didn't work out well, though, he thought that particular cop's head would wind up on a platter. The vice president herself might see to that. Or maybe Marlene Flower Moon might come up with some other ghastly fate for him.

The patrol cop saved John the trouble of asking the obvious question. "You got everybody's names, addresses and phone numbers, right, Lieutenant?

"Jesus Christ, of course, I did. Verified by drivers licenses." Knowing John was in the patrol car, the lieutenant asked, "Your passenger got anything to say?"

John shook his head.

"Negative, sir."

There was a moment of silence, as if the lieutenant regretted not being able to use an argument he'd devised to defend himself against the visiting big shot. "Okay, then. All the bank people will be here tomorrow, if he wants to talk with them. Metro will round up the customers for him, at his request."

And that was that. The first step in John's investigation had bit the desert dust.

He asked his driver, "You have a local hotel you can recommend?"

The cop nodded. "I'll set you up somewhere nice. Make up for the aggravation."

He took John to the J.W. Marriott Resort & Spa, got him a room with a mountain view, all for a price that worked with his per diem. The cop explained, "Places here discount the rooms because they make their money in the casinos."

John had never wagered on anything except his own athletic abilities.

Hadn't even done that for a while.

He told the cop, "That business model works for me."

John was unpacking his suitcase when his cell phone rang. Marcellus Darcy was calling from New Orleans. "We've got three mugs we like, Edmee and me, for the robbers' scout. All the shots were taken by the bank's security cameras."

Edmee, John thought. The beginning of a beautiful friendship?

"Any of them connected to trucking?" he asked.

Marcellus chuckled. "Our favorite is an independent operator with his own rig."

"Promising. You have a picture of the truck?"

"Edmee found one. I'll send it with the mug shots."

"Great." John thought he'd forward the pictures to Captain Grunwald and Deputy Director DeWitt.

"I'll email them to you right now," Marcellus said.

John said, "One more thing. You and Edmee up for a little more digging?"

"Sure."

"This trucker, see if he has any education in computer programming." John thought it would be a point of efficiency for the gang's ninth *Indian* to have more than one skill set. He might be reaching, but what the heck?

Marcellus also thought it was a stretch. "A trucker who knows computers?"

"Maybe plans bank robberies, too," John reminded him.

John's view of the mountains was enhanced when he went out to take a seat on the room's balcony. He stared into the distance trying to find the clue that had eluded him: Why did that one robber's sign language seem familiar. It wasn't American Sign Language; he'd checked that out on the flight from Washington.

Another thought occurred to him.

He took Ellie Booker's card out of a pocket and called her.

She answered by asking, "You have something for me, Special Agent?"

"Yes, a question. You interested in doing some legwork for me? The payoff might not be immediate but there could be a big credit in the future."

"You're asking me to work on spec?"

"Only if you want to; only if you think I'm being straight with you."

After a moment of silence, Ellie asked, "The credit would be with you?"

"Me at a minimum. Possibly someone high up in the FBI."

A longer pause followed. It ended with Ellie asking, "What do you want?"

"Over a period of say the past twelve months, can you find out if a Chinese national lost a large sum of money at a Las Vegas casino?"

Hearing from the Metro cop how the hotels subsidized their room rates made him remember stories he'd read about big-time gamblers getting all sorts of freebies because they dropped so much money. That tied in with DeWitt's strong suspicion that China could be the country that might be behind the cyberattacks. Unlike John, the Chinese had a reputation for loving to gamble.

Ellie confirmed that. "With the money the Chinese have these days and the way they like to hit casinos, there could be more than one."

"Okay, give me the top three and the amounts they lost, if you can find that."

"Anything else?"

A second consideration came to John's mind. "Yes, see if any of these guys who lost a fortune, if they exist, has an Ivy League connection."

"You know you're making me crazy, right?" Ellie said. "Wondering how all this ties in to the bank robberies."

On a bit of roll for the moment, John decided to take a risk.

"You have access to all sorts of entertainment databases, don't you?"

"Yeah. Movies, TV, theatre, even commercials."

"Great."

John thought the African-American robber's face might have been deleted from the NCIC, but what if his likeness had found its way into another digital archive?

"You going to tell me why you want to know that?" Ellie asked.

"I'm going to send you a copy of a picture. I'd like to see if you can find out the man's name. Check newspaper files, too, if you can."

"All this does tie in somehow, doesn't it? With the robberies, I mean."

John said, "We're back to the area where I can't comment. You decide if it's worth your time."

Tulane University, New Orleans, Louisiana

Louis Mercer, sitting in his tiny TA's office, was supposed to be busy preparing for the media classes he would teach that fall term.

He also had his doctoral dissertation to think about. Think about? Hell, he had to start *writing* the damn thing … though, given his area of study, he thought it might be cool to do a short film instead.

But what really lit up his prefrontal cortex just then was thinking about the return to campus of one of his students from last year, Dana Bang, a Danish-American beauty from Tangletown, Minnesota. She would be both a senior this year and twenty-one years old. Louis was very careful about dating women in the student body. Seventeen was the legal age of consent in Louisiana, though you could get married at sixteen with parental approval, but Louis saw teenage girls as nothing but trouble for a man planning a career in academia.

A twenty-one-year-old woman, however, was fair game.

Not that he'd ever speak of a woman as someone to be hunted.

Still, he felt sure some other guy would snap her up if he didn't move fast.

At the moment, however, he was unable to either plan his seduction or meet his scholarly obligations because his literary agent was talking to him on his cell phone.

"I didn't have the time to do exactly what you wanted; I've got to make a living."

"Yeah, David, we all do. Nothing special about that."

"Paying the rent on Midtown office space and the mortgage on a Manhattan apartment is very special, Louis. You hustle all the time or you disappear without a trace."

"You ever think of moving somewhere else?"

"Louis, there *isn't* anywhere else."

"I thought half of New York had moved to L.A."

"Yeah, the half that couldn't cut it here. You want to hear what I have for you or not? We can call it quits, if you're not satisfied."

Considering that Louis had conned the agent into conducting a search for him in the first place, he felt it would be smart to play along.

"Okay, David, what do you have for me?"

"Every nonfiction publishing proposal that has been submitted to a Big Five publisher for the last three months."

"Wow! Wait a minute. If the bank robbers sent in the idea for their book that far in advance, wouldn't that be giving themselves away?"

"Only if they gave an exact time and location. Otherwise, banks are always thinking they might get robbed anyway, aren't they?"

"Yeah, I suppose."

"There's another thing."

"What's that?"

"You know how many of these proposals were never read?"

"No."

"Well, neither do I, but you can be damn sure it was most of them."

"How many are there?" Louis asked.

"Eight hundred and ninety-two."

"Jesus."

"Yeah, be glad everything's electronic or you'd have to pay me a ton for the postage. Let me know if you find what you need to complete a front list title."

Front list meaning a best seller. Or don't bother calling back.

That point was made clear when David ended the call without saying goodbye.

It took Louis almost ten minutes to download David's email attachments.

Christ, eight hundred and ninety-two proposals. No wonder publishers called their unsolicited submissions a slush pile. He didn't have the time to wade through all that shit. Classes were about to start. Dana would arrive tomorrow. So what could he do?

He found the card John Tall Wolf had given him.

Forwarded David's email to the special agent.

Let Tall Wolf be the one to get eye strain.

It was his damn idea.

— CHAPTER 25 —

Mirage Hotel, Las Vegas, Nevada, Saturday, August, 24th

Captain Eric Grunwald of the Metro Police apologized to John at 8:00 a.m. that morning when the federal agent arrived at the hotel in his rental car. "Lieutenant Hoskins, who let everybody go home from Desert Mountain National Bank yesterday, was informed that he'd made a serious mistake."

"Did you hear from Washington?" John asked.

Grunwald nodded. "Never had a woman talk to me like that before."

"The vice president?"

"Uh-huh."

"I heard she played ice hockey in college," John said.

"Must've been the enforcer."

"Just so you know, it wasn't me who complained."

The Metro cop gave John a long look. The special agent momentarily lowered his sunglasses so Grunwald could see his eyes. "Okay, if it wasn't you, then who?"

Ellie Booker came to John's mind.

He had seen her on TV interviewing Marlene Flower Moon. He had no doubt Ellie had also cultivated more than one source of information inside the local police department. Thing was, he didn't see what she'd gain from ratting out Hoskins. And he pegged Ellie as someone who always acted to gain personal advantage.

He told Grunwald, "I don't know, but I'll try to find out."

Not that he was sure he'd succeed. If Coyote was involved, it might not be possible.

Grunwald led him into the hotel and then a small conference room.

A quick head-count told John there were thirty-four people there, not counting two people from the hotel setting up a coffee urn and platters of pastries.

Grunwald told John, "This is everybody who was in the bank during the robbery, staff and customers. Thought we'd try to save you some time that way."

Rather than speak to each person individually, John had the witnesses sit in two semi-circular rows with the chairs staggered so he could see everyone and they could see him.

"Everyone comfortable? Good. I'll ask a question and any of you may respond if you have something to say, but please wait until I call on you so we're not talking over each other and have to repeat things. The first thing I'd like to know is how you would describe the robbers in terms of their physical appearance."

Every hand went up.

John pointed to the woman nearest him, matronly but upscale.

"Indians," she said.

John said, "Real Native Americans or masquerade Indians? A show of hands for real."

The matron kept her hand up and was joined by two more people. Several of those who thought otherwise rolled their eyes. After everyone else dropped their hands, a woman in the second row held hers up.

"Yes?" John said.

"I'm a makeup artist. I worked revues in this town for fifteen years. These guys all wore makeup and it wasn't well done. It was too thick. The warpaint markings looked like something from a kid's storybook. You, you're Native American. They didn't come close to your skin tones."

"Thank you."

A man raised his hand.

"Yes?"

"I don't know anything about makeup, but I thought these guys were just about perfect in everything else they did. The one that clocked that poor guard who went for his gun? He moved quicker and smoother than some of the stiffs I've seen in boxing rings here."

John asked, "Everyone agree with that?"

Heads bobbed in both rows without any dissent.

"Did any of the robbers speak to anyone?"

This time every head shook.

Another man raised his hand and John recognized him.

"They had written signs for us and little hand motions for each other."

Just like New Orleans, John thought.

He felt a spark of intuition. "Did these hand motions the robbers used look anything like the ones soldiers use in combat situations where they need to communicate silently?"

Only four of the witnesses had been in the military; none had seen combat.

They were unable to answer John's question.

One man, speaking without being recognized, said, "I can tell you what they looked like to me: a well-oiled team."

That might make them military, John thought.

Then, in a darker turn of mind, he considered that they might even be cops.

A renegade SWAT team, say. Wouldn't that be a kick in the pants?

John wondered if he'd get anything new or useful. He could see that his audience, polite to a fault thus far, was getting restive.

A woman at the far end of the front row raised her hand.

"Yes?" John said.

"I work in entertainment, too. I'm a choreographer. I like to watch how everyone moves, not just dancers. After I went home yesterday, I drew sketches of how the robbers moved. They were fluid. Not like dancers, though. More like athletes."

John had heard that before, too.

Then the woman said, "I also noticed the one robber signaling the others. It reminded me of jazz hands, only his palms were facing him not his men. I sketched his hands, too, if you'd like to see them."

Couldn't hurt, John decided. "Yes, please, I'd like copies of all your drawings."

Grunwald said he'd see to it John got the sketches.

John thanked everyone for their help.

As the last of the witnesses departed, John shook hands with Grunwald.

They were about to leave when Deputy Director DeWitt entered the room.

The Strip, Las Vegas, Nevada

Despite the growing heat of the day, John and DeWitt decided to go for a walk along Las Vegas Boulevard South past the ranks of hotels and casinos. DeWitt's car with two FBI agents inside idled along in the curb lane fifty feet back. There was no one else on the sidewalk.

DeWitt looked around, as if to be sure no one was pointing a directional mike their way.

Before getting down to business, he said, "Never saw the appeal of this place. Every game the casinos run, except for Twenty-One, is stacked in the house's favor. And they don't let you count cards in Twenty-One. Always thought that was a mistake. Letting a few sharp cookies win would encourage a lot of chumps to think they could do the same. They couldn't, of course, and the house would —"

John heard a small voice buzz in DeWitt's earbud.

"Okay, we're good," he told John. "No one's trying to eavesdrop."

"From a parked vehicle or a hotel room?" John asked.

"Yeah."

"Things have gotten to the point where the bad guys might be doing counterintelligence?"

"Word has come down: Don't make any mistakes. That suggests an abundance of caution is in order."

"That's why you came to see me?" John asked.

"That and to tell you the spooks say there's no doubt the Chinese are behind the robberies and the infrastructure attacks."

"Are you supposed to share that with me?" John asked.

"I was *told* to share it. You seem to have won the vice president's favor."

John felt a chill run down his spine, and not because the vice president was a looker. He'd made keeping a low profile the signature of his career at the BIA. He left the politics to Marlene Flower Moon. Now, if he was on the vice president's radar, he had the uneasy feeling he wouldn't like what might come next.

Disappoint Jean Morrissey on this investigation, she might be the one to ask for his resignation. On the other hand, if he tied up the case with a ribbon and a bow, he might get a promotion as his reward. He wouldn't mind a bump in pay, but he wanted to remain an investigator not become an administrator.

DeWitt said, "I would have told you anyway. So you'll be in step with what comes next."

John nodded. "I'd do the same thing in your place."

The deputy director smiled. "Kindred spirits, that's what we are. We ran the photo of that robber your mother unmasked through our databases."

"I tried it on NCIC without any luck," John said.

"We struck out there, too. Then we ran it through military records, passport files and some other electronic archives I really can't mention. No luck anywhere."

John shared his idea that maybe the hackers working for the other side might have lifted the robbers' file from any government records where they might normally be found.

"I thought of that, too. Caused quite an uproar when I

mentioned it. People are checking that right now."

"I had another idea," John said.

He told him about asking Ellie Booker to check popular media sites to see if there was a match for the robber's face in a place the other side might not think to look.

"You think they might turn up in IMDb?" DeWitt asked with a smile.

Referring to the Internet movie database.

"I don't know. Thought it couldn't hurt to look."

"Yeah, you're right about that. Our tech people used the picture your mother gave us as an example of the right way to strip away the warpaint and makeup from the other robbers. That and add appropriate skin shading. I should have the results within the hour. Let me know if you get anything from Ms. Booker. If you don't find anything, we're going to put all the robbers' images on TV and the Web. Ask the public for help finding these guys."

More than anything else, that told John how much pressure was coming down from the top.

DeWitt gestured to his car and asked if he could give John a lift.

He accepted a ride back to the Mirage to pick up his car.

John checked his phone for voice mail or texts from Ellie Booker.

Hoping for but not receiving any information on her database searches.

Captain Grunwald, however, left a message saying the sketches done by the choreographer had been dropped off at John's hotel.

— CHAPTER 26 —

J. W. Marriott Resort & Spa, Las Vegas, Nevada

John felt like going for a swim. His talk with DeWitt had made him tense, feeling a sense of urgency he'd never known before. Not as a special agent for the BIA anyway. He still got night sweats sometimes when the terror of being left out in the wilderness as an infant to die, almost consumed by a coyote, fought its way past the intervening years and found him again.

He'd heard from many people how they couldn't remember their early years.

He wished he could forget his earliest day. Not that he had detailed recall. But the sense of mortal dread remained undiminished.

PTSD from the cradle onward.

Swimming would be a pleasing way to relax the tension, but he'd have to wait until the blazing desert sun was no longer directly overhead and he could take his sunglasses off. The radiance was barely tolerable even with his Ray-Bans on. He'd wait until twilight. See if he had the time for a dip then.

The hotel had an Irish pub called J.C. Wooloughan. John stopped in for lunch and found a table in a quiet corner. He ordered a corned beef sandwich on rye and a bottle of Arrowhead sparkling water. He opened his laptop. The lighting in the pub struck a happy medium, comfortable on his eyes and adequate for reading from his laptop screen.

He called up his email and found a message from Louis Mercer with multiple attachments containing eight hundred and ninety-two proposals for nonfiction books.

Comprehensive, John thought. Would have been nice if Louis had narrowed things down for him a little. He couldn't complain, though. He'd been delegating tasks to a lot of other people throughout this case. Getting a pile of work handed back to him, he could hear his father's voice.

"Son," Haden Wolf had told him, "what goes around comes around."

He hadn't understood at first. Mom clarified it for him in biblical language, "As ye sow, so shall ye reap."

Both parents had taught him not to complain when he had to do the heavy lifting. He started by creating a file that combined all the individual proposals under one heading. Then he did global searches for the words bank robbery, thefts, stealing and cyberattacks.

Bank robbery brought up no returns. Theft brought up one that was off topic. Stealing returned a proposal that included stealing bases, a baseball book. Cyberattacks produced twenty-three hits.

John paid his lunch tab, leaving a handsome tip for not being disturbed as he'd occupied the table for hours.

He went up to his room to read the proposals on cyberattacks.

To see if anyone thought of using them to facilitate other crimes.

After reading the book proposals and speaking with DeWitt earlier that day, John's thinking about the bank robberies began to crystallize. Eight so-called Indians were the public faces of the crimes. A ninth accomplice drove the truck that carried off the cash, costumes and motorcycles. Behind those guys, according to DeWitt, stood the People's Liberation Army of China. They were the ones who bore the official responsibility of doing that country's computer hacking.

DeWitt had told John the PLA had already hacked its way into the Pentagon and any American tech firms worth mentioning. It was as if the Chinese had backed up a gigantic truck to the USA and were heisting every piece of the country's intellectual property worth having. On top of that, the bastards ran an annual multibillion dollar trade surplus with America going back, roughly, to the Pleistocene.

It was enough to —

Make John laugh when he looked at it from the perspective of a Native American. A bunch of damn foreigners was stealing the country out from under the noses of the locals? How dare they? The irony might be comical, but most of the continent's original inhabitants wouldn't be any more pleased to have the Chinese running the show than they were now.

It'd be a long damn time before they got their buffalo back from those people.

John wondered if the robbers knew for whom they were working.

He doubted it. They were more likely driven by the profit motive than the struggle for the triumph of the proletariat. Knowing the robbers were probably good capitalists might give him some leverage in the end. But wait a minute …

There had to be one guy — the truck driver? — who was the interface between the domestic crooks and the foreign commies.

He might be motivated by both money and ideology.

John had read those were common traits among the elite in Beijing these days.

He got up from his computer and went out on the balcony to look at the mountains. He let his eyes relax with a bit of long-distance focus. The peaks were brown and red in the lowering sunlight. He glanced down to look at the lush gardens and adjacent golf course surrounding the resort. It was amazing what a hundred million dollars could do to rehab a desert landscape.

Create a reasonable facsimile of Eden with low humidity. The pool down there, a vast expanse of crystal blue water, looked quite inviting, too. Time for a swim, John thought.

Then he'd come back to his room, order a room service dinner and look over the choreographer's sketches of the robbers. He'd pay attention to the static images of the way they moved, and how that one guy used his reverse jazz hands.

First, though, not having packed for water sports, he had to call down to the hotel gift shop and see if they had swim trunks in his size. As big as he was —

They did. He said he'd be right down.

He didn't get there. Byron DeWitt called.

"My people checked out Penn to see if Carl Gugasian, the Ivy League bank robber, had any acolytes or groupies. Turns out he did. Sort of."

John sat down to listen.

— CHAPTER 27 —

The Hook & Plow, Seattle, Washington

Corey Price drove a subcompact rental car up I-405 from Tacoma to Seattle. He was on his way to meet Lamar Dekker in the gastropub of a waterfront hotel that was a lot fancier than the economy motel he was staying at down the road. The hotel valet had to force a smile when he took the key to Corey's little tin bucket.

That left Price trying to decide whether he should tip the kid big when he picked up his wheels, show him he was a sport, or just stiff the condescending little prick. When Price walked into the pub, he saw Dekker sitting in a booth at the back with two glasses of beer in front of him and two more on the other side of the table. Happy hour.

Price slid into the booth feeling anything but cheerful.

He downed half of his first beer anyway.

"What the hell is a *gastro*pub?" he asked.

"Means they serve craft beers, the kind of beef you don't get in chain places and fish that came out of the water this morning."

The beer was damn good, but Price wasn't about to let that settle him down.

"I'm done," he said.

"Because you never could stand prosperity, right?"

Price finished off his first beer, thinking there was a good deal of truth to Dekker's gibe.

Dekker just sat there looking at him until Price had to concede, "We have made some good money, but that asshole with the cell phone in New Orleans and the wannabe hero guards in both banks —"

"They got you nervous, huh?"

"It's different when you're on the field, Lamar, not just watching from the stands."

Dekker said, "That picture-taking prick in New Orleans? I'm thinking about maxing out all his credit cards. Show him there's a price for everything."

That made the two of them laugh, but Price stopped first.

"I suppose you could do the same to me," he said.

"Yeah, I could, but you'd know who did it."

Price took a sip of his second beer. Looked at Dekker over the top of his glass.

"You've learned a hell of a lot since I first met you," he said. "You keep surprising me what you can do with a computer."

Dekker shrugged. "I give it all I've got. Just like I do with everything. That's the only way I've ever accomplished anything. You know what I mean. You're the same way."

"I've always *overdone* everything," Price said.

"Your leg still bothering you?" Dekker asked.

"Not so much. I had this little Japanese massage therapist work on me last night. Felt a whole lot better until she gave me the bill. I looked at the number and asked if she was charging me in yen."

"Didn't get your knob polished, too, did you?" Dekker asked.

"Strictly therapeutic. Made me think I should take some massage classes myself. Pays damn near what we've made the past few days."

Dekker took a roll of cash out of a pocket and peeled off three Ben Franklins.

Price let the money sit on the table.

He said, "I hope you're not dipping into other people's money. Living high off our earnings."

"Sticking strictly to my share."

"You'd better, because I can still stomp you flat."

Dekker grinned and took a sip of his beer. "Would've been interesting, we both got into it when I was younger. But you've got the edge now. I ever get wind you're coming for me, I'll head straight home. You'd never find me there."

Price caught the eye of a waitress. Ordered another round and drained his glass.

He looked at Dekker. "You've tasted the big time, Lamar. You have to spend your life hiding out in the woods, that'll be punishment enough." He pushed the money to the other side of the table.

Dekker let it sit there. "We have just one more job planned. The take for this one could be as much per man as the first two combined. That'd make a nice bundle for all you guys to take into whatever you want to do next."

Price sat silent and thought about that.

Dekker went on, "I'll make out okay regardless. You probably won't do too bad for yourself. Maybe find a niche in one of the towns on the circuit. The others probably won't be as lucky as us … and you know they won't do another job without you. Who else would tell them what moves to make?"

Price did know that. He felt responsible for the others. Dekker had approached him; he'd been the one who got the guys to go along.

Still, he said, "After the last two, it's gonna be harder to surprise anybody."

Dekker smiled. "Wait 'til you see what I have planned this time."

Price put up a hand. "I don't want to know. Not until I have to."

What scared him, what he didn't want to admit even to himself, was the idea there was someone a whole lot smarter than Lamar Dekker standing in the shadows. Playing all of them for suckers. Ready to cut and run, leave the chumps for the cops to catch, if things got too hot.

"It's gonna be all right," Dekker said. "We'll all walk away with better than a hundred grand each. Tell me where else you could get that kind of money."

Nowhere else, Price thought. "One last job, then we go our own ways."

Dekker nodded. "Won't bother you if I buy dinner, will it?"

Price shook his head.

"I promise," Dekker said. "We won't have any reunion parties."

Price grinned and said, "Yeah, fuck you, too."

"Never figured you'd be the guy who got the jitters."

"Me neither."

What Price wasn't about to tell Dekker or anyone else was that his agent had called again that morning. The movie producer who'd optioned his book got the money to finance his movie of Price's story faster than he'd ever expected. They looked good to go for filming. The book deal, as a result, was going to kick in a six-figure bonus as soon as the movie deal was announced. Price sure as hell didn't want to screw all that up.

If he hadn't been so close to the other guys for so long ...

If they all hadn't shared the same frustrations and disappointments ...

But they had, and Price couldn't let himself be the guy to fuck them over one last time.

So he went along with the plan and let Dekker buy him the best damn steak he'd ever eaten. They'd placed their orders when the waitress had come back with four beers instead of two. She'd said, "Good timing, you just squeaked this order into the last minute of happy hour."

Dekker raised his glass and said it was a good omen.

Price joined the toast.

Their meals came and they ate and drank and talked of better days to come.

Leaving the pub just minutes before the national news started on the TV behind the bar.

Showing a spot-on picture of Tut Warren and identifying him as one of the robbers who had struck banks in New Orleans and Las Vegas.

— CHAPTER 28 —

J. W. Marriott Resort & Spa, Las Vegas, Nevada

DeWitt told John that a Chinese graduate student at Penn, working on his Ph.D in sociology and criminology four years ago, had compared the modalities of organized crime in the United States and China. His dissertation had included a prominent section on Carl Gugasian and how an individual malefactor might organize his illegal activities in a fashion more common to larger criminal enterprises.

John said, "Maybe there's a place of higher education for crooks, like that old movie 'School for Scoundrels.'"

DeWitt picked right up on that. "Sure, they could confer MCA degrees."

"Master of Criminal Administration?"

"You got it."

What they both had now was the grad student's name: Cheng Zou.

Cheng's research might have been nothing more than honest intellectual inquiry, but neither John nor DeWitt was willing to give him the benefit of the doubt. If the scholar was still in the United States, he'd soon be talking to federal agents. If Ellie Booker's research turned up Mr. Cheng as a fellow who'd gambled and lost big in Las Vegas, the questioning would be intense.

Not five minutes after John's call with DeWitt had ended, his room phone rang.

Captain Eric Grunwald was in the lobby and had information for John.

"Come on up." He gave the Metro cop his room number.

John met Grunwald at the door and ushered him into the room.

The Metro cop looked around. "Nice digs. You hit the casino yet?"

"That's not my thing. I've been trying to get in a swim, but haven't managed to do that yet."

"Well, you stay out of the casino, you're ahead of the game in this town."

Words of wisdom that made John think of Cheng Zou again.

Reinforced the feeling the Chinese doctor of philosophy had played a part in the robberies.

"You were right," Grunwald said.

"About what?" John asked.

"NVEnergy, our power company, told me there was a small-area power failure that began thirty minutes before the robbery at Desert Mountain and lasted thirty minutes after it was over."

"So your patrol people are going to canvas the area where the surveillance cameras and the lights went out?"

"I have units doing that right now, but my thinking is they're more likely to find someone who spotted the truck during the workday on Monday. Saturday night and Sunday, the people who might have seen it are likely to be somewhere else."

"You're right," John said. "If I didn't mention it before, we're searching for a semi-trailer rig that might look just like this."

He used his laptop to pull up the photo of the truck belonging to the guy that Marcellus Darcy and Edmee LaBelle liked for the scout on the New Orleans robbery, and explained how he got it. Then he forwarded the jpg. file to Grunwald's phone.

The Las Vegas cop smiled. "You know, we might be getting somewhere with this case. I'll pass the picture along to patrol officers."

"I've got another photo," John told him. "The guy who owns the truck. It was taken in the bank in New Orleans that was robbed."

Grunwald beamed. "Better and better."

"Not so much. He was wearing a baseball cap and eyeglasses. Had big muttonchop sideburns, too. You take away all that stuff, you might not recognize him."

The idea of changing appearances spurred a thought for John. He told Grunwald he needed to make a call.

"No problem. The news about the blackout is all I have for the moment."

John asked him to stay. "What I'm thinking might help your people."

"Okay."

John called Marcellus Darcy and said, "That guy you like for the robbers' scout, the one with the truck?"

Marcellus said, "I was just about to call you about him."

"Yeah?"

"Yeah. I wasn't happy with that picture of him in the bank."

John smiled. "Great minds think alike. Neither was I. Did you see if he has any educational background in computers?"

"You're gonna spoil all my fun, ain't you? He went to the University of Arizona for one semester, then switched to online classes."

"Don't suppose you have a list of this guy's classes and his GPA."

There was a long silence.

"I did spoil all your fun, didn't I?" John asked.

"Just about."

"So I shouldn't ask you if you found a student photo of him?"

"Damn," Marcellus said.

"I'm sorry," John told him.

He could have taken matters a step farther, but he didn't want to hurt his friend's feelings.

"That all you got?" Marcellus asked.

"It is," John lied.

"Good. 'Cause Edmee and me went one more step."

"What's that?"

"We pulled the man's current driver's license outta the computer. Got a picture of what he looks like now."

That was what John was about to suggest.

"Good idea," he said. "You and Edmee are doing great work. Can you send me everything you've found?"

"Just sent the email."

John thanked him and said goodbye.

Grunwald asked, "You got cops everywhere working for you?"

"Marcellus is a postal inspector, another fed, but, yeah, I like to be inclusive. Let's take a look at what he's sent."

John opened the email. Two photos, headshots of the same guy looking like they'd been taken some years apart, judging by a receding hairline and growing jowls.

Grunwald said, "If that guy isn't the one we want for the bank robberies, I'd bet my house he's in some other racket."

"Let's see if he's been caught for anything," John said.

He pulled up the NCIC website and entered the man's name: Lamar Dekker.

The query came up negative, no record found.

Grunwald said, "I still say he's wrong, and maybe you're right about the system being hacked."

John said, "Maybe. I'll send the pictures to the FBI anyway."

After Grunwald left, John looked at the sketches of the Desert Mountain National Bank robbery made by the choreographer who'd seen it. The drawings had been done in pencil, outlining the robbers' shapes against minimally rendered backgrounds. The figures of the robbers themselves were simple line drawings with no details to the faces beyond the placement of eyes, noses and mouths.

Omitting the makeup, warpaint, wigs and feathers actually helped John to see things differently. Removed the distractions. He knew by now the robbers weren't Native Americans but the stripped down renderings started to help him see other possibilities.

What the choreographer captured, logically enough, was a sense of flow.

A still life rendering of men in motion.

One guy running, caught in midstride, both feet off the ground.

Another one vaulting the tellers' counter.

These guys were athletes, just as the choreographer had said.

Athleticism was a distinguishing mark of elite soldiers, of course, but John felt these guys were civilians. Teammates. The only question was what sport they played.

He looked at the sketches of the robber who made the hand gestures. There were sketches of three hand signals. Individually, they still didn't give John the answer he'd been seeking. He held the pages with a thumb and index finger and riffled through them like an animation flipbook. That sparked something, but didn't quite bring it all the way out of hiding.

He repeated the exercise two more times. He kept inching closer to the answer. He put the sketches down and working from memory duplicated the gestures the choreographer had drawn. He knew he was right on the edge of finding his answer now.

The best thing to do at that point was to relax and just let it come.

He called down to the hotel gift shop to make sure it was still open. He hurried down and found a pair of swim trunks he liked in his size. He paid with his personal credit card.

Marlene Flower Moon often criticized his expense account, but she'd never been able to find anything of substance that could cause him real grief.

Ten minutes later, after changing in his room, he was in the hotel pool. It was huge. Had its own waterfall. When John arrived there was a young couple with two small children splashing in the shallow end of the pool. They left shortly after he'd entered the water.

He had the whole pool to himself. He lay back and floated, looking up into the dark sky. The resort was off The Strip, surrounded by golf courses not neon signs. So the stars didn't have to fight a blast of light pollution to be seen. They sparkled like a Cartier display case set against the ebony sky.

Suspended in water that was only marginally cooler than the balmy night air, John felt at peace. If not at one with nature, he was well content to view heaven's light show. He watched the constellations wheel through the sky above him.

As if communicating with the stars, John began duplicating the hand gestures the choreographer had sketched. At first, there was no cosmic sign of acknowledgement. But the third time he ran through the sequence, he saw a shooting star. It raced through the darkness in a long graceful arc that reminded John of —

A curve ball. As if he'd just called for a breaking pitch.

That would make him the catcher.

Making the robbers baseball players.

— CHAPTER 29 —

Cashman Field, Las Vegas, Nevada

The stadium was the home field of the Las Vegas 51s, the Triple A minor league affiliate of the New York Mets. A Google map showed John where it was located in North Las Vegas. There was no game that night, but the ballpark's security team was on duty. John only had to ring a bell at the main gate to get their attention in the person of the chief officer, a gray-haired fellow whose name tag said Lathrop.

John showed his ID and said, "Federal officer, is there someone who —"

Lathrop squinted. "You're from the Bureau of Indian Affairs?"

"Yes."

"I don't think we have any Indians on our team."

"It's not the home team I want to talk about."

"So none of our guys is in trouble?"

"Not with me."

"That's good. So why are you here?"

"You think you might let me in?" John asked.

"Look, I'm not trying to give you a hard time, but my job is to keep people out of the ballpark and, no offense, I've never heard of your outfit before."

"How about the Metro police? You know them?"

"Sure."

"Here's my local contact." John handed him Grunwald's card.

Lathrop scanned the information. "You won't take it wrong if I call Captain Grunwald."

John shook his head. "Always good to be careful."

The call and confirmation of John's bona fides took less than a minute.

Lathrop opened the gate and let John inside. Returned Grunwald's card to him.

"What can I do for you, Special Agent Tall Wolf?"

"You have somewhere we can talk?"

Lathrop took John to his office.

A trained observer, John noticed a photo of a younger Lathrop in a baseball uniform on the wall behind the security chief's desk. The two men took their seats. Lathrop tried to make up for his perceived lack of respect for John's official status.

"Sorry about not recognizing your law enforcement credentials. Captain Grunwald gave me a quick earful about that. You like a soft drink or something?"

"I'm good, thanks, and the BIA isn't a high profile agency."

Lathrop seemed to relax a bit, hearing that John bore him no ill will.

"What is it you do? Your regular job, I mean."

"I work at the intersection of Native American and mainstream cultures. If there's a four-car pile-up, I try to sort things out."

Lathrop nodded. "That sounds like a good idea, but what does that have to do with this baseball team? Wait a minute, you did say it wasn't our guys, right?"

"Right. I'm hoping maybe you can tell me about the visiting team that just came through."

"San Bernadino? What've they got to do with anything?"

"You know about the big league steroid scandals, of course."

"Damn right, I do. They should never let any of those bastards into the Hall of Fame."

"Well, all I can say is what I'm working on is worse than that."

Lathrop sat back in his chair and said, "Damn. And it's got something to do with In — I mean, Native Americans? I don't think there's a one on the San Bernadino roster."

"No?" John thought about that and asked, "Is their team name the Indians?"

"Unh-uh. It's the Serranos."

John asked Lathrop to spell that for him.

He tapped "Serrano tribe California" into his smart phone.

He read aloud the information that came up. "The Serranos are a native tribe centered in the San Bernadino Mountains."

"Sounds kinda Spanish to me," Lathrop said.

John nodded. "That's the name the colonial missionaries gave them."

"And you had to look that up?"

John asked, "You know how many tribes there are in this country, Canada and Mexico?"

Lathrop said he didn't.

"That's okay, neither do I," John told him, "but it's a lot. By any chance, do you have a program for your team's series with the Serranos?"

The security boss opened a desk drawer, took one out and handed it to John. He leafed through it. The full rosters of each team were provided with a picture of every player, his position and season batting and pitching statistics, as applicable.

There was also a column for the league standings. The 51s were in second place, a game out of first. San Bernadino was dead last. Twelve games behind the leader.

"Looks like the Serranos are having a rough season," John said.

"They were before they came here, before they hit New Orleans. Now, they're on a tear, a four-game winning streak. Won those games by an average of seven runs."

"Really?"

Successful bank robbing must be a real pick-me-up, John thought.

"Too damn late to do the poor bastards any good," Lathrop said.

"Wait until next year?" John asked.

"Not even that for those guys."

"Why not?"

"This is San Bernadino's last season. They've been bad a long time. Basically, it's where guys have gone to end their careers. They can't fill their stadium for love or money. Heard the owner is going to declare bankruptcy. If more than one or two players on that team catch on anywhere else, I'd be amazed."

"Well, hell," John said.

"Yeah." The empathy was clear in Lathrop's voice.

John looked at the picture of him in his baseball uniform.

"It's pretty tough to let go of the dream, isn't it?"

"Damn right, it is. You tell yourself you'll get over it, but you never do. I haven't anyway. There's never been a major league player my age, but there isn't a day I don't wake up and think I could still pound the ball against half the bums I see taking the mound in the big leagues."

"Is that anger talking?" John asked.

"It was at first. Now, it's just wishful thinking."

"Thanks for all your help," John said. "There's just one more thing I need to know."

"What's that?"

"Where do the Serranos play next?"

Lathrop didn't even have to look it up. He was a true baseball lifer.

"Tacoma."

Traveler's Rest Motel, Tacoma, Washington

Corey Price's room was no bigger than anyone else's on the team and with eight large men occupying the space, it felt like there wasn't enough air to breathe easy. An antique window air-conditioner couldn't keep up with the body heat the guys generated. Everyone was sheened with sweat, though some of that had to do with tension. The small window in the bathroom was open, but all that did was admit a stale odor from the creek behind the property.

The only good thing was, the team manager and the coaches had worries of their own. They were content to leave the players to their troubles. The skipper had suggested the team stay together for a blowout after their last ever game. Everyone had agreed, but without any great enthusiasm.

Nobody really expected the entire roster to show up.

Price had returned from Seattle with two coolers filled with beer.

After everyone had popped a can, he let them know how he felt.

"Dekker said we can expect to make as much money from the Seattle job as the other two combined but, personally, I have a feeling the shit is about to hit the fan."

Jack O'Grady, who played center field like he was channeling a young Willie Mays but couldn't hit a ball off a tee, said, "It was bound to, wasn't it, the kind of luck all of us have. Still, it was fun while it lasted."

Everyone agreed and most of them grabbed another beer.

Price said, "I told Dekker I was thinking about blowing off the last robbery."

Tut Warren, who could hit but couldn't field a ball if you let him use a fisherman's net, asked, "You sayin' we're done robbin' banks, Corey?"

Tut was one of the few guys who thought he stood a chance of finding a slot on another team, one that was affiliated with an American League club, so he could sell himself as a designated hitter and wouldn't ever need to worry about playing the field.

Price shrugged. "I told Dekker I'd go through with it, but that was only to shut him up. If it was up to me, I'd say to hell with it. But if the rest of you guys want to do it, I'll be right there with you. So let me see a show of hands. Who wants to do one last bank job?"

Six of them did. Only Price and Tut thought otherwise.

Tut gave the other guys, including Price, something to think about.

"If this is the last job an' it's a big haul, who's to say Dekker doesn't just keep all the money and our bikes, too. Disappear without a word. Maybe even tell the cops who done it."

O'Grady pointed out, "He rats on us, we rat on him."

Tut said, "They got pictures of us doin' a robbery, man. What they got on Dekker?"

"How would they even know where to find him?" Eloy Garcia asked. "He gets in that truck of his, he could drive all the way to Panama."

Exactly where Eloy, a third baseman who demonstrated brilliance in all aspects of the game just often enough to stay on the payroll, planned to go with his stolen loot. He said once he got home he knew places nobody would ever find him.

Eloy shifted to Price and Tut's side, and the debate was on. Voices rose and gesticulating hands flung beer across the room. Price had to intervene twice between guys who verged on throwing punches. He whistled down shouting matches several more times. They didn't want to get busted for creating a disturbance at the motel, he reminded them.

When he decided the jawing had gone on long enough, he stepped to the center of the room and held an open hand out to each side. "Let's take another vote."

The result this time was an even split, four to four.

Each side glared at the other.

Price said, "I got something I want each of you to think about. Let's say we rob this one last bank. We get away clean with the big money Dekker promised. What do we do then?"

The others all looked at him like that was as dumb a question as they'd ever heard.

O'Grady was the one to answer. "Well, Corey, I believe what we'd do then is take our money and head our separate ways."

Price nodded. "Uh-huh. So we get on our motorcycles and go. Only don't you think, by now, every cop in the country knows what kind of bikes we ride? And what about the cash? Are we going to put it all in duffel bags and strap them to our backs? Don't you think that might be just a bit obvious? Wouldn't the sleepiest state trooper in the world sit up and take notice?"

Nobody in the room had ever heard of the Socratic method but they all got Price's points.

"Well, shit," Tut said.

"Here are the two biggest questions of all," Price told them. "How come with all the planning Dekker handed us, he never gave us a final getaway plan? One that might take us all home. You think maybe having us come to a bad end was part of the deal all along?"

"That sonofabitch," O'Grady snarled.

The others seconded the opinion with their own profanities.

In the end, when their venting lost steam, they turned to Price.

"One last vote," he said.

Eight-zip against doing the last bank robbery.

"Driving back here from Seattle," Price told the others, "I just couldn't accept that the Lamar Dekker I've known for ten years is smart enough to pull off all the shit he's done on his own. He's got somebody else behind him, and that's what really worries me. We don't know who the hell that is, but I don't think whoever it is gives a rat's ass about us."

O'Grady asked, "What're you saying, Corey? We not only forget about doing the last job, we walk away from the money we already stole?"

Price shook his head. "No, we risked our asses for that money; it's ours. What I think we do is take the money Dekker says he's holding for us — say a prayer he hasn't stashed it in some foreign bank — and take Dekker's share, too. Then we leave all this stuff behind. Never say a word about it to anyone. Be careful we don't flash the money we stole. Spend it slow and easy."

O'Grady asked, "What about that problem? Ridin' off on our bikes with all that money."

"Well," Price said, "what I was thinking is we'll need another big truck. One we rent. Anybody here know how to drive one?"

Harris, a pitcher with a big arm and control problems, said

he did.

Price smiled. "Good. That's one problem solved. Now all we've got to do is get our money back, rip off Dekker and do one more thing."

"What's that?" Tut asked.

"Beat Tacoma these last two games. Go out winners."

J.W. Marriott Resort & Spa, Las Vegas, Nevada

Once John learned the robbers were professional baseball players, he made the very short intuitive leap to think that Lamar Dekker, the guy he felt sure had trucked off their stolen loot and motorcycles, could well be a member of the same fraternity.

He called the campus police at the University of Arizona, where Marcellus Darcy had told him Dekker had taken classes. At that hour, he figured they'd be the only ones at the school picking up a phone. He was right. Now, he'd have to persuade the cop on the line that the BIA was indeed a part of the U.S. government and he was a federal officer.

He caught a break, though, when the call was answered by a voice saying, "University police department, Sergeant Tall Elk speaking."

John had heard that name before, in Goldstrike, California. He'd worked a case there with Chief of Police Ron Ketchum, who had gone on to become the town's mayor. A guy named Tall Elk had been a cop there before leaving for another job.

"Sergeant, this is Special Agent John Tall Wolf of the BIA."

"No kidding. *Ya-ta-hey.*"

Diné — or Navajo — for hello. *Ya-at-ééh* in the original iteration.

John asked, "Are you the Tall Elk who worked on the Goldstrike PD?"

"Yeah, that's me. How'd you know that?"

John told him he'd worked a case there and had heard his name mentioned.

"Yeah, it was a good place to work, but I was ambitious and I knew Sergeant Stanley would be running the day-to-day operations as long as he wanted. So I came here. What can I do for you, Special Agent?"

"I'm wondering if you might have access to a database that can give me some information about a former student, Lamar Dekker." John spelled the name.

"He do something bad?"

"Looks like something real bad."

"In a way, that's good. For me to find him, I mean. If we have him on record as a troublemaker here, we might have imported his academic standing. A kid on probation for poor classwork, he's closer to getting a fond farewell if he screws up than a good student who steps out of line just once. Give me a minute while I look, okay?"

"Sure."

John finished the last of his packing while holding the phone to his ear. Sad to say, DeWitt had taken his plane back, and John would have to fly commercial. He was booked on the first flight out in the morning.

Sergeant Tall Elk came back and said, "Got him. He's in our records for creating a public disturbance. His only offense and he got off with a reprimand. His high spirits were excused because he'd just found out he'd been drafted by a pro baseball team. You'll like this, it was the Cleveland Indians."

"No kidding?" John said. "Were you able to see what kind of student he was?"

"Yeah, straight-C average." Matched the GPA that Marcellus had found on the guy. "Respectable for an athlete. He left school after his freshman year and then came back twelve years later for one semester. After that, he finished his degree online."

"What was his major?"

"Physical education. Thought you might have guessed."

"Did he have any math or science classes?"

"Rocks for jocks and … I don't believe this. Computer science?"

"You have a grade for that last one?"

"Yeah, he got a B in it. Looks like his high-water mark."

"But it's an introductory course, right?

"Uh-huh, that's just what it is. Don't see any follow up. Does any of this help?"

"I think it does, helps fill in a picture for me. Thanks for your help, Sergeant."

"Glad to do it. Us tall guys have to stick together."

With the information Sergeant Tall Elk had provided, John was able to go online and with a bit of sleuthing find *Total Baseball: The Ultimate Baseball Encyclopedia.* The eighth edition was the most recent, published in 2004. That was good enough to cover the six years Lamar Dekker played in major league baseball. From his stats with the Cleveland Indians, Texas Rangers and Seattle Mariners, John could see that he'd started out as a good glove, weak bat second baseman.

He was respectable enough to make the big leagues, but he didn't stand out enough to stay more than two years at any one club. Both his batting average and fielding percentage dropped year by year. A note at the end of his stint with the Mariners said his rights had been traded to a team in Osaka, Japan, the Orix Buffaloes, as the player to be named later.

Regarded as an afterthought at the end of his career, Dekker had been sent into exile.

A guy could become bitter about something like that, John thought. Especially if he came back from overseas hoping for re-demption only to see his baseball future die in the minor leagues. Where he met more guys who were just scraping by and had never gotten a chance to see the big time.

All of which was speculation, John knew.

He dug farther, hoping to see if he could find out anything about Dekker's days in Japan. An hour later, he found a story about Dekker in *The Japan Times,* a newspaper published in English. The sports section ran the headline GLORY AT LONG LAST above a photo of a smiling Lamar Dekker in a dirt-smeared uniform.

Dekker had been named the MVP of a three-game exhibition

series, leading his team to a 3-0 sweep. He'd hit .455, made several spectacular plays in the field and had scored the winning run in the final game by stealing home. Hence the dirty shirt.

What especially interested John was where the series had been played: Taiwan.

The Chinese fans had idolized Dekker for his unlikely heroic performance. So much so that he was hired to do TV commercials for a local beer, a gig that lasted five years and paid Dekker far more than his baseball career ever had. None of which prevented him from coming home and giving American baseball one last try.

As John had suspected, his career fizzled out in the minors, double-A ball.

The story in *The Japan Times* concluded that no one should feel sorry for Lamar Dekker because he still had friends in both Osaka and Taipei. Any time he wanted to come back to either city, he'd be warmly greeted and well compensated.

John closed his laptop and went out onto his balcony and stretched his muscles. He took out his cell phone and looked at the time: just after one a.m. If Deputy Director DeWitt was anywhere in the country east of Las Vegas, it would be even later for him.

He made the call anyway.

DeWitt picked up on the first ring and asked, "You have something good?"

John stepped back into his room. He had the team roster Officer Lathrop had given him at Cashman Field open on the desk he'd been using. He'd scanned the pictures of the players and sent them to his mother. She'd picked out the guys John wanted.

"Thought you might like the names of the eight bank robbers and the guy who's in cahoots with them."

"What I remember from law school, cahoots is a serious crime," DeWitt said.

"Generally is, yeah. I can tell you the city they probably intend to hit next, too."

"Special Agent, you've made me glad I didn't turn my phone off."

"One last thing," John said. "This ninth Indian?"

"Yeah?"

"He played baseball in Taiwan."

"Hot damn, a Chinese connection," DeWitt said. "I do believe you've earned an attaboy from the vice president."

— CHAPTER 30 —

Lincoln Park, Seattle, Washington, Sunday, August 25th

John's flight from Las Vegas landed at nine-fifteen a.m., ten minutes after DeWitt arrived from Los Angeles. The deputy director had gone to the City of Angels to meet with Vice President Morrissey who was in town to raise campaign cash. Never having been married to a billionaire, as the president had, Jean Morrissey needed to raise her own funds, and three years ahead of the next presidential election was not too soon to start.

DeWitt had called John en route to Seattle and the two men met at the car the local FBI office had provided for the visiting bigshot. John dumped his suitcase in the trunk and got in the back seat. The deputy director asked him, "You feel like stretching your legs a bit?"

"Always."

DeWitt had his driver take them to Seattle's Lincoln Park, a green space on Puget Sound not far from the airport. They strolled down the paved walkway alongside the beach. Though the sky was blue and the air mild, the park was uncrowded. The good people of the town might have been sleeping off their Saturday nights or bending their knees in the hope of salvation. In any case, the two feds were able to speak openly without fear of being overheard.

John explained how he put things together to find out the robbers' identities.

"Your mom strikes again," DeWitt said.

"She's never let me down."

"I think you've got someone else in your corner, too. After we spoke last night, I took the chance of calling the vice president. She was still up. Plotting with her brother, Frank, to make certain she's the next president."

"You sure I need to know this?" John asked.

"I think you'll be interested. When I told her what you'd come up with, she asked me what I thought of you. I said you're smart, self-assured and not worried about your next career move."

John nodded. He could live with that assessment.

DeWitt continued, "Madam Vice President told me you don't have to worry about your career because she has plans for you."

John stopped dead in his tracks. "What?"

DeWitt came to a halt and turned to look at John. "Those were her exact words."

"I like the job I have." Something he'd never admit to Marlene.

The deputy director told him, "Some are born great, some achieve greatness —"

"I don't want *anything* thrust upon me," John said.

DeWitt held his hands out, then let them drop. "You'll have to find a way to elude the plans of the mighty, if that's the case."

John looked at the deputy director for a moment and said, "You've faced this kind of situation, haven't you?" Off DeWitt's nod, he asked, "How'd you avoid it?"

"I managed the feat only up to a point. I told my betters I'd stay with the Bureau only if I could keep a foot in each world. I do my share of the administrative grind, but I work cases, too. I use my perks, like the personal aircraft, to lighten my psychic load. I also put up a serigraph of Mao Tse Tung in my office as a caution against any future promotion."

That made John smile. "Maybe I could get a print of Crazy Horse. Use that as a totem."

"Whatever works. I just wanted to give you a heads-up."

The two men resumed their walk.

John said, "The robbers are Indians in a way, San Bernadino

Serranos. A triple-A baseball club."

"I've heard of the tribe but not the team," DeWitt replied, "and I'm a California native."

"That's part of the team's problem. They aren't much of a draw. This is their last season before they fold their tent."

DeWitt gave John a look. "Desperate characters?"

"I ran their names through NCIC. Nothing more than a drunk and disorderly on two of them. The others have no criminal records at all. Going from a clean sheet to bank robbery makes me think they feel aggrieved at the least."

"Yeah. But are they far enough gone to shoot it out with us when we come for them?"

John said, "Maybe a few of the younger players hold out hope they can catch on with another team. The older ones have to know the dream is over. Hell, the Serrano people themselves have enrolled in different bands of Native Americans: the Morongo, San Manuel and Soboba."

DeWitt mulled that over. "You probably couldn't ask for men more ready to do something stupid."

John said, "Not all that stupid. They've gotten away with a big chunk of money from each of the two banks they've hit. We could arrest them in the next ten minutes, but getting convictions wouldn't be a sure bet."

"So it would be better to … what? Catch them coming out of a bank? We've all been lucky so far that no one has been killed. Third time could be the fatal charm. I guess the best thing would be to intercept them going into the next bank. They resist, it's all over for them."

John thought about that for a quarter-mile or so.

Then he said, "It's all over for them anyway, isn't it? I don't see the Chinese letting them live. It'd be much smarter to kill them."

DeWitt told John, "After I spoke with the vice president last night, I called a friend at one of the spook shops in DC. Passed along the information you gave me. What my friend said was the only chance for these guys to survive would be for us to arrest them. Because, yeah, he's sure the Chinese will get rid of them. As a matter of housekeeping, if nothing else."

"So you're working on some brilliant plan, right?" John asked.

"To the best of my meager abilities, but superior minds are involved as well."

"Meanwhile, I'm good to keep going?"

"Unless and until Acting Director Nelda Freeland says otherwise." DeWitt grinned. "I wouldn't worry about that, though."

"Good," John said.

J.W. Marriott Resort & Spa, Las Vegas, Nevada

Ellie Booker showed up at the posh hotel that Sunday morning, uncharacteristically one step behind the events of the day. She lost more ground when she stopped to look around at the opulent decor and furnishings of the huge lobby. It wasn't lost on her that the cost of a room there, subsidized by the casino, wouldn't get you into a Holiday Inn in Midtown Manhattan. Still, if Tall Wolf wound up jerking her around somehow, she could see bringing a camera and a microphone back there and letting middle America see where a government employee working on their dime had lain his head to rest.

The WorldWide News audience would scream that they couldn't afford such luxury.

They'd be right, too. It'd take a casino, an amusement park and a state fair to underwrite their visits to digs like this.

Ellie walked over to the young supermodel-in-waiting working at the reception desk. She asked for directions to the nearest house phone. Said she'd like to speak with a guest.

"If you'll tell me the guest's name, perhaps I can help you," the sweet young thing said. Her name tag said Persephone, the goddess of springtime. That made Ellie wonder if the young woman's mother was educated or had just heard the name in a beauty parlor and liked it.

Given the proper spelling, Ellie had to concede a measure of book-learning. Then again, it was shocking the jobs even Ivy League grads had to take these days.

Ellie said, "I'd like to speak with Special Agent John Tall Wolf, please."

"I'm sorry, but he checked out early this morning."

Ellie's face turned red with an infusion of blood, heat and anger.

The SOB *was* playing games with her. He'd conned her into doing his errands and —

Ellie saw the young goddess was enjoying her discomfort. As stoically as possible.

Then, just as Ellie was about to tear into her, she asked, "Are you Ms. Booker?"

"I am."

"May I see some ID, please?"

"Why?"

"Special Agent Tall Wolf left a message for Ms. Booker."

Ellie almost reached for her driver's license. Then she thought why show the goddess just what an old hag she was. All of thirty-seven. Instead she handed over her business card from WorldWide News. The one that listed her job title as Executive Producer followed by a parenthetical *inter alia*. Latin for: among other things.

Ellie was pleased to see envy flash in the goddess's eyes.

And annoyed when the younger woman smiled, clearly having understood the Latin.

Perhaps she had gone to a good school.

"Your message from the special agent, Ms. Booker," Persephone said handing Ellie a slip of paper.

Ellie's anger retreated. Tall Wolf hadn't screwed with her.

He'd gone to Seattle. Didn't say why, but there had to be a new development in the case. She could call him on his cell or fly up and they could talk in person.

So he hadn't frozen her out.

Probably still had ways to use her.

She decided Tall Wolf was the slickest operator she'd encountered since James J. McGill. The special agent had earned her a hundred grand bonus when she'd told Hugh Collier, the network's CEO and largest shareholder, that she'd not only scooped the rest of the media on the Indian bank robber story, she had a source inside law enforcement who'd give her details no one else would get.

Of course, if Tall Wolf didn't come through with sensational tidbits, she wasn't above indulging in a little creative journalism. It wouldn't be the first time WorldWide News had run with something like that. As long as no media watchdog prig caught her, she'd be okay.

But she thought she could negotiate a legit *quid pro quo* with Tall Wolf. She'd found the three biggest Chinese gambling losers to hit Las Vegas in the past year. One, by far, had burned through more cash than the other two. Could be a real big story behind a Chinese national blowing ten million bucks in Sin City. Ellie would bet the guy had been pissed off all the way back to Beijing. Might even have had some explaining to do once he got home.

Getting the dirt had cost her a quarter of her bonus money.

The cost of doing business.

Just as going to Seattle would be part of the job.

She fished her AmEx Centurion Card out of her wallet. She wasn't about to wait for a seat on a commercial flight. She was going to charter her own wings. Only there was no concierge on duty at the moment. He or she might only have stepped away for a whiz, but Ellie was not prepared to wait.

She turned back to Persephone at the registration desk and put her black card down.

"I need to charter a jet to Seattle as soon as possible. I'll also need a good room in whatever Marriott up there is the equivalent to this one. Can you do that for me?"

"Of course, Ms. Booker. Won't take long at all."

There was still a hint of envy in the younger woman's eyes, but she handled herself professionally. Acted like she'd seen a black card before. Didn't plead for help landing a media job because she really wasn't meant for the hospitality industry.

Ellie liked all that, and was impressed by how efficiently Persephone accomplished her tasks. She said, "Do you have a business card?"

Envy was replaced by suspicion, but it lasted no more than a heartbeat before a completely professional demeanor took over. For someone that young, she was really pretty good, Ellie thought. Still, there was room for one last test.

"Is there a car that might take me to the airport?" Ellie asked.

"I took the liberty of arranging a limo for you, Ms. Booker. It's waiting with the motor running."

Ellie smiled. "The next time you're in Washington, DC, give me a call if you're interested in a career change, and don't worry. There won't be any funny stuff involved."

She left at a jog.

Thinking she couldn't remember the last time she'd made such an offer.

Probably wasn't one.

She wondered if Tall Wolf's sly cordiality was rubbing off on her.

Henry M. Jackson Federal Building, Seattle Washington

The local FBI special agent in charge set Deputy Director DeWitt up in the largest conference room in the three floors the Bureau occupied. Sandwiches, pastries, herbal tea, orange juice and bottled water were provided for sustenance. Coffee, which had made Seattle famous, along with alt rock, had been declined by both DeWitt and Special Agent Tall Wolf.

John had spent the morning walking through the city's downtown area from Union Street to James Street, from Western Avenue to Sixth Avenue, looking for a bank he thought might be a likely target. Problem was, he found too many possibilities. Choosing one over another would be nothing more than guesswork. No tingle of intuition made him think *this* was the one.

Forsaking banks as his objects of scrutiny, John turned to looking for trucks. He knew what Lamar Dekker's semi-trailer looked like and had the plate numbers. Maybe the guy was parked nearby, waiting to pick up a bundle of stolen money and eight motorcycles. But he couldn't find the truck either.

Shortly before he would have chucked both efforts as pointless, DeWitt called.

"You hungry?"

"Now that you mention it, yeah."

"I've had some food sent in, and I've heard from Washington. Come on in."

"Right."

Now, the two feds sat across a conference table from one another.

John faced the near door to the room. A stack of federal arrest warrants rested on the table between them. John looked at the notes he'd made on his laptop about the two previous bank robberies. He had the feeling he was overlooking something important.

DeWitt glanced at his watch and said, "Ten minutes, then we grab these guys."

FBI Director Jeremiah Haskins had suggested it would be a good idea to take custody of the bank robbers while they were still breathing. Haskins didn't say so, and DeWitt didn't ask, but the undercurrent suggested that the idea of bringing the bad guys in alive was also shared by the vice president. Hearing the news, John had asked what the attorney general thought. Would one of his prosecutors be able to make the case?

DeWitt said, "I think that question is best left to those far above our pay grades."

What the deputy director did say was he'd been able to find the Tacoma motel where the San Bernadino Serranos were staying.

Hearing that was what had made John feel he was missing something.

He also told DeWitt another interested party would be heard

from soon.

"Who?"

"Marlene Flower Moon."

"How would she even know about any of this?"

"She's Coyote," John explained

DeWitt knew of the myth, and John connected it to the circumstances of his birth.

"Interesting," the deputy director said. He was a firm believer that not everything in the world could not be explained empirically. "We've got people watching the Serranos so another half-hour shouldn't hurt, if you want to wait for Ms. Flower Moon."

John used the time to review his notes.

DeWitt felt the need to ask again, "You're certain she's going to come?"

"I am."

"How can you be sure?"

"You keep tabs on the people who work for you?"

"Generally, but you've been very open and sharing."

"Not me. Your FBI minions."

"I allow more flexibility than most managers, but I stay on top of things."

"Who's your contact person with Nelda Freeland," John asked.

"Special Agent Christopher Panopoulos."

"Young or old? Well, that doesn't matter. Gay or straight?"

DeWitt said, "Young and straight, as far as I know."

John told him, "My money says Nelda has him eating out of her hand. Not that she'd be obvious about it. But what's the big deal? The two of them are both federal officers. And Nelda's higher up the ladder. And beautiful. And at least feigning an interest. You see where I'm heading?"

"I do. I should have seen it sooner," DeWitt said.

"Not a big deal. Neither of us has done anything wrong. But every word Nelda has heard from your man has been passed along to Marlene."

"I haven't told Chris about the vice president's interest in you."

"That's good."

DeWitt laughed. "You don't think you're feeling maybe just a bit paranoid?"

"It's not about me, not primarily. Marlene has grand ambitions and she wants to make sure some of the credit for cracking this case will go to her."

"How can that be? What has she contributed?"

"It's what she *will* contribute."

"You'll have to explain that one to me."

"If we go out and arrest the robbers in the next few minutes, we'll have them, but they won't be able to confirm that they're working for the Chinese. At the very least, we'll have to catch Lamar Dekker for that. Maybe even that wouldn't be enough."

"What do you mean?"

"Maybe there's another cutout between Dekker and the big bad guys."

DeWitt saw it now. "Maybe someone Dekker met during his time in Taiwan."

"Yeah, like that." John smiled. A light just went on in his head.

"You just thought of something," DeWitt said. "What is it?"

John held up a hand and went back to check his notes. He nodded to himself.

"The robberies in New Orleans and Las Vegas? They happened the afternoon before the Serranos played a night game ... the night before the team left town."

DeWitt said, "That's some nerve, robbing a bank and then going out to play baseball in front of thousands of people."

"Smart, too. Who would expose themselves like that other than innocent men? The next morning they get up early and catch their flight to the next town on their schedule, just like any good businessmen would do."

"I think I see where you're going here," the deputy director said. "The Serranos play a game tonight and another tomorrow. So tomorrow is when they'll hit the bank."

John said, "That gives us a day to work with. If we grab the robbers now, and Dekker expects to hear from them but doesn't, we might have a hard time finding him."

"That could be a problem. But a bigger one is we don't know who the killers are, the people hired to kill the Serranos."

John lapsed into silent thought. It looked to DeWitt like he might be closing in on something good. The deputy director stayed quiet, not wanting to cause a distraction. After a long moment, John raised his right hand as if reaching for a tangible object.

He twisted his wrist and formed a fist. He had what he wanted.

"Maybe we do know who the would-be killers are," John said. "The Serrano baseball players aren't true Native Americans, but who was it that claimed credit for the bank robbery in New Orleans?"

DeWitt knew whom John meant. It took him just a second to come up with the name.

"Red Nation Rising."

John nodded and said, "What could be smarter than to hire hit men who *are* real Indians?"

The door to the conference room opened and Marlene Flower Moon entered.

As if she'd been listening to every word that had been said, she asked John, "How many times do I have to tell you, Tall Wolf, that the politically correct expression is Native Americans?"

With a smile both beguiling and chilling, she turned to look at DeWitt and say, "My movie just wrapped."

Displaying an aplomb that made John want to applaud, the deputy director replied, "Hooray for Hollywood."

Rain Shadow Meats, Pioneer Square

The place was a butcher shop that featured locally sourced meats. It had high ceilings and brick walls. Then taking things one step farther, it had an open kitchen and dining tables up front. Craft beers, wine and soft drinks were available. The three feds went out to eat and talk because Marlene was hungry.

She had the Zuni sandwich, thin slices of roasted pork shoulder and arugula on toasted sourdough, and a glass of red wine. John and DeWitt had fed themselves earlier on far less artisanal fare. The deputy director allowed himself a Northcoast Scrimshaw Pilsner; John made do with a bottle of San Pellegrino mineral water.

Marlene told DeWitt, "Tall Wolf doesn't drink alcohol."

"I watch my consumption," he said. "Usually look at beer as one more course in a meal."

"He won't open any email I send him."

"Have to be careful about spyware," DeWitt said with a nod.

John told the deputy director, "I'd recommend you do the same, if she sends something your way."

He didn't let himself be bothered by the glare Marlene directed at him.

"Noted," DeWitt said.

"If I'm not wanted here," Marlene said, looking at both men, "I'll go. I thought I might be of help."

John looked at her. "You go, you won't get any credit. I'll find out what I want to know. Might take me a little longer, but I'll get it."

Marlene amped up her glower, but took a folder out of her large handbag and tossed it on the table in front of John. He lifted the cover and glanced at the contents.

"This list is arranged in most likely to least likely order?" he asked.

She nodded. John passed the folder to DeWitt and said, "If I'm right about the Chinese hiring Native American killers to do their dirty work, these are the people we want to watch for."

Marlene, sly as the Trickster that John thought she was, had figured things out, too.

DeWitt studied the names and photos in the file and then looked at both of his companions.

"These people are white and two of the top three are female."

"Makes sense," John said. "Women can get closer to athletes more easily than men, and my guess is that all of the people on the list are either 1/32 or 1/64 Native American. They get away with the hit, they're Red Nation Rising; they get caught, they're white people."

"White *racist* people," Marlene elaborated.

"Huh," DeWitt said.

Marlene told him, "Do you know Tall Wolf refuses to work on reservations?"

The deputy director shrugged and said, "I try to stay out of New Jersey."

— CHAPTER 31 —

Marriott Waterfront Hotel, Seattle, Washington

John had made his reservation at the hotel on his flight north; law enforcement personnel comprised one of two classes of passengers allowed to use a cell phone in flight. The other was flight crews. The Seattle hotel didn't have a casino as a profit center and the room rates were higher than his BIA per diem, even with the discount given to federal employees.

In such cases, John made up the difference out of pocket. At his height, he'd lose a night's sleep if he went for lodgings with a bed that left his feet hanging over the edge. He didn't mind the expense. For the most part, he lived modestly and had recently saved enough money to buy a third share of Berkshire Hathaway, BRK.A, $173,389 per share that day, up $904 from the last time he checked. Warren Buffett appeared to be in good health and continued to work hard to increase John's minor wealth.

When he checked in that evening — the arrests of the Serranos having been postponed as discussions between the FBI and the vice president regarding the best way to bring matters to a conclusion went on — the desk clerk gave him a verbal message.

"You've been invited to dinner at The Hook and Plow."

Taking a guess, John said, "The hotel restaurant?

"Yes."

"By whom?" John wondered if Marlene had some trick in mind. Washington might change its plans, but Marlene, DeWitt and

John had left things with the idea that FBI personnel would watch the ballplayers until tomorrow morning. Make sure they didn't attempt any thievery that night, and protect them from Chinese and/or Indian assassins. Move in fast if skulduggery or mortality looked imminent.

The desk clerk told John, "Ms. Ellie Booker extended the invitation. She's currently a guest of the hotel."

John met Ellie in the restaurant. The hostess led them to a quiet table with room to carry on a confidential conversation. John had no doubt Ellie had selected the table personally. Probably tipped the hostess to keep other diners away for as long as possible. Well, John thought, she undoubtedly had a bigger expense account than he did.

She handed him a sheaf of stapled papers from what looked like a courier's bag.

"The information you wanted about Chinese visitors to Vegas incurring big gambling losses."

John smiled at her and said, "Thanks."

He read every word she provided, but he might have stopped after reading the first profile in bad judgment. The name Cheng Zou flew right off the page at him. The Chinese doctoral candidate at Penn. The scholar whose research included a study of Carl Gugasian's bank robbing techniques.

The amount of money Cheng had dropped was impressive.

"Ten million dollars," John said, "that had to sting."

"Maybe not too much. What I was told, he dropped another quarter-mill in tips on his way out the hotel door."

"Saving face?" John asked.

"Maybe. That or it's small change to the guy. I spent a bit of money myself before I left Vegas and heard from one person who might have it right that Mr. Cheng is a billionaire."

John said, "He still had to look like a putz losing that much. His ego got egged."

Ellie laughed. "Putz, huh? Didn't know that was an old Indian word."

"Native American," John said.

"Yeah. As long as I was looking into people, I took a quick run past your public reputation. You're not the politically correct type."

"That's true. So did you make out monetarily for the scoop I promised you? Get a nice bonus?"

Ellie was usually reticent about things like that.

A typical newsie, she loved to snoop but was fiercely protective about her privacy.

But she told John, "Yes, I did."

"Might have something more for you, if you'd care to do some more digging."

Ellie nodded. She was interested.

"Lamar Dekker," John said, and explained Dekker almost certainly was the robbers' outside man, driving the truck that made off with the stolen cash and the gang's motorcycles. "Dekker also played professional baseball in Taiwan, made business connections there."

"You want to know if I can find any connection between Dekker and Mr. Cheng," Ellie said.

"You're a smart lady. The connection might be that Dekker and Cheng had occasion to gamble in the same casinos in Las Vegas or, say, Macau. Maybe Cheng covered some of Dekker's losses. Could be one way to start a beautiful relationship."

Ellie sensed a great story in the offing, but it was her nature to be suspicious.

"How come you're not doing this legwork yourself?"

John said, "Hey, if the Pentagon can use private contractors, why can't the BIA?"

Ellie didn't buy that, but she didn't object.

What wasn't John telling her?

Even though the answer was simple enough, she didn't see it.

If something went wrong on her end, it would be harder to blame the Indian.

Alone in his room after dinner, John called Rebecca Bramley.

"Miss my voice?" she asked.

"That and everything else. Plus, I'm almost back in Canada."

"Where are you?"

"Seattle."

"I still have one vacation day and a few personal days I can tap."

John said, "I think the case I'm working should wrap up soon. Meet you in New Orleans?"

"I'd like that."

John took a deep breath. "Would you mind if my mother and father join us for dinner?"

"You want me to meet your parents?"

"I think you'd like each other."

"Okay, if you'll meet my parents, too. Say within the next year."

"Only fair, provided it's not Nunavut in January."

Rebecca laughed. "How about South Florida on New Year's Eve?"

"That sounds good."

They left things there, happy but wondering how their relationship would turn out.

Living and working in different countries.

Before she went to bed that night, Ellie sat down at her laptop and wrote a detailed summary of her meeting with John Tall Wolf. She included having found Cheng Zou per Tall Wolf's request and how the special agent had asked her to look for a connection between the Chinese billionaire and the bank robbers' outside man.

She sent the document to a secure cloud server. In the event that she died unexpectedly, her lawyer would open an envelope that would provide a password to access all of Ellie's confidential files. Some would be used to sell stories to WorldWide News or other media outlets to maximize her estate. Others would be made public to destroy her enemies.

Before closing down her computer, Ellie used an app that had been written specifically for her. It allowed her to access the guest registry files of a dozen major hotel chains, including Marriott. She liked to know if anyone special was staying under the same roof where she lodged. You never could tell where a story might be found, she thought, especially if two celebrities who thought they were being discreet were getting carnal just one or two floors away from her.

No such luck. Not that night at the Marriott in Seattle.

But, damn, if she didn't spot the name Tall Wolf had just given her.

Lamar Dekker had been a guest in the hotel.

Had checked out just that morning.

Ellie put off going to bed.

Thought how she might get information about Dekker from the hotel staff.

See if she might find the bastard before Tall Wolf did.

Wouldn't that make a great story?

— CHAPTER 32 —

Traveler's Rest Motel, Tacoma, Washington

Corey Price was drowsing in his motel room when a loud knock at the door all but lifted him off his bed. He'd been watching *A League of Their Own* for the ninety-ninth time. He'd always liked it, but that night he could relate to the movie more than ever. With his own team about to disappear, he truly knew the deep disappointment the women in the All American Girls Professional Baseball League must have felt when their careers ended.

If anyone told him there was no crying in baseball, he'd bust their nose for them.

Sipping his third bottle of Rainier Beer, still in uniform except for his cap and spikes, his mind had drifted back and forth between the film and that night's game. The Serranos had won 1-0. The two teams had three hits between them; there'd been a combined twenty-eight strikeouts and no walks. The game was over in an hour and forty-nine minutes. You went to the men's room with sluggish bowels in the first inning, you missed it.

Price had his team's only hit, a decisive home run.

He'd never felt so sad about winning a game in his life.

Tomorrow would be his last game, the last time he'd ever play professional ball. He could all but feel his heart breaking. Emptying the bottle of beer, he turned his eyes and his mind back to the TV screen. Maybe that's what he'd do, start a new women's baseball league. Begin with two recruits who looked like Geena Davis and

Madonna. The way they did in the movie.

He started to doze and dream of his plan coming true.

Geena and Madonna were there, both begging him for uniform number 1. They'd do anything to get their way and —

Then the knock at his door had almost given him a heart attack.

The skipper poked his grizzled head in the room.

"Come on, get up! Shower and get changed. The Tacoma boys are gonna show us they're real sports. We're going out to eat and drink on them. In honor of us playing our last game against them tomorrow."

Price sat up and asked, "Shouldn't we wait until *after* we play our last game?"

The skipper said, "Win or lose, how do you think we'll feel tomorrow? That wouldn't be a party; it'd be a wake. Besides, there's a big storm front coming in. We might get rained out tomorrow. You think they'll reschedule for us? We might've already played our last game, goddamnit."

The thought hit Price like a sucker punch. He rolled off the bed.

"I'll be out in ten minutes," he said.

The four FBI agents assigned to watch the Serranos at their motel that night had been bored silly, until a motorcade of eight taxis pulled up to the place. Players and coaches poured out of motel rooms. Two old guys, had to be the manager and a coach, got in the first cab. Three guys got into each of the following seven cabs. Then they all took off.

"Where the hell are they going?" asked Baldwin, the senior agent on the detail.

Nobody had a clue.

The only thing the feds could do was get into their two cars and follow.

Baldwin was about to call for help, suspecting something akin to a mass jailbreak, when the taxis pulled into a parking lot outside a sports bar in a little town down the road from Tacoma.

The Burning Onion, Gig Harbor, Washington

The guys on the Tacoma team competed as hard as anyone in baseball, but that night they stepped up as brothers to the Serranos. The team that would hear the magic words, "Play ball," next spring opened their hearts and wallets to the guys who would never again have the chance to "wait until next year."

Food and drink came in large quantities; the guys from Tacoma were generous hosts. They weren't alone in the spirit of good will. The owners of the place had a professional photographer take pictures of each team and the two of them together. The fans of the Tacoma team patted the backs of the guys on the opposing team, told them to come back and visit any time.

Price, as the Serranos' hero that night, was singled out. He signed dozens of autographs on baseballs, bats and game programs. He shook hands with people, had his back patted and was kissed by more than a few women who looked good enough to be in either real movies or the ones in his dreams.

He did everything he could to enjoy the moment.

Laughed at the weakest jokes.

Said, "Yeah, you're right," more times than he could remember.

Managed to keep his eyes dry most of the night.

Having waited outside the sports bar for hours, Baldwin finally lost patience.

"I'm going in," he said.

The three junior members of the detail had all taken turns watching the back entrance to make sure nobody tried to slip out that way. Nobody did. Several people, all of them fans or people simply dining out that night left the place. The number of cars in the parking lot thinned to the point where the FBI cars were now isolated, obvious to anyone who cared to look their way.

One of the agents asked Baldwin if he could bring some take-out food and soft drinks back with him. He said no. But once he came back they could take turns going inside to use the men's room. Muttered expressions of mock gratitude followed. Baldwin pretended not to hear them.

He went inside and was surprised by the quick attention he got from a waitress.

"You order over there, sir," she said. "Then we bring your order to your table."

Pegged for an outsider from the get-go, Baldwin thought.

He wasn't off to a good start. Trying to recover, he asked, "Can I order food to go?"

"Of course. Same way. You order, we deliver."

"Thanks." Gourmet burgers seemed to be the specialty. He ordered four with colas. Then he took a table where he could watch the players partying. Those guys weren't limiting themselves to soft drinks. Beer was everywhere. But nobody was getting testy. Just the opposite. The guys who weren't laughing seemed to be comforting one another.

Baldwin's headcount put the number of ballplayers from both teams at forty. They all seemed to look alike. Not in skin color or facial features necessarily but the fact that they were all extra large, had arms, shoulders and chests you didn't find on normal people. Some had quick reflexes, too. A couple of guys off to one side were doing a juggling act, tossing five salt shakers back and forth between them.

Never dropped one.

Not while Baldwin was looking anyway. He was distracted when the waitress came back with his order, far faster than he'd expected. He'd already paid, so there was nothing left for him to do but leave. The waitress told him to have a nice night. He summoned a smile that was half genuine only because she was such a sweet kid.

The other agents were surprised and pleased when Baldwin passed out the food and drinks, stunned when he didn't ask to be reimbursed. Dumbfounded when he didn't start talking until everyone finished eating.

"I saw forty guys in there, either ballplayers or coaches. I couldn't pick out the eight we want, and I was sitting no more than thirty feet from most of them. When the party breaks up and these guys start filtering out, any of you think you'll be able to tell who's who?"

Baldwin gave them a team program for the Serranos versus Tacoma game.

He'd found it at his table.

The photographs of the home team were two inches square; the visitors' pictures were maybe an inch-and-a-half square. Players on both sides all wore baseball caps. At best, the images gave hints of appearances.

Identifying the wanted individuals across a parking lot, even using binoculars, would be a very good trick indeed. And they didn't have binoculars.

"We could stop everyone coming out the door," the junior agent said.

Baldwin pointed out, "We haven't been told to make any arrests yet. Your way might just hint to the bad guys that something was up."

The number two man said, "If we can't tell who they are, anybody looking to kill those guys won't be able to do any better."

"Yeah, unless they pull up with automatic weapons and take out everyone just to make sure," Baldwin said.

He decided it was time to call in for guidance from above.

He punched Deputy Director DeWitt's number into his phone.

He was waiting for the call to go through when the party finally broke up and people started pouring out of the bar.

Not quite everyone left. The eight Serranos who'd moonlighted as bank robbers stayed behind, not wanting the night to end. With them was the manager of the Tacoma team. He and Corey Price sat at a table off to themselves.

Walt Wooten, the Tacoma manager, put a hand on Price's arm, not so much from sentiment, more like a guy checking out a cut of beef. He nodded. Approved of what he'd found.

"I think you still got it, kid."

Wooten was old enough to call someone who was thirty a kid.

"Got what?" Price said.

"Enough bat speed to get around on a ninety-six mile per hour fastball. That's what you hit out of the park for your home run tonight."

Hearing that made Price smile. That pitch had looked like a beach ball floating in when he'd swung his bat. The fact that Wooten knew just how fast the pitch was told him Tacoma could afford a radar gun to clock the speed. The Serranos didn't have anything like that.

Wooten continued, "I think if you play first base instead of catching your legs would last another five years, too."

"So you think I have a future?" Price asked.

The manager leaned forward, "I don't think you'll make it to The Show."

The big leagues.

As much as he tried to be a realist, it still hurt Price to hear that.

"Then what?" he asked.

"I think you could show the young guys coming through Triple-A how to improve their chances of becoming big leaguers."

Price laughed. "Yeah? That and five bucks will get me a latte, right?"

Wooten sat back in his chair. "Tell me something. The day you signed your first contract, did you do it for the money?"

"I wasn't a bonus baby. Well, not more than a $5,000 bonus baby. I signed because somebody showed interest. Was willing to pay me *something*."

"So you played for the love of the game, basically."

"Yeah."

"Figured the big money would come when you earned it."

Price nodded.

"You still think the big money's gonna come?"

"No."

"You still love the game?" Wooten asked. "Some guys get bitter."

"None of them could hit a ninety-six mile per hour fastball, I bet."

The Tacoma manager laughed. "Damn few of them anyway. So you still love the game. What I'm offering you is a chance to play for us next season. You do what I think you can, down the road, I could see you managing a team. Maybe even become a coach or a manager in the big leagues. I believe you've got the smarts. That's how I can see you getting to The Show ... if you're interested."

Price glanced up. The nearest TV had the local weather forecast on. A radar image showed the storm front getting close. Heavy rain was predicted to last for two days. Looked hopeless that they'd get their last game in.

Wooten followed Price's gaze, saw the forecast, too.

"If you're *not* interested," the Tacoma manager said, "at least you'll go out like Ted Williams, hitting a home run in your last at-bat."

Price looked at Wooten in disbelief. Then he laughed so hard he almost fell off his chair.

"Me and Ted Williams, mentioned in the same breath. That's the funniest damn thing I've ever heard."

Wooten shook his head and started to rise.

"Wait, wait a minute," Price said.

The manager sat back down.

"What about any of the other guys?" he asked.

"Your teammates over there?" Wooten shook his head.

Price sighed and asked, "If I sign with your team, will you give me a bonus?"

"I might get you something real modest, enough to keep you

in lattes for a while."

"I was thinking of something else. How about you let me and the guys go back to your park and take one last turn at batting practice together?"

Wooten was touched by that. He asked, "You want me to get my pitching coach to throw to you?"

Price shook his head. "Nah, a pitching machine is good enough."

"Okay. We got a Casey 3G. Spits 'em out up to a hundred miles per hour, if you want. Throws breaking balls, too. You set it up the way you want. I'll have the security boys put it out. They'll let you and your friends into the ballpark. That do it for you?"

"That'd be great," Price said.

The two men stood. Wooten extended his hand. Price took it.

"The offer to join my team is good for a month," Wooten said.

— CHAPTER 33 —

Puget Sound Stadium, Tacoma, Washington

John Tall Wolf got a call from Deputy Director DeWitt, explaining the situation that the FBI detail watching the San Bernadino Serranos had encountered: the San Bernadino team's trip to the sports bar, the party with the Tacoma team, groups of ballplayers going off in different directions, the FBI agents being unable to follow all of them.

"In other words," John said, "we don't know where our Indians are."

"No. The best we can say is we're working on it."

John respected the man's candor.

"You have any ideas?" DeWitt asked.

"Maybe one. If that doesn't work, then I don't know," John told him. He added, "I'll need a couple of your people to help me. You want to come along?"

"I would, only I'm not in Seattle at the moment."

"Where are you?"

"On my way back from San Francisco, the next stop on the vice president's fund-raising tour."

Better you than me, John thought.

He said, "My idea works out, you want me to call you?"

"Yes, no matter how late," DeWitt said.

John told the deputy director, "Have your people meet me at the Serranos' motel."

Two FBI agents met John at the Traveler's Rest Motel and the three feds went looking for the team's manager. They found him unconscious in his room. The motel desk clerk had to let them in. The two FBI agents got the manager stripped and into the shower. They wrapped him in towels and poured coffee into him.

Five minutes later, he was telling his story.

"Best damn party I've been to in the past twenty years. Jesus, I'm gonna miss this game." He started to cry.

John got down on one knee in front of him.

"Sir, this is really important. We need your help. We're trying to save the lives of eight of your players. Will you help us do that?"

The manager looked at John as if he was crazy. Then he started to get angry. The guy was still inebriated and emotional.

"Somebody's tryin' to hurt my boys? I'll kill *them*."

John got him settled down, told him the names of the players he wanted.

"That bunch? The best of them is Corey Price. Why, I gave the Tacoma manager permission to talk to Price about joining their team next year. He won the game for us tonight. Came back to this dump still wearing his uniform. I had to tell him to change for the party."

John said, "What's your best guess where Price and the others might be right now?"

The man's eyes went blank for a moment as he tried to think.

Then he smiled as if he should have known the answer all along.

"You want to find a ballplayer, I'd say the best place to look is a ballpark. Could be he went back to where he hit his final home run tonight."

The FBI agents took the manager from the motel to spend the rest of the night in better lodgings downtown. John didn't want him talking about his interview to anyone else. Especially not Corey Price and his seven teammates.

He headed off to Puget Sound Stadium.

He hadn't wanted to get his hopes too high.

He expected to find the ballpark dark.

But the field lights were on.

And John heard the distinctive sound of a wooden bat hitting a baseball.

John called the Tacoma PD, made his way up the ranks to Captain George Abe, the man in charge of the Patrol Division that night. He identified himself to the captain and gave him some background on the robberies in New Orleans and Las Vegas. The local cop already knew the publicly reported details.

"Are you saying these guys intend to hit Tacoma next?" Abe asked.

John thought it was more likely the target would be in Seattle but he didn't want to hurt local pride. "Here or that town up the road," John said.

"Yeah, it could be there, I suppose. But what's the connection between Tacoma and those other towns? New Orleans and Las Vegas have a lot more flash."

"Your town like the others has a Triple-A baseball team."

"That's it?"

"Yeah. The robbers are ballplayers."

"Our guys?" The captain's voice was filled with disbelief.

"No, the San Bernadino Serranos."

"Oh, them." Feelings about Californians weren't always warm in Washington state.

"Yeah, anyway I'm at the ballpark right now. The lights are on and it sounds like someone is taking batting practice. I'd like to go inside and make an arrest."

"You want to bring in eight guys by yourself?"

"Well, as long as you'll be talking to stadium security about letting me in, I thought you could send a few cars over to transport the prisoners."

Captain Abe paused before saying, "I sure to hell hope this isn't one big practical joke."

"How about this?" John asked. "I'll give you the personal phone number of FBI Deputy Director Byron DeWitt. He can vouch for me. But please get someone to open the stadium for me, because there's one more thing to think about."

"What's that?"

"There's a real chance there might be people out to kill these guys to keep the robberies from being connected to higher-ups. If there is a shoot-out in your town tonight, it would look better for everyone to have the good guys win."

"Holy shit. If that's true ... I'll call the deputy director right away."

"Open the gate for me first," John told him.

A security guard whose nameplate read Johansen came to the third base gate and said to John, "May I see your ID, please?"

John showed him his BIA credentials. The guard nodded.

The sounds of batting practice continued in the distance.

Johansen unlocked the gate and let John in.

"Hard to believe ballplayers are crooks," he said, relocking the gate.

"People get desperate when they lose their jobs."

"Ain't that the truth? You want some help?"

"Thanks, but no. I don't want to put anyone else at risk. Let the Tacoma police in when they come, but keep everyone else out."

"Everyone else?"

"There might be some bad guys around. They'll probably have guns. Don't give them a chance to fire at you."

The security guard's eyes went wide. He bobbed his head in agreement. He wasn't going to play the hero. That pleased John. He didn't want any regrets about how he was handling things.

He walked quietly up into the grandstand and through the cheap seats down to those near the home team dugout on the third base line. He took a seat and looked at the man standing to the left of home plate in the batting cage, swinging at balls from a pitching machine. The batter looked up at John, letting a ball go past unchallenged. It hit a sheet of heavy canvas with a thunk.

Then the batter turned his attention to the next ball the machine hurled his way. He swung hard and made solid contact. John followed the flight of the ball as it cleared the stadium wall in center field, above the number 425. The seven men sitting across the field in the visitors' dugout also tracked the ball, until they turned to look at John.

None of them, by their expressions, seemed to think he was just a guy who happened to wander into the ballpark. Not even after John applauded the batter's long drive. Men with guilty consciences, they figured him for just what he was, a cop.

But they stayed put, maybe trying to decide their next move.

More likely, they'd chosen to let the man in the batting cage take the lead. He let another pitch from the machine go by and then walked over to stand on the field not ten feet from where John sat. John held up a finger and used speed dial to call Byron DeWitt.

He said into the phone, loud enough for the guy with the bat to hear, "I found them at the ballpark in Tacoma. Yeah, eight of them. No, just me. Did you get a call from Captain Abe? Good. Help's on the way? Good. No, I don't think so. Let me ask."

John lowered the phone and looked at Corey Price. He said, "I'm on the phone with the deputy director of the FBI. He wants to know if he should send a SWAT team to help me out. You think he should?"

Price said, "You've got your own gun, don't you?"

"I do."

"None of us is armed."

"You're holding a bat."

"None of us is that stupid."

"You sure?" John pointed his chin toward the opposite dugout.

The seven other men were stepping out of it, each of them holding a bat.

All of them were staring at John as they approached.

John took out his Beretta and said to Price, "I might have to shoot a few of you. Also, being a real Indian as well as a federal officer, I'm licensed to take scalps."

Price said, "What?"

Johansen was watching the third base gate from the cover of a deep shadow under the grandstand. Keeping the ballpark safe at night was no harder than keeping the dearly departed in a cemetery from going for a moonlight stroll. You didn't believe in ghosts, you had no worries. Just like his job. No worries at all.

Tonight, though, he'd been told by a federal officer to watch out for guys with guns coming to shoot ballplayers who were bank robbers. Jeez. The bank robber part was awful enough. Guys wanting to kill them, maybe kill him, too, if he made the wrong move, he wasn't being paid near enough to get in the way of any of that.

If any of it was true, of course.

But then the guy from the BIA — he'd never heard of that outfit before tonight — had known it was the Serranos not the home team taking batting practice. That was what Captain Abe had said. He'd also said some cars from the Tacoma PD would be by soon, too.

Crazy as everything was sounding, having some cops on hand would be reassuring.

Johansen saw headlights turn into the stadium parking lot, but it wasn't a patrol unit. His guts started to churn until he saw who got out. Not any guys with guns. Just one woman. Kind of skinny. Short spiky hair. But she had a cute foxy face.

What the hell did *she* want?

Johansen decided to emerge from the shadows and investigate.

Ellie Booker approached the security officer standing behind a barred gate she presumed was locked. Guy looked pretty nervous for seeing one small woman walking his way. Ellie carried both a knife and an expandable twelve-inch steel baton. She knew how to use both weapons, but most guys, including the likes of the one looking at her now, took her at face value.

So why did the security guard look so nervous?

As she stopped on the other side of the gate, he told her, "The stadium is closed."

She saw his nameplate: Johansen.

Ellie said, "The lights are on, Officer Johansen."

"Closed to the public," he explained.

"That's okay, because I'm not a fan. I'm the media."

She showed the guy her WorldWide News ID.

"No press after hours."

Ellie said, "I'm not talking newspapers. I do TV. Don't you want to be on TV?"

In her experience, nine out of ten people did. If only to alert their family and friends to the appearance. Especially if they got to say something. Meant their lives wouldn't end without any public notice.

That was cynical, she knew, but true, too.

Johansen, however, just shook his head.

He was beginning to annoy her. She wanted to rap his knuckles with her baton. But she kept her cool.

"Listen," she said, "I didn't want to have to say this, but I'm working with the federal government."

She saw the reaction in the guy's eyes. Knew she had the right fix on things.

"You just let a federal agent inside your stadium. I saw him."

The guy's jaw dropped. She had him now.

"I was parked over there," she hooked a thumb at the access road to the stadium. "I was waiting for some information before I joined him. You gonna make me call him? He has to come back to the gate, you're gonna look pretty silly."

Johansen didn't like that. Made a stab at seeing how smart she was.

"You're with the FBI guy?"

Ellie grinned. "Nice try. Special Agent Tall Wolf is with the BIA." Johansen said, "Shit."

He let her in. Ellie moved ten feet into the stadium. If the guy changed his mind and tried to shove her back out, she'd sooner duck and run than pulp him. Johansen followed her but kept his hands to himself.

"Which way did he go?" Ellie asked.

He pointed the way. "You gonna put him on TV? Him and the bank robbers?"

They were here, too? Ellie almost swooned at the idea of shooting some video.

As usual, she had her Canon PowerShot Elph on her, as well as her weapons. The little beauty shot both stills and video. Worked great in low light. Had built in Wi-Fi so she could upload her footage in a snap.

She said, "You bet. Maybe even include—"

You, she was about to say when she saw a black sedan roar into the parking lot.

Ellie knew trouble when she saw it.

She told the security guard, "Lock the gate, take cover and call the cops."

"They're supposed to be on the way," Johansen said.

"Tell 'em to hurry."

Ellie looked over her shoulder as she ran.

The security guy stood paralyzed when he saw who poured out of the car.

Four guys with assault rifles — dressed like Indians.

Johansen might have reached the gate in time to slam it shut.

Just in time to have the muzzles of the automatic weapons poke between the bars and shred his precious heinie. He had neither the courage nor the daring of the bank guards in New Orleans and Las Vegas. He bugged out.

Deciding if he survived the night he'd have no trouble living with his choice.

Price told John, "You're bullshitting, about taking scalps."

"Yeah, but not about shooting you guys, if I have to."

The other robbers now stood in a cluster behind their leader.

"You with the FBI?" Tut Warren asked.

John shook his head. "Bureau of Indian Affairs."

Jack O'Grady asked, "They sent you because —"

Price cut him off with an upraised hand.

John told him, "That was one of the things that put me on to you. The way you use hand signals. Took me a while, but I finally figured out you're a catcher. Right?"

Price nodded.

John saw a couple of the men behind Price, bats in hand, were edging out of the group. He wasn't sure whether they meant to run or intended to come at him from different directions. He was fairly certain he could shoot both of them. If the others charged while he was engaged with the first two, though, things were going to get bloody fast.

He'd have to shoot to kill.

But if one of them got through and hit him with a swing like the one Price had used to hit the ball over the fence, he was going to have some headache.

John said, "Don't even think about taking a run at me. I might not get all of you, but the Tacoma cops are on the way, and if they see you've killed a federal officer …"

He shrugged. Let them decide if they'd be taken in alive.

Seven of the robbers turned to Price for a decision.

Before their leader could act, John gave them something else to think about.

"We know about Lamar," he said. "What I'm wondering is whether you guys know he's working with the Chinese government. Those tricks he played with the green lights in New Orleans and the casinos in Las Vegas? That wasn't just to help you rob banks. People in Washington think it was a trial run to see how cyberwarfare might be used against our country."

Price looked as if he'd just had a question answered.

The others were affronted.

"You think we're traitors?" O'Grady asked.

John said, "I'm waiting for you to tell me. My guess is you guys were just trying to grab some decent money to take with you into your retirement from the game. Maybe you're not working for Beijing, but Lamar is."

Price said, "I wondered how Lamar had learned all that stuff."

"He had good teachers, for any part he had to do himself," John said. "But the heavy lifting was done from back in China. That's the way things work with computer warfare. There's one more thing you should know. Washington thinks the Chinese have decided to tidy up after themselves by killing all of you. We think that will happen soon."

Tut said, "A bunch of commies are gonna kill us? Shee-it."

"Maybe even commies dressed like Indians," John replied.

O'Grady wasn't buying that. "Is that right? Bull —"

Ellie Booker burst into view.

"Guys with rifles coming!" she yelled. "Dressed like Indians!"

Now, everyone believed.

John told them, "Keep your bats. Grab as many balls as you can and follow me."

The four killers masquerading as a combination of Halloween Indians and outlaw bikers pushed through the third base gate. They were the ones who locked it behind them. There was no hand release on the lock that they could see. They'd have to find a key. Ought to be one on the chickenshit security guard they'd seen run off.

They'd been told to kill eight unarmed baseball players. Now, they'd have to ice some broad and an unarmed rent-a-cop, too. Shouldn't be too hard. They were the ones with the assault rifles, and the lights were on out on the field.

Only thing was, the place was pretty big. Might have more than a few places to hide. That and everybody and his dog had a cell phone these days. Somebody might've called the cops already. So they couldn't afford to dawdle.

They split up into two teams of two men each for broader coverage.

Before they went their separate ways, the chief said, "Remember, this is a Jim Morrison."

Meaning no one there got out alive.

Except for them, of course.

John made what he hoped was the correct assumption: the hit squad had entered the stadium the same way he had, through the third base gate. He paired that notion with the battle proven wisdom that it was always best to fight from the high ground; worst to have to fight your way uphill. Following that thinking he led Ellie and Price and the others up the first base side of the grandstand.

Along the way and on the fly, he pointed out hiding places for the player-robbers.

Leaving it to them to best work out their ambushes with bats and balls.

Thinking it ironic how quickly even the most unlikely alliances could form.

He, Ellie and Price took up positions in the stadium's broadcast booth.

Down on the field, the pitching machine still spat out baseballs from the huge bin that supplied it. The horsehide balls hit the canvas backstop with loud thunks. The sequence repeated itself like some misplaced metronome.

In the best sniper fashion, John and Ellie exposed as little of themselves as possible, peeking above the booth's broadcast console. They could see the entire field and every seat in the single-deck ball park. John glanced at Ellie and saw she had a knife in one hand and a baton in the other. He liked her attitude but not her odds against rifles, especially if they were military style weapons.

He leaned over and whispered into her ear, "Do you know how to shoot?"

She nodded.

He gave her his backup weapon, a Smith & Wesson J-Frame revolver, small and light with an internal hammer. Only five shots, but .357 Magnum loads. She smiled her thanks.

John looked over at Price. He had his entire head exposed about the console. He was using hand signals to position his team-mates. Like he was saying, "This batter pulls the ball with power. Play deep. Put yourselves here, here and here."

That or he was conducting their movements like the maestro of a symphony orchestra.

Either way, the guys down below would have to be skilled enough to pull off their parts.

John gestured to Price, told him in a quiet voice, "The first thing is, we all want to get out of here alive. But if we can take the guys with the guns alive, too, things might go somewhat better for you and your friends."

Price responded with a soft laugh.

"Just a suggestion," John said, "if you can communicate that to your friends."

"Yeah, okay."

The two men sensed Ellie watching them. She wasn't only looking their way. With the Smith in her right hand, she held a small camera in her left hand and was using it to shoot video. John thought a visual record might come in handy, especially if the bad guys cleaned the slate. He didn't object and the camera kept whirring.

"For you feds," Ellie whispered, as if she'd read John's mind.

But she was really thinking of the fortune Hugh Collier at WorldWide News would pay for the video. Might get a ton of gold from SportsCenter, too.

Keeping his voice down, John asked her, "You followed me from the Marriott tonight, didn't you?"

She nodded. "Followed you all the way here. Didn't spot me, did you?"

"No. You're quite the sneak."

Ellie beamed. As if she'd received a high compliment.

Then Price cleared his throat. The hit squad had entered the stadium.

John and Ellie held their positions and their fire. You didn't hit targets at more than a hundred feet with a semi-auto or short-barrel handgun except by pure luck. John saw now that the hit squad did have assault rifles. The effective range of those weapons was measured in hundreds of yards. Given the disparity in armament, potshots would only tell the bad guys where to direct their fire.

John was glad Ellie seemed to know that and held her fire.

Price moved to the broadcast booth doorway on the right side of the space.

He squatted with a comfort that came from years of practice. John saw he was repositioning his friends, based on the bad guys' movements. The killers had gone to the far ends of the seating area, one of each pair climbing to the concourse above the top row of seats, the other working the walkway between the box seats and the grandstand.

The killer on the upper concourse of the right field grandstand moved toward Tut Warren and Jack O'Grady, who were sheltering behind a refreshment stand on the same level. In less than a minute, the killer would cross in front of the players. If that happened, their only chance would be to have the bastard looking the wrong way when he got there.

As the killer drew near, though, Tut followed Price's signals and rolled a baseball down the stairway that led up to the refreshment stand. The thunk, thunk, thunk of the ball bouncing down the concrete steps drew the attention of the asshole with the assault rifle. He turned his back on the players' position. O'Grady, in a crouch not seen since the playing days of Jeff Bagwell, swung his bat with all his might.

Had he aimed for the guy's head it might have come off. Instead, he went for the back of the SOB's knees. The guy went down fast and face-first, his eyes glazed with shock even before he did his face plant. By the grace of the gods of baseball, his weapon didn't discharge.

Tut and O'Grady pulled the unconscious man into the lee of the refreshment stand.

Each of them looked to Price to see what they should do next.

He clenched a hand into a fist and then held it palm out.

That was just what they did. Grabbed the asshole's gun. Waited for further instruction.

The other killers had all heard the baseball bouncing down the cement stairs. They tried to track it. Then came the heavy thud. All of them knew what that was. The sound of a body dropping. By the time they tried to pinpoint where it fell, the source wasn't apparent.

What was clear, though, each of them could see only two other guys.

They were down a man, and an assault rifle, too.

Things weren't looking quite so easy as they did a moment ago.

The ballplayers had struck first. What they didn't know was, the killers were all members of the same family. They'd taken the job for money. Now, they had vengeance in mind, too. The three remaining killers opened fire on full auto in the general direction of where they'd last seen Cousin Bob.

The air filled with a hail of death and noise.

Tut and O'Grady thought it only fair to take shelter behind their victim. John, Ellie and Price pressed themselves into the floor of the broadcast booth, wrapping their arms around their heads. Shards of the structure around them turned into shrapnel and drew blood.

As soon as the shooters ran through their first clips, John combat crawled over to Tut and O'Grady and took possession of the weapon they'd captured.

Neither ballplayer thought to contest him for it.

Price was back in action, too. He peeked over the remnants of the booth's control board and signaled to four of the players who'd worked their way down to a point just outside the restrooms on the third base line. The four of them hurled baseballs high in the air.

The killer closest to those players responded by ducking and diving out of the way of the misperceived threat. When he rolled over he saw four angry faces looking down at him. The athlete's reflexes were better than his. Terry Foy, a third baseman with a cannon arm and a complete inability to lay off of pitches out of the strike zone, grabbed the assault rifle from the guy. Tony Theodore, the back-up catcher to Price who bounced throws to second base on steal attempts, dropped a knee on the killer's chest, taking him out of the game.

The two shooters on the lower level of the grandstand reacted to the balls in flight as if they were skeet. The fusillade they put into the air knocked down three balls. But now they'd burned through two clips of ammo, and when they looked back into the higher reaches of the seating area, Cousin Billy was gone, too.

They had to assume their would-be victims now had two assault rifles.

The desire for vengeance dimmed precipitously.

The instinct for self-preservation began a steep climb.

Even so, they were professionals. They cut and ran now, they'd never work again. There'd be a lot of explaining to the family to do, too. Leaving kin behind. The two remaining killers pulled together. Standing shoulder to shoulder, they charged up the stairway that led to the broadcast booth.

John took the lead in the counterattack. He opened up with the captured assault rifle. He could have taken out both killers, no problem, but as he'd explained to Price it would be more helpful to take them alive. You can't interrogate dead men. He'd fired his three-round burst into the infield dirt to the right of the oncoming killers.

They responded logically, turning toward the direction of the incoming rounds.

Looked desperately to find a target they might take out.

No sooner had they swiveled their heads than a hailstorm of baseballs filled the air.

The killer on the left took one smack on the skull and dropped like a dead man.

John couldn't fault whoever threw the ball.

He might have been a pitcher sending a message to the other team.

The remaining shooter emptied his final clip without doing any damage. That was all the ammunition he had. The killing crew had never anticipated needing more than three hundred and sixty rounds between them to kill eight people.

The remaining bad guy dropped his weapon and ran toward the exit staircase on his left. He hadn't gone ten feet before a loud boom sounded. Johansen, the faint-hearted security guard, appeared. He'd located his courage and a shotgun. He'd run up the stairway the killer had intended to use for his exit. Cut off from that avenue of retreat, the killer ran onto the playing field, clearly hoping to put distance between himself and everyone who was shooting at him.

Johansen fired his second barrel.

The killer cut across the infield in front of home plate, moving from the third base side to the first base side. John laid down a round to keep him in fair territory. The guy turned and headed back the way he came like a tin figure in a shooting arcade. Then he realized that wasn't a good choice. He came to a dead stop, looking left and right.

Then he turned his head and looked straight ahead.

Directly at the still functioning pitching machine.

He had but a split-second to try to figure out what he was looking at.

Then a one-hundred-mile-per-hour fast ball hit him right between the eyes.

The players in the stands thrust their fists in the air and cheered.

Ellie got footage that would wind up earning her an Emmy.

John hoped he had at least two bad guys who were still breathing.

— CHAPTER 34 —

Twelve Tacoma cops and ten FBI agents had heard the battle taking place inside the ballpark, but had been unable to force their way into the stadium. They'd just brought in a guy with an acetylene torch to cut through the bars when they saw Johansen running their way, still carrying his shotgun. Everyone with a badge shouted at him.

"Drop the weapon!"

Some of them emphasized the order with profane adjectives.

Johansen skidded to a stop and let his shotgun clatter to the ground.

"Ballpark security," he yelled back. "Lennart Johansen. I've got a key to let you guys in."

Johansen was told to approach slowly without his weapon.

He did and allowed the forces of law and order to enter.

The welder didn't mind; he got paid just to come out.

"Come on," Johansen told the others, "I'll show you where everyone is."

They let him take the lead but not pick up his shotgun.

Ellie recorded Johansen showing the way to the cops and feds.

John told her, "You might want to be discreet where you point your camera. Those guys look a little tense."

John saw Deputy Director DeWitt appear a moment after the others. He felt better immediately. He wore his BIA badge on his belt now. That didn't mean it would be easily accepted by those unfamiliar with his niche of law enforcement. There might even be a yahoo or two, local or federal, who'd demand he remove his sunglasses.

That would mean trouble.

DeWitt's presence would prevent that problem.

The pitching machine had been turned off and the hit squad lay in a row on the infield grass. Two were conscious, two weren't. All of them were still breathing. Corey Price and his teammates stood in a lineup behind the supine figures as if they'd just been introduced to the crowd before a ballgame. They'd been speaking quietly to one another, but fell silent when they saw the cops and feds approach.

Price raised his hands in a formal gesture of surrender and the others followed suit.

John waved that off and they lowered their hands.

DeWitt made his way to the crowd of lawmen and took control of the scene.

Then he walked over to John. He glanced at Ellie.

"Would you mind giving us a minute?"

She looked at John. He nodded, whispered into her ear. She thought about what she'd heard for a moment. She stopped her camera and stuck it in a pocket. Returned John's Smith & Wesson to him. Moved ten feet or so away from John and DeWitt. Hoping John would fill her in on anything good.

He'd just told her if she wanted to have a mutually beneficial relationship with him in the future, she'd play along now.

There were cops and feds flanking both the hit squad and the ballplayers now. They'd allowed themselves to dial back their adrenaline a notch. The bad guys had all been disarmed; their weapons — assault rifles and baseball bats — had been piled at John's feet.

"You took down all these guys by yourself?" DeWitt asked John.

He shook his head and told DeWitt what happened. Giving

credit where it was due. Remembering to include Johansen's late-inning appearance.

He explained to the deputy director, "The ballplayers only recently became criminals and were never less than loyal Americans or honest foreigners. Once I told them how they'd been used, they were happy to help me put up a fight."

"You also told them they were targeted for death?" DeWitt asked.

"Yes."

"No doubt that helped motivate them," DeWitt said.

"Sure, but their hearts were in it, too."

"They used to *be* the guys with the automatic weapons."

"Now they know how it feels to be on the wrong side of that. It doesn't excuse what they did, but I think they're truly sorry."

"You didn't make any promises to them, I hope," DeWitt said.

"Only that I'd testify how they helped me."

"So they know they're going to prison."

"Yeah, but they should get some consideration at sentencing for what they did tonight. That and I'm going to request that wherever they get locked up they be allowed to play baseball to the extent possible. Who knows, these guys might help other inmates find a better way."

DeWitt nodded. "The baseball part sounds reasonable."

"They helped me take the hit squad alive. That should be valuable."

The deputy director stepped closer to John and lowered his voice.

"We got Cheng Zou, too."

John smiled. "Where?"

"Hawaii. Talking to people posing as tourists."

"The tourists weren't so innocent?"

"Our Honolulu office thinks they're part of a ring snooping on military facilities in the islands. We decided it was time to bring Mr. Cheng in for a prolonged chat, which we're able to do under the Patriot Act."

"He doesn't have diplomatic immunity?"

DeWitt shook his head. "He's ours for as long as we want him. We'll give him back eventually. Probably in trade for someone the Chinese are holding or some poor sap they arrest in retaliation."

"There's something more you should hear about this guy," John told him.

He waved Ellie over. She told DeWitt about the Chinese gambler who lost ten million dollars in Las Vegas: Cheng Zou.

John said, "If this guy was playing with money he'd come by illicitly and the people he answers to didn't know about it ... well, they actually execute people over there for committing economic crimes, don't they?"

"They do, indeed," DeWitt said. "If we can hold all this over Mr. Cheng's head, he might be a good deal more forthcoming. Tell us enough to earn permanent residency here. Nice work, Special Agent. Nice work, Ms. Booker."

"There's just one more guy to grab," John said, "the ninth Indian, Lamar Dekker."

Ellie said, "I have an idea where he might be."

"Where?" DeWitt said.

"Alaska or on his way there."

John asked, "How do you know that?"

"Turns out he was staying at the Marriott in Seattle, just like you and me. He checked out the morning before we checked in. I talked to a cocktail waitress at the hotel. Dekker chatted her up. Said he had this great piece of land up there. And a nice house. And his own little lake. And a float-plane to get there. The waitress wasn't interested, but it sounds like a hideaway to me."

DeWitt wanted to know, "How did you find out Dekker had been at the Marriott?

Ellie hesitated before responding, "It's a crime to lie to a federal agent, right?"

John and DeWitt both nodded.

"Then I have nothing more to say."

In light of all the help she'd provided, neither fed pressed her on the matter.

But John asked to have Price brought over to them.

He asked the former ballplayer, "How well do you know Lamar Dekker?"

"You're looking for him, aren't you?"

"Yes."

"I won't ask what I can get in trade for this information. I'll just hope that you'll remember my cooperation."

"That's fair," John said.

"Dekker's from Alaska. There were a couple times we didn't see things eye to eye. He said if I ever got it in mind to pound on him, that's where he'd run. Out in the wilderness somewhere."

"Thanks," John said.

"The bastard was supposed to hold our share of the money we stole. Now, he's going to keep it for himself." Price shook his head in regret.

John asked, "How do you think he'd get up there?"

"From here in Washington? His truck, no doubt about it."

"That would take him through Canada," John said.

DeWitt said, "I'll call the authorities north of the border."

John told him "No need. I know a Mountie."

— CHAPTER 35 —

Eisenhower Executive Office Building, Washington, DC
Monday, August 26th

The question of why John Tall Wolf had remained on the case after the robbers were determined not to be Native Americans was answered the day after the culprits had been arrested.

John and Marlene Flower Moon took a red-eye flight across the country in Deputy Director DeWitt's aircraft to meet with Vice President Jean Morrissey in the capital. The vice president offered coffee to both of them. Marlene accepted. John was tempted. He could have used a stimulant given the few hours of sleep he'd had. But he decided to get by with a little fructose.

He asked for and received a glass of orange juice.

"I want to commend both of you for your roles in capturing the gang of bank robbers masquerading as Native Americans and, more important, helping the government to understand the defense posture it must adapt to deal with cyberwarfare. There will be changes made in foreign policy as a result of what has happened in the past several days. The result will be that our country will be better able to protect our critical infrastructure. The administration owes a debt of gratitude to both of you."

John expected to see Marlene smile.

Instead, she regarded the vice president with a look of open suspicion.

As if she might fall into a trap if she wasn't careful.

She said, "Madam Vice President, my part in this matter was all but negligible. The most that can be said of my contribution was that I recruited Special Agent Tall Wolf."

Jean Morrissey told her, "A sharp eye for talent is no small virtue. So is an undivided loyalty to one's job. Tell me, Director Flower Moon, is your leave of absence concluded? You've helped Mr. Steadman make his movie and you're ready to resume your duties full time?"

"I am, Madam Vice President."

"Good, but the Secretary of the Interior, in consultation with the president and me, has decided to restructure the BIA's Office of Justice Services to allow for greater efficiency and flexibility."

Marlene sat stone-faced and mute.

John was the one who felt a chill. "I beg your pardon, Madam Vice President. What kind of changes are you talking about?"

"For one, you're no longer Special Agent Tall Wolf; you are Deputy Director Tall Wolf."

John couldn't help himself. He winced.

"Something the matter?" the vice president asked.

"I'm very flattered, Madam Vice President, but I'm not an administrator. I'm a field man."

"Just what we have in mind. You'll be the chief investigator. The only time you'd be called on to act in any other capacity would be if Director Flower Moon might need to step away from her desk again or should pursue other opportunities on a permanent basis."

The light dawned. Nelda Freeland's days of filling in for Marlene were over.

John nodded. "Yes, I suppose I could do that."

Marlene looked as if she'd been paralyzed.

"As deputy director, you'll also decide which of the pending cases at the Office of Justice Services need your personal attention," the vice president said.

John bobbed his head. He liked that, too.

"And you'll have full responsibility for deciding which of the recruits Director Flower Moon finds will be chosen to become special agents. Do you think you can do all that?"

"Yes, ma'am, I think I can."

"Good. Madam Director, do you have any questions?"

"None," Marlene said, having no desire to prolong her humiliation.

She turned to John and said, "Congratulations."

But the look in her eyes promised only new and more dangerous confrontations.

"Are we done here, ma'am?" Marlene asked the vice president.

"You are. I'd like Deputy Director Tall Wolf to stay a minute."

John wasn't sure the vice president noticed, but he heard Coyote snarl as she left.

"Deputy Director DeWitt of the FBI recommended you for your promotion," Jean Morrissey told John. "He said you would handle it well. I'm trusting him on that, though from what I've seen I have to agree."

So, John thought, another powerful woman would be keeping her eye on him.

"DeWitt also said that anytime your workload at the BIA hits a lull your services should be made available to the FBI or other government agencies. Are you up for that?"

"I already help out at the Environmental Protection Agency," John said.

"Yes, well, we're thinking of a broader portfolio."

"Wherever I'm needed, ma'am," John told her.

"Good. There's someone who has heard of your contribution to resolving our recent difficulties and would like to meet you."

John's scalp began to tingle and, instinctively, he came to his feet.

Jean Morrissey opened a door and the most famous woman in the world appeared.

"Madam President, it's my pleasure to introduce you to John Tall Wolf, the new deputy director of the Office of Justice Services, Bureau of Indian Affairs."

Patricia Darden Grant extended her hand and John took it.

The president said, "I like your Ray-Bans."

— CHAPTER 36 —

Gallatoires Restaurant, New Orleans, Louisiana
Saturday, September 21st

John Tall Wolf and Rebecca Bramley sat at a table for four. Their two dinner guests would be arriving shortly. Rebecca sipped a glass of Lillet. John chose ginger ale as his aperitif.

They'd arrived in town the previous night and celebrated John's promotion with Marcellus Darcy and Edmee LaBelle at the Krazy Korner. They listened to Dwayne Dopsie and the Zydeco Hellraisers. They talked and danced and laughed into the wee hours. Rebecca amused everyone with her Alberta accented French, laughing when they said she spoke French like a Texan.

John told the others what he'd recently heard from Ellie Booker. The publishing arm of WorldWide News had paid a seven-figure advance for Corey Price's baseball memoir, *Take the Extra Base*. It told the story of a player who had all the talent needed to make the big leagues but kept setting himself back with injuries because his irrepressible nature forced him to try to stretch singles into doubles. Doubles into triples. Tearing up his hamstring.

Federal law prohibited convicted persons from profiting from their crimes, but Price's book was about baseball not bank robbing, and he'd had interest in the book from a publisher before his role in the robberies was known. A judge said the deal could proceed.

With WorldWide's investment in the book, the movie money grew exponentially.

Corey Price could have been a rich man when he got out of prison, but he settled for being affluent. His lawyer set up a trust giving each of his seven teammates an equal share. A decision that when made public would boost both book and movie ticket sales.

For no fee whatsoever, Price gave Ellie the exclusive insider's story of the bank robberies.

Diminishing Louis Mercer's opportunity to exploit his story to the vanishing point.

When John and Rebecca got back to the Renaissance Arts Hotel that night they were tired but still found the energy to make up for the time they'd spent apart.

Saturday night was planned to be a more refined affair.

Then John made the mistake of bringing up political speculation.

As to whom would succeed Patricia Darden Grant in office.

"You really think Jean Morrissey will run for president?" Rebecca asked.

"Of course, she will. That's what politicians do. They take their oath and plan their next campaign. Where else can she go but the Oval Office?"

Rebecca bobbed her head and smiled. "I like her."

"Sure, she played college ice hockey and she's from Minnesota. She could be your cousin."

"Will you introduce me? Will you be working out of Washington full time?"

John hadn't thought of that. Wasn't sure he liked the idea.

What was he going to do, though?

Say reservations weren't the only place he wouldn't work?

Rebecca asked, "When Jean becomes president, do you think she'll have a bigger job for you?"

John told her, "The only way I'd take over the BIA would be if your PM made you ambassador to the United States."

Rebecca slapped his back, laughed loudly and said, "Wouldn't that be a hoot?"

There was no end of places in New Orleans where such behavior would fit right in.

Gallatoire's, however, wasn't one of them. Other diners glanced their way.

Their looks said John and Rebecca might be more at home in a honky-tonk.

Rebecca blushed and settled down. "Can't take me anywhere." Lowering her voice, she added, "Still, I'm really jazzed thinking about the future."

Then, in a sense, the future arrived in the form of John's parents.

Their disapproval of Rebecca wouldn't be a deal-breaker.

But John was hoping for a warm and mutual embrace.

They greeted each other effusively, propriety be damned.

Ten minutes later, they were old friends.

Hayden and Serafina sat spellbound as John told them of his recent case.

They beamed when he said, "Rebecca was the Mountie who slapped the handcuffs on Lamar Dekker."

As the first test of the perks of his new job, John had pulled the strings for that.

And it worked, giving him more of a thrill than he'd ever expected.

He decided in that moment he would have to be careful.

Drinking wasn't the only bad habit that could bring a man down.

ABOUT THE AUTHOR

Joseph Flynn has been published both traditionally — Signet Books, Bantam Books and Variance Publishing — and through his own imprint, Stray Dog Press, Inc. Both major media reviews and reader reviews have praised his work. Booklist said, "Flynn is an excellent storyteller." The Chicago Tribune said, "Flynn [is] a master of high-octane plotting." The most repeated reader comment is: Write faster, we want more.

Contact Joe at Hey Joe on his website: *www.josephflynn.com*. You can also read excerpts of all of Joe's books on his website. All of Joseph Flynn's novels may be purchased online at *amazon. com*.

The Jim McGill Series
The President's Henchman, A Jim McGill Novel [#1]
The Hangman's Companion, A JimMcGill Novel [#2]
The K Street Killer, A JimMcGill Novel [#3]
The Last Ballot Cast: Part 1, A JimMcGill Novel [#4]
The Last Ballot Cast: Part 2, A JimMcGill Novel [#5]
The Devil on the Doorstep, A Jim McGill Novel [#6]
The Good Guy with a Gun, A Jim McGill Novel [#7]
The Echo of the Whip, A Jim McGill Novel [#8]
The Daddy's Girl Decoy, A Jim McGill Novel [#9]

The Last Chopper Out, A Jim McGill Novel [#10]
The King of Mirth, A Jim McGill Novel [#11]
McGill's Short Cases 1-3

The Ron Ketchum Mystery Series
Nailed, A Ron Ketchum Mystery [#1]
Defiled, A Ron Ketchum Mystery [#2]
Impaled, A Ron Ketchum Mystery [#3]

The John Tall Wolf Series
Tall Man in Ray-Bans, A John Tall Wolf Novel [#1]
War Party, A John Tall Wolf Novel [#2]
Super Chief, A John Tall Wolf Novel [#3]
Smoke Signals, A John Tall Wolf Novel [#4]
Big Medicine, A John Tall Wolf Novel [#5]
Powwow in Paris, A John Tall Wolf Novel [#6]

The Zeke Edison Series
Kill Me Twice, A Zeke Edison Novel [#1]

Stand Alone Novels
The Concrete Inquisition
Digger
The Next President
Hot Type
Farewell Performance
Gasoline, Texas
Round Robin, A Love Story of Epic Proportions
One False Step
Blood Street Punx
Still Coming
Still Coming Expanded Edition
Hangman — A Western Novella
Pointy Teeth, Twelve Bite-Size Stories